# Ghostly Getaways: Mystery in the Sonoma Vineyards

Kelly Greer

ISBN: 979-8-218-67702-2

# DEDICATION

To my incredible family, thank you for your unwavering support, your patience through every plot twist (on and off the page), and for always bringing me back to what matters most.

To my amazing friends, you continue to be the heart behind these stories. Your joy, honesty, and adventurous spirits are a constant source of inspiration and laughter.

This second getaway wouldn't have happened without you all. Here's to friendship, mystery, and a good glass of wine.

# CONTENTS

# ACKNOWLEDGMENTS

Thank you to the incredible people behind the scenes who helped shape this story from a spark of an idea into a book I'm so proud to share. Your thoughtful edits, encouragement, and attention to detail made all the difference.

To those who offered feedback, shared their love for Leigh and her friends, or simply cheered me on from the sidelines, your support continues to mean more than words can say.

Every page of this journey is better because of you.

# 1 CATCHING UP OVER COFFEE

The familiar aroma of freshly brewed coffee wafted through the cozy Omaha café, mingling with the soft sounds of conversations and the occasional clink of ceramic mugs. Sunlight streamed through the large windows, casting a golden hue across the room and illuminating the warm, earth-toned decor. Leigh leaned back into the worn leather chair tucked into the corner, cradling her latte in both hands. The warmth of the cup seeped into her palms, grounding her amidst the bustling energy of the café. She took a deep breath, savoring the rich aroma of her coffee and the comforting familiarity of the space, this haven, was where she and her friends always reconnected, slipping easily into their long-standing camaraderie whenever life's chaotic schedules allowed for it.

The peaceful hum of the café surrounded her as she glanced around the table at her friends, Kay and Alice, relishing this circle of friendship that had been years in the making, built on countless shared memories, late-night heart-to-hearts, and most recently, their spontaneous, whirlwind adventure to Savannah. The memory remained vivid in her mind, the old southern cobblestone streets, the Spanish moss-draped trees, and the unexpected thrill of mysteries both past and present. Leigh still chuckled at how they stumbled, quite literally, into a mystery that turned them into amateur detectives. At first, she'd been hesitant, clinging to the safety of her routine like a lifeline. But being thrust into that whirlwind of intrigue had been an unexpected thrill, pulling her out of her comfort zone in a way she hadn't realized she needed. She learned something about herself in Savannah, that she craved adventure more than she'd ever admitted. She recalled how exhilarating it had felt to be caught up in something bigger than her everyday life.

But Sonoma would be different. This time, it wasn't about ghosts or mysteries; it was about slow mornings, good wine, and uninterrupted girl time. A low-key escape, or at least that was the plan. Leigh had a sneaking suspicion that with this group of women, "low-key" might be asking too much, but she was determined to savor the trip nonetheless.

The café door swung open, pulling Leigh from her thoughts, and Marie strode in, her usual grace tempered by visible fatigue. Marie always appeared polished, always put together. Today, though, there was a certain dishevelment to her, her sleek, tailored blouse was slightly creased, and her normally flawless makeup showed faint signs of wear. Leigh doubted anyone who didn't really know Marie would ever notice. She still, of course, managed to look chic, her oversized leather tote stuffed with fabric samples and notes from her job, recently being promoted to head buyer for a well-known fashion design firm. But Leigh could tell, Marie was drained.

"Sorry I'm late," Marie muttered, sliding into the chair beside Leigh and letting out a sigh so heavy it seemed to release a week's worth of tension. She dropped her bag to the floor with a dull thud and leaned back, her fingers absentmindedly massaging her temple.

Leigh raised an eyebrow. "Long day?"

Marie's smile barely touched her lips. "Try a long week." She tucked a loose strand of hair behind her ear, a gesture that Leigh knew was her way of trying to pull herself together. "It's been one thing after another, flying between showrooms, arguing with suppliers over exclusive fabrics, managing back-to-back deadlines. New releases are coming up, and I feel like I'm drowning in it all."

Leigh studied her friend, noting the faint smudge of eyeliner under Marie's tired eyes, something that would normally never escape her meticulous attention to detail. Marie was the type who thrived under pressure, always calm and composed, but today there was a vulnerability in her voice that was rare.

"You need this trip," Leigh said gently, her voice carrying both warmth and resolve. "No emails, no meetings, no fabric negotiations. Just wine, sunshine, and maybe a little gossip. You've earned it."

Marie's smile appeared more genuine this time, though it didn't reach her eyes. "I've never needed a vacation more in my life," she confessed, leaning back in her chair. "I need to remind myself what it feels like to breathe."

Leigh nodded, sensing the underlying exhaustion that Marie tried so hard to hide. Her friend was a master at maintaining the perfect exterior, but even she couldn't outrun the toll her demanding career was taking on her. Leigh wanted this trip to be exactly what Marie needed, a break, a moment to recharge.

Leigh's eyes wandered over to the barista counter, where Hunter, one of Marie's twin boys, stood tall, wiping down the espresso machine with a mix of casual efficiency and youthful energy. His trademark grin was firmly in place, the kind that could brighten even the dullest of days. His blond hair was slightly tousled, likely from a busy morning shift, and he moved with the confidence of someone who'd mastered his routine. The sight of him made Leigh's heart warm, not just because Hunter had become such a responsible young man, but because she knew how proud Marie was of her boys, though she didn't always get to see them as much as she liked.

Marie spotted him too, and her tired expression softened in an instant. "Oh, there's Hunter," she said, her voice lifting with unmistakable affection. Her eyes lit up in a way that only a mother's could. Without hesitation, she grabbed her oversized tote and made her way toward the counter, her earlier exhaustion all but forgotten. Leigh smiled, watching her friend's stride transform from weary to purposeful.

Leigh watched as Marie approached her son, her face breaking into a wide smile. She hadn't even had a chance to go home and see her family after her last-minute work trip, and it was clear she was itching for a moment with one of her boys, even if it was only a few minutes here in the café. Hunter looked up just in time, his grin matching hers as they exchanged a few words. Leigh couldn't hear what was being said, but she saw the way Marie gently squeezed his arm, the motherly affection spilling over despite the hectic day. It was a snapshot of everything good and grounding amidst their otherwise hectic lives.

After a moment, Hunter strolled over to their table with Marie, a damp cleaning rag still clutched in his hand. "Hey, ladies," he said, his warm, familiar voice carrying an easy confidence. He leaned casually against the back of Marie's chair, towering over the group in his apron, every bit the composed, good-natured young man Leigh had watched grow up.

"Hunter!" Kay chimed in, her green eyes sparkling with playful mischief. "Still the coffee king, huh? How's life in the caffeine business treating you?"

Hunter chuckled, shaking his head. "You know, just keeping Omaha caffeinated one latte at a time. What would this city do without me?"

Leigh smiled as the ladies laughed with him, appreciating how easily he spoke with their group. Hunter had always been good-natured, and even though he was still in high school, he'd developed an easy rapport with his mom's friends over the years. He had inherited Marie's easy going charm, no doubt about it.

"So, what's the next big trip?" Hunter asked, folding his arms and leaning in closer, his curiosity piqued. "I heard all about Savannah. You guys thinking of moonlighting as detectives now or something?"

Leigh laughed, a wave of nostalgia washing over her at the mention of their Savannah adventure. "Nope, just wine this time," she said with a wink. "Sonoma is strictly for sipping, relaxing, and enjoying life. No mysteries allowed."

Hunter raised an eyebrow, clearly not convinced. "Yeah, right. You all get into trouble wherever you go."

Marie rolled her eyes, though her lips twitched with amusement. "He's not wrong."

"I want a full report when you get back," Hunter teased, his grin widening. "Wineries, shenanigans, whatever drama finds you, don't leave anything out. And don't forget to bring me back a souvenir. Something fancy, okay?"

He gave Marie a quick squeeze on the shoulder, the kind of affectionate gesture that showed just how close they were despite their busy lives. Then, straightening up, he tossed the rag over his shoulder and flashed another grin. "Alright, I better get back to it. This place doesn't run itself." With a final wink, he turned and strolled back toward the counter, leaving the table to bask in the easy warmth he'd brought to their conversation.

Leigh watched Hunter go, a fond smile tugging at her lips. It was always heartwarming to see how much he had grown into such a kind, responsible young man. Everyone knew how much Marie cherished every moment with her boys, even the brief ones like this. As Hunter disappeared into the back of the café, the familiar sound of the bustling space filled the quiet that remained, coffee grinders whirring, the low murmur of conversations blending into each other. Leigh wrapped her hands around her warm drink and turned her attention back to her friends. She took another sip, savoring the comforting flavors, and settled deeper into the rhythm of their gathering.

Marie, visibly lighter after seeing her son, chatted animatedly with Kay. Kay's boundless energy was infectious, and her excitement about their upcoming trip seemed to pull Marie further out of her earlier weariness. Kay leaned forward, her eyes sparkling as she gestured wildly, recounting a story about a vineyard she'd researched. Leigh smiled as she listened, content to let the conversation flow around her.

But on the other side of the table, Alice remained unusually quiet. She sat with her hands folded neatly in her lap, her eyes downcast as she absently twisted a napkin between her fingers. The motion was subtle, but Leigh caught it immediately. Alice's stillness, once a comforting presence, now felt charged with tension. It wasn't like her to withdraw like this. Alice had always been the grounding force of their group, the calm in the storm, the friend who could offer sage advice with just a few thoughtful words. But something had shifted. Lately, she seemed distracted, as if she were carrying the weight of something she hadn't shared.

Leigh's gaze lingered, watching the way Alice's fingers fidgeted with the napkin, picking at its edges as if trying to unravel its fibers. Her shoulders were hunched slightly, her posture betraying an inner turmoil she couldn't quite hide.

"Everything okay?" Leigh asked gently, her voice soft enough to keep the question private but firm enough to convey her concern.

Alice blinked, her fingers stilling as she looked up, as though Leigh's voice had pulled her from a deep fog. For a brief moment, she hesitated, and Leigh noticed the flicker of something unreadable in her eyes. Then Alice forced a small smile, the kind that didn't quite reach her face. "Yeah, just…stuff," she murmured, her voice barely above a whisper.

Leigh's heart tightened at the vague response. Alice had always been reserved when it came to her own struggles, preferring to focus on others rather than herself. But this felt different, heavier. Leigh couldn't help but wonder what "stuff" meant. Was it something at home? A personal struggle she hadn't confided in them about?

Leigh decided not to press, at least not now. Alice wasn't one to open up easily, and Leigh knew from experience that pushing too hard could make her retreat even further. Instead, she leaned in slightly, her tone warm and reassuring. "You know we're here for you," she said softly, her smile steady and inviting.

Alice nodded, her expression a mixture of gratitude and hesitation, her guard still firmly in place. Leigh could see the struggle in her friend's eyes, the way she was fighting to hold it all together. It wasn't the time to dig deeper, but Leigh made a mental note to check in later, privately, when the moment felt right.

The conversation at the table continued, Kay's vibrant storytelling filling the space with laughter and energy. But Leigh's mind lingered on Alice, her heart aching for whatever her friend was going through. She resolved to be there when Alice was ready, knowing that sometimes, the most important thing was simply letting someone know they weren't alone.

Leigh laughed, grateful for Kay's infectious energy. She was the spark that always kept their group lively, the one who could brighten any mood. But even Kay's excitement seemed different today, more intense, almost frantic, like she was chasing something she couldn't quite grasp.

"You're unusually hyped," Leigh teased, a playful glint in her eyes. "Even for you."

Kay grinned, though there was a flicker of something behind her smile, an unspoken need for more. "I just really need this trip," she said with a sigh. "Life's felt…stuck lately. Boring, maybe. I don't know." Her gaze drifted for a moment before snapping back. "I'm ready for some fun."

Leigh sensed there was more to Kay's restless energy than just boredom, but she didn't push. They all needed this trip for different reasons, and Leigh had her own need for this time away. Her kids had recently left for college, and while she was endlessly proud of them, the empty nest had left her adrift. The bustling, purpose-driven life she had built around raising her children had grown quieter, the days stretching long and unfamiliar. It wasn't sadness exactly, more like a strange hollowness, a question mark lingering in the stillness of her home.

That's when planning trips became her unexpected lifeline. What had started as a way to create a wonderful trip to Savannah with her friends had blossomed into something much bigger, a venture that combined her love for travel, organization, and adventure into one fulfilling hobby-turned-business. Leigh hadn't realized how much of herself she'd put on hold during those years. It wasn't that she regretted it, she adored being a mother, and taking care of her family had been one of the greatest joys of her life. But somewhere along the way, she had forgotten to nurture her own identity.

"I've been planning like crazy," Leigh said, her voice brightening as she shifted the conversation. "It's kind of become my thing. I'm starting to organize trips for other friends and even some clients. It's been fun researching new places."

Kay smirked, a knowing glint in her eye. "Of course you are. You're so good at it, you made Savannah's mystery seem like it was planned."

The group laughed at the memory. Their adventure in Savannah had been thrilling, like stepping into one of the mystery novels Leigh loved so much. From the eerie charm of the Mercer-Williams House to the twisty ghost tour that led them to unexpected clues, the trip had been more than they could have imagined. While they hadn't planned on playing detectives, that spontaneous adventure had ignited something inside her.

It wasn't just about solving mysteries or taking trips anymore; it was about rediscovering the parts of herself that had been buried under years of caring for her family. Planning had become more than logistics, it was an outlet for creativity, a way to dream again. Before Savannah, she had only thought about destinations in terms of what her kids or her husband would enjoy. Disney, the Grand Canyon, and countless sports tournaments had been wonderful, but they weren't her dreams.

Now, for the first time in what seemed like forever, Leigh was creating a bucket list just for herself. The

Sonoma trip, the hiking tour in Oregon she was eyeing next, and even the idea of planning a writers' retreat in a tucked-away cabin in Maine, they were all hers. These destinations were chosen with her own curiosity and sense of adventure in mind, and she loved it.

There was something freeing about having a bucket list that wasn't centered on anyone else's needs or schedules. It wasn't selfish; it was self-affirming. The more she planned, the more she realized how vast the world felt, and how much there was still to discover. Each destination she researched made the list grow longer, and for once, that didn't feel overwhelming, it felt like an invitation.

Kay's voice pulled her back to the present. "So what's next after Sonoma? You must have something lined up."

Leigh grinned, unable to hide her excitement. "I'm thinking of a hiking trip to Oregon with Tom. It's been on my list for a while, and now we have the time to actually do it."

Kay raised an eyebrow. "Hiking? You?"

Leigh laughed. "I know, right? But it's funny how your own interests can surprise you when you finally have the time to explore them."

"But for Sonoma it's just peaceful activities right? We're leaving the sleuthing behind this time," Marie said firmly, shaking her head as if to ward off any lingering thoughts of their last escapade. "Sonoma is about wine, relaxation, and nothing else."

Leigh smiled, glancing around at her friends. They had been through so much together, through the whirlwind of raising kids, navigating careers, and finding their identities beyond their day-to-day roles. This trip felt like a wonderful pause, a chance for all of them to breathe, reconnect, and simply be. The crisp Omaha air greeted them as they finished their drinks and stepped outside, a gentle reminder of the world waiting for them.

But as Leigh walked to her car, a strange feeling tugged at her chest. Despite their best-laid plans, she couldn't shake the sense that Sonoma wouldn't be quite as peaceful as they hoped.

And secretly, part of her was okay with that.

# 2 ON THE ROAD TO ADVENTURE

Just a few days later Leigh was zipping up her last suitcase when her husband, Tom, walked in, hands casually tucked into his pockets, a mischievous gleam in his eye. "So, what's the big plan while I'm away?" she teased, glancing over at him with an eyebrow raised. She already knew his answer would be a mix of dry humor and playful exaggeration, the kind she had grown to appreciate even more now that the house was emptier and quieter than it used to be. The absence of their children had left space for moments like this, small exchanges that seemed more precious than ever.

"Oh, nothing too wild," he replied, drawing out his words dramatically, a grin already forming. "Maybe I'll perfect my competitive TV-watching skills, start a championship nap league… or dust off one of those woodworking projects I packed away ages ago." He paused, contemplating, his grin widening as he said, "The championship nap league could be my ticket to fame, though. Don't you think?"

Leigh chuckled, her eyes brightening. "A championship nap league, huh? I'll have a trophy made. 'Tom Greyson: Nap King of the Midwest.' Has a nice ring to it."

"Hey, naps take skill," he said, raising his hands in mock protest. "But seriously," he continued, his voice softening, "maybe I'll finally organize the garage or get started on those shelves I keep promising. And there are still boxes of old photos we've been meaning to go through. It might be nice to dive into those, maybe rediscover some memories along the way." He nodded to himself, already imagining the projects, and Leigh smiled, grateful for his steady companionship and the new rhythm they were finding together. After years of juggling the chaos of kids, schedules, and work, these quieter moments carried a different fulfillment, one marked by a deep appreciation for each other's presence.

Since the kids had gone off to college, they'd filled the empty spaces with weekend getaways, leaning into Tom's love of spur-of-the-moment adventures balanced by her knack for planning. Last spring, they took a drive to Winterset, Iowa, a destination chosen on a whim because they had wanted to see the historic covered bridges, with Tom pointing out every charming roadside diner and unexpected scenic spot along the way. Once, on a whim, they pulled into a small town fair that neither of them had heard of, simply because Tom was curious about the laughter they heard drifting through the car windows. Her organized notes had ensured they didn't miss a guided tour or a must see spot, but Tom's relaxed pacing meant they lingered, soaking in the charm without rushing.

On another trip, they'd found themselves winding through the Blue Ridge Parkway, stopping at bed and breakfasts they spotted along the way, none of which had been in her plans. Tom's spontaneity had led them down country roads, past vineyards they hadn't expected, with scenic overlooks Leigh would've bypassed in favor of the next scheduled stop. And somehow, it worked. The balance between his whimsy and her structure allowed them to discover experiences neither would've had alone. While family trips with the kids had always been fulfilling in their own way, full of laughter, shared discoveries, and memories Leigh cherished, these recent getaways felt like a slower, deeper kind of joy. There was something uniquely peaceful about having the freedom to linger as long as they wanted, letting the days unfold at their own charming pace.

Though she had tried to embrace Tom's way of traveling, Leigh still found herself slipping a printed itinerary into her bag, "just in case." Tom would joke about it, calling it her 'map to adventure,' and she'd laugh, agreeing that some habits were too hard to break. She was learning, bit by bit, to appreciate the freedom that came with not knowing every detail. And deep down, she loved that their trips always had the best of both worlds: the thrill of exploration with just enough guidance to keep them from getting lost along the way.

Leigh tried to remind herself about her enjoyment of the detours she'd taken with Tom as she added a few last items to her suitcase. She glanced down at her Sonoma itinerary with a flicker of anxiety. Her mind went into overdrive, running through a mental checklist: travel guides, tickets, chargers, everything down to her favorite pen for jotting down memories. But this time, she knew she needed to make sure she didn't put too much pressure on herself. Her friends enjoyed spontaneity just as much as Tom, and certainly didn't expect her to know it all. They'd planned this trip as a chance to unwind and reconnect, not to follow a rigid schedule. She closed her eyes, taking a deep breath, grounding herself with the mindfulness techniques she'd recently been practicing. She whispered quietly, "It doesn't have to be perfect, just fun," reminding herself that letting go, even a little, brought just as much joy as the best-laid plans.

Tom noticed her moment of hesitation and stepped over, resting a reassuring hand on her shoulder. "You've got this," he said softly, his voice warm and steady. "You've planned every detail, like always, and now it's time to enjoy all the work you put into it. Besides," he added with a playful glint in his eyes, "if anything goes off script, just blame it on me. That's what I'm here for, right?"

Leigh laughed, feeling the tension ease a bit. "I might just take you up on that," she replied, looking up at him with a smile. "I keep telling myself to relax, to let it flow a little more, but I guess some habits die hard."

Tom chuckled. "Hey, I'm really proud of you, Leigh, for putting yourself out there. And you know," he leaned in a little closer, "I'm also kind of proud of you for learning to take a few deep breaths along the way."

Leigh squeezed his hand, her anxiety fading as she let herself lean into the excitement of the adventure ahead. "Thanks, Tom. Really. It means a lot."

On the way to the airport, they picked up Alice. As they pulled up to her house, Leigh spotted her friend standing on the front porch, balancing a few bags and glancing anxiously over her shoulder. Normally, Alice radiated calm, a serene presence in any setting, the one who could find her keys without thinking, pack an entire suitcase in minutes, and always seemed unruffled, no matter how chaotic things got around her. Today, however, her movements were hurried, her normally composed face slightly flushed as she tried to manage her bags and check something on her phone at the same time.

"Sorry, guys," Alice murmured as she approached the car, her voice softer than usual, with a hint of something Leigh hadn't heard from her too often, fatigue. "It's just…there seems to be so much to juggle lately." She glanced down, avoiding Leigh's eyes, as if afraid that one look might unravel her carefully guarded composure.

Tom got out to help with her bags, and as he did, Leigh caught sight of Alice's husband, Zach, standing in the doorway. He waved, then motioned Leigh over. "Hey, Leigh," he whispered, leaning in with a slight smile that didn't quite reach his eyes. "Alice has been… well, overwhelmed. I don't think she's really letting it show, but I can see it. Make sure she actually relaxes this trip, okay? She needs it."

Leigh gave him a small nod, her heart squeezing as she looked back at Alice. She could see the weariness in the set of her friend's shoulders, the slight slump that seemed foreign to someone usually so collected. Leigh made a mental note to give her the space she needed and save the deeper questions for later. For now, she offered Alice a warm, reassuring smile as she slipped into her seat, hoping to ease a bit of the burden Alice was so clearly carrying.

There would be time during the trip for genuine conversation, for giving her friend a place to exhale. But right now, Leigh decided, was the moment for light-heartedness and friendship, the very things she hoped would help Alice feel the weight start to lift.

At the airport, they spotted Kay and Marie waiting near the entrance to security, both waving with big smiles as soon as they saw them approach. Kay's colorful scarf and bright laughter added a spark to the usual drabness of airport surroundings, and Marie's chic, professional style hinted at her nonstop work life, though she looked more than ready for a break. The friends embraced in a flurry of hugs and excitement, their laughter echoing across the terminal as if no time had passed since their last adventure together. Even strangers couldn't help but glance at their joyful reunion, smiling at the infectious energy they brought to the moment.

As they approached the gate, a small hiccup surfaced in the form of a seating issue. Their tickets had them scattered around the plane, miles apart by airplane standards. "Oh, leave it to me," Marie said, a glint of confidence in her eye. With a wink and a flip of her hair, she marched up to the gate agent, not missing a beat as she began chatting up the agent with effortless charm. Leaning casually over the counter as if they'd known each other for years, Marie's friendly laugh and animated gestures seemed to relax even the weariest of employees.

Leigh and the others watched in awe, stifling giggles as Marie pointed toward their group with a pleading look, her hands clasped as though negotiating a peace treaty. After a bit of back and forth, the agent finally chuckled, nodding in agreement, and handed Marie a fresh set of boarding passes. Marie sauntered back with a proud grin and four seat upgrades in hand, waving them like golden tickets.

"Voilà! Problem solved," she said, holding out the passes with a triumphant flourish.

"You've outdone yourself, Marie," Leigh laughed, taking her ticket and patting Marie's arm. "They should honestly put you in charge of every airport across the country."

"Don't tempt me," Marie replied with a smirk. "I'd have this place running like clockwork."

When they landed in Las Vegas for their layover, the sparkle of slot machines greeted them almost immediately, each one flashing in vivid colors and chiming with enticing jingles. As they made their way through the terminal, Kay spotted the row of slots and lit up like a kid in a candy store.

"It's a new tradition," she declared, striding up to a

nearby machine with a wink. "I can't walk through here without testing my luck." She slipped a dollar in, gave the lever a tug, and watched as the symbols spun…only to fall into mismatched lines.

"Ah, better luck next time," Leigh teased as they continued to the next gate, but Kay wasn't done yet.

"One more!" she laughed, dropping another dollar into a different machine and, once again, coming up short. "Just warming up!" she said with a grin, shrugging at her friends' amused glances. Her small army of one-dollar bills quickly vanished, each machine returning her enthusiasm with a disappointing clang.

"Kay, you're on your ninth dollar!" Leigh teased, shaking her head with an affectionate smile.

"Last one, I swear," Kay replied, though the glint in her eye said otherwise. She reached for the lever with dramatic flair, muttering something about beginner's luck and luck in numbers. And just as they all laughed and prepared to move on, the machine lit up in a wild symphony of flashing lights and cheerful dings, signaling a small jackpot.

The girls erupted in laughter and cheers, drawing curious glances from other travelers as Kay threw her arms up in victory. "Ladies, I told you! Sign of good luck!" she declared, clutching her handful of winnings and twirling around in excitement.

Marie held her hands up, chuckling. "Kay, it's not even that much, but I swear, you'd think you hit the lottery."

Kay's face was alight with glee as she clutched her prize. "Oh, don't ruin the moment! I was born to be a high roller," she said with an exaggerated wink, striking a pose that had them all laughing until their sides hurt.

Kay's antics drew a small crowd of amused onlookers who clapped as she waved her winnings in the air like a trophy. "I wonder if I should quit my job and make this my career," she joked, pretending to toss her winnings in the air like confetti.

Leigh wiped a tear from the corner of her eye, leaning in to hug her friend. "Well, if this is how the trip is starting, we're in for a memorable one."

Kay pocketed her winnings with a proud grin. "Good thing we are leaving now or Vegas may never have recovered from my amazing gambling skills."

As they sank into their seats for the final leg of their journey, Leigh couldn't shake the unease that had been creeping up on her since their takeoff from Omaha. The hum of the engines, the faint rattle of the overhead compartments, and the flickering cabin lights all seemed to heighten her nerves. Airplanes always made her feel trapped—no escape routes, no quick way out. She clasped her hands tightly, focusing on her breathing, counting each inhale and exhale, hoping to calm her spiraling thoughts. In…out… She repeated the mantra, reminding herself that turbulence was normal and that soon, they'd be in Sonoma, ready to relax and enjoy the adventure.

Lost in her thoughts, Leigh almost didn't notice Alice's hand reaching over to rest gently on her arm. She turned to see Alice's calm, soft expression and an understanding smile that spoke volumes without saying a word.

Alice's eyes, usually so focused and steady, seemed to carry a quiet strength, a grounding energy Leigh hadn't expected, especially given how much Alice herself had been managing lately. That simple, unspoken gesture, Alice's hand on her arm, brought Leigh back from her worry, anchoring her in the present moment.

Leigh was touched by her friend's silent support and found herself even more determined to make sure Alice got the rest and relaxation she deserved on this trip. For so long, Alice had been the steady rock, always there to lift others up. Now, Leigh wanted to be that anchor for her friend, returning the favor.

Settling back into her seat, Leigh focused on the warmth of Alice's hand and the calm it brought, her nerves beginning to ease.

As the plane climbed into the sky, Leigh's heart steadied, and she looked out the window at the sea of clouds below. The days ahead promised laughter, adventure, and a much-needed escape—a chance for all of them to recharge, reconnect, and, as always, lean on one another.

# 3 WELCOME TO SONOMA VALLEY

The moment Leigh and her friends stepped off the plane and into the warmth of Sonoma Valley, it seemed like all the layers of responsibility they hadn't even known they were carrying were gradually falling away. A soft radiant California sun, warmed her skin as a gentle breeze drifted over them, carrying the earthy scent of vineyards mingled with wild lavender. Leigh closed her eyes, letting the fragrance sink in, and for a heartbeat, the constant noise of her restless thoughts grew quiet. She opened her eyes to see endless rows of vineyards stretching toward the horizon, their leaves shimmering in the glow of the sunlight. It was a picture-perfect scene, and the promise of a relaxing, indulgent escape finally began to feel real.

She looked over at her friends, each of them taking in the scene with that same quiet sense of awe. Kay had her sunglasses perched on top of her head, a wide grin spreading across her face as she scanned the landscape. Marie, with her signature red lipstick and contagious energy, was already chatting about the wines they'd try first. Alice stood quietly beside her, her expression softening as she gazed out at the vineyard. For a second, Leigh caught a flicker of peace in Alice's eyes, something she hoped would grow as the trip went on. They were all absorbing the surrounding beauty, and for the moment, they weren't in a rush.

At the car rental, their laughter echoed through the lot as they spotted the sleek red convertible that would be their ride for the weekend. "Ladies," Kay announced with her hands on her hips, "clearly, this car was meant for us." She and Marie shared an impish grin, and without another word, they both volunteered themselves as the official drivers for the trip.

"This is going to be wonderful," Marie said, slipping her scarf around her head in an attempt to protect her long hair from the wind.

With Kay at the wheel and Leigh slipping into the passenger seat, Alice and Marie hopped into the back, already giggling as they adjusted their scarves and sunglasses. Before Leigh could say a word, Kay pushed the button to lower the top, letting the sun pour over them. "Let's roll!" Kay shouted, revving the engine. "I'll get us there in style, top down, of course!" she added. A chorus of laughter erupted as the wind immediately tangled their hair, making any attempt at neatness futile.

"You do realize the top is going to destroy any attempt we make at looking glamorous, right?" Leigh quipped, trying and failing to untangle her curls.

"Who needs glamour when you've got freedom?" Kay shot back with a laugh, gunning the car onto the highway.

As they cruised down Highway 101, the wind whipping through the open car felt like freedom itself. Leigh caught sight of Alice in the rearview mirror, her short pixie cut barely moving, unlike Leigh's own wild curls, which whipped across her face in a tangle of frizz. "At least one of us looks dignified!" Leigh shouted over the wind to Alice, a grin on her face as she tugged her own hair from her eyes. Her laughter mingled with the shouts and squeals of her friends, a soundtrack of pure joy filling the car.

Alice, though unusually reserved so far, couldn't help but laugh, a sound Leigh was grateful to hear. "This haircut was my best decision yet!" Alice teased, her eyes sparkling. Still, Leigh noticed a flicker of that quiet tension underneath. Leigh hoped that with each mile, Alice would find herself relaxing a bit more.

They fell silent as the Golden Gate Bridge rose in the distance, its towers piercing the sky with a fiery red that glowed against the clear blue. Kay, with an almost reverent look, pulled over at a vista point, and for a moment, they all stared at the iconic structure, feeling small yet alive in its shadow. The bridge seemed to hum with its own energy, a place where countless people had begun their journeys, dreams stretching as far as the eye could see.

"We have to capture this!" Kay exclaimed, fishing out her phone and urging everyone out of the car. The four of them stumbled out, windblown and laughing, each trying in vain to smooth their hair. Leigh chuckled as Kay tried patting down her red tresses, only for them to bounce right back up into a cloud.

"Forget it, ladies this is the look of freedom!" Marie announced, snapping a selfie of the group. They struck playful poses, the red towers of the bridge towering behind them, a symbol of the freedom and adventure they hoped to capture on this trip.

As they climbed back into the convertible, their sounds of joy lingered, echoing off the hills as they drove deeper into wine country. The promise of the weekend seemed as vast as the landscape before them, and Leigh knew that whatever lay ahead, they were exactly where they needed to be.

Finally, they reached Sinclair Winery, and the sight of

it took their breath away. The estate sprawled across rolling hills, each one covered in neat rows of vines that seemed to stretch endlessly, bathed in the warm glow of the afternoon sun. The winery looked like it belonged in a storybook, with ivy-covered stone walls, vintage wooden doors, and rustic charm spilling from every corner. Their cottage for the week sat right at the edge of one of the vineyards, a cozy retreat with wooden floors that creaked warmly beneath their feet, sprawling windows that framed the lush greenery outside, and a porch practically begging for them to sit and sip wine as the sun dipped below the hills. A small garden bursting with vibrant flowers lined the walkway, and an old wooden swing hung from a nearby tree, its ropes weathered but sturdy. It was the kind of place where time almost seemed to pause.

"This," Kay declared, extending her arms as if to embrace the entire landscape, "is exactly what I hoped for." Her voice held a note of admiration, and the others nodded in agreement. Leigh let her fingers brush against the rough wood of the porch railing, breathing in the scent of grapevines and soil, mingling with the faint sweetness of ripe fruit in the air. The place felt like a world away from deadlines and obligations—a cheerful oasis where even the most serious worries seemed to lose their grip.

After settling in and freshening up, they made their way to the Sunflower Caffé, drawn in by its cheerful yellow facade and lush greenery spilling over the outdoor dining area. The café was a slice of pure joy, with bright yellow chairs scattered across the patio and tiny pots of herbs on each table, filling the air with the fresh scents of basil, rosemary, and mint. String lights crisscrossed overhead, their soft glow mingling with the sunlight filtering through the trees, creating an atmosphere that was both lively and intimate. It was like stepping into a vibrant, sunlit oasis that welcomed them with open arms. Leigh marveled at it all, and the warmth seemed to seep into her bones as they found a table in a cozy corner.

Leigh ordered the roasted squash salad, each bite a mix of earthy, caramelized squash, crisp greens, and a tangy dressing that brought everything together. The toasted seeds added just the right crunch, that hinted at the care poured into every ingredient. Across the table, Kay's sunflower grilled cheese was pure comfort food, with golden melted cheese spilling out of the perfectly crisp bread as she took a hearty bite. Marie's smoked ham and grilled cheese, layered with fresh herbs, earned appreciative nods all around the table. Alice, however, sat quietly with her kale and chicken Caesar, her fork moving absentmindedly as she stared into the distance.

"Hey, are you sure you're okay?" Leigh leaned over, keeping her voice low. She could see the faraway look in Alice's eyes, and something in her heart twinged with concern.

Alice offered a faint smile, her gaze flickering back to the present. "Just…a lot on my mind. But this place is beautiful. I'll be fine." Her words were calm, but Leigh could sense the weight lingering in them.

They lifted their mimosa glasses in a toast, each glass a different shade reflecting their personalities. Kay's guava was bold and tropical, Leigh's lavender mist soft and fragrant, Marie's classic orange bright and traditional, and Alice's blueberry thyme a deep, rich hue that seemed to suit her contemplative mood. They clinked glasses, laughing as the sunlight danced through the sparkling liquid, and in that moment, the rest of the world faded away. Here, in this little café, surrounded by good friends, it was just them, sunshine, and a promise of adventures still to come.

After lunch, they strolled toward Sonoma Plaza, their footsteps lighter with each step as they took in the allure of the historic square. The Spanish-style buildings that framed the plaza seemed frozen in time, their warm terracotta roofs aglow beneath the late afternoon sun. Quaint, colorful storefronts lined the cobblestone pathways, each one brimming with character and charm. Kay pointed out a small artisan shop with a window display of handcrafted jewelry—delicate earrings and intricate rings that glinted in the sunlight. Across the way, Leigh's attention was drawn to an antique bookstore. Bookstores always caught her eye; after all, no one could ever have too many books. She felt a familiar pull, imagining herself wandering through its shelves, savoring the scent of old pages and uncovering hidden gems. The last time an antique bookstore had caught her attention, she and her friends had been swept into a whirlwind of a mystery during their trip to Savannah. It had started with a simple curiosity and unraveled into an unforgettable adventure, one that still sent a shiver of excitement down her spine whenever she thought of it. What stories, she wondered, might be waiting here in Sonoma?

Their next stop was the Sonoma Cheese Factory, where they sampled creamy wedges of cheese that melted on their tongues, each one paired with sips of local wine. They giggled, pretending to be seasoned connoisseurs as they exchanged tasting notes. Marie insisting that the Brie had hints of wildflower, while Kay swore it had a nutty undertone. Beyond the cheese shop, the square was filled with life. Musicians played gentle tunes on acoustic guitars, their melodies winding through the air like the fragrance of fresh-cut flowers spilling from a nearby flower stall. There was a faint murmur of voices, locals and tourists alike, laughing, chatting, and enjoying the sunlit square.

From there they made their way toward a tour at Mission San Francisco Solano, the final stop on California's historic Mission Trail. The adobe walls, heavy and weathered with age, seemed to hold secrets that had lingered through the centuries. Leigh marveled at the thick adobe structure, a blend of Spanish and Native craftsmanship, and imagined the early settlers and indigenous peoples who had once walked the same ground. Inside, dim corridors stretched around them, shadows dancing along the walls as if the past were alive, breathing alongside them. The mission had been established in the early 1800s, a final link in a chain of settlements meant to extend Spanish influence across California. The weight of history seemed to wrap around them, filling the silent halls.

Their guide, Robbie, a local with a voice as rich and magnetic as the pages of a gothic novel, gathered them close as he began a tale seemingly meant for twilight hours. "Many say this place isn't as empty as it appears," he murmured, his eyes gleaming with the thrill of the story. He spoke of Sem-Yeto, a Pomo Chief, whose people had endured great suffering with the arrival of Spanish settlers. According to legend, Sem-Yeto's spirit had been seen wandering the shadowed corners of the mission, guarding the memory of his people's heritage, a restless sentinel ensuring their story was not forgotten. Leigh listened intently, the vivid imagery weaving its way into her imagination. She could almost feel the presence Robbie described, a spectral guardian watching over the mission grounds, unwilling to let time erase the struggles and triumphs of the past.

A chill ran down Leigh's spine as cool air brushed her skin. She glanced at the empty lot behind the mission, where the shadows seemed to shift unnaturally, bending and stretching as if unseen figures stood just beyond her vision. Marie, usually brimming with confidence, clutched her arms close to her chest, her grin replaced by a wary glance over her shoulder. "Why do I feel like something's watching us?" she whispered, her voice trembling slightly.

Alice, who loved history and mystery as much as the next person, was unusually tense, gripping Leigh's arm with more force than usual. "Maybe we should've stuck with wine tasting," she muttered, her calm facade giving way, just for a moment, to the unnerving sense that something unseen lingered around them.

Leigh gave her arm a reassuring squeeze, her own pulse still racing. "Don't worry," she whispered, forcing a smile that she hoped was calming. For now, she was just grateful that the combination of mystery and history had done the trick, pulling Alice out of her worries and into the thrilling unknown of a shared ghost story.

As they made their way back to the winery, the golden light of the late afternoon cast long, soft shadows across the vineyard, painting the landscape in hues of amber and ochre. The gentle rustling of grapevines in the breeze and the distant sounds of laughter from the winery created a melody that seemed to echo the wonderfulness of the day. Leigh felt the magic of it all settle into her heart, the vibrant plaza, the haunting beauty of the mission, and the laughter and camaraderie of her friends.

When they finally reached the cottage, its cozy porch filled with the glow of the setting sun, Leigh paused. She looked at her friends, Kay's face bright with excitement, Marie's laughter ringing out as she recounted the cheese shop antics, and Alice's thoughtful smile as she replayed the guide's stories in her mind. This day, Leigh realized, wasn't just a collection of moments; it was a treasure. Sonoma had already wrapped its welcoming arms around them, offering beauty, history, and the promise of adventures still to come.

# 4 THE ENGAGING EVELYN SINCLAIR

Upon their return to the winery, the ladies found themselves greeted by Evelyn Sinclair, the matriarch of the estate, a woman whose presence alone commanded attention. She stood with a grace and poise that Leigh could only compare to someone from a bygone era, a woman whose life had seen love, loss, and, perhaps, secrets. An elegant twist held Evelyn's silver hair, with a few loose strands framing her lined but soft face. Her eyes, sharp as they were kind, held a twinkle that suggested she had lived long enough to have her share of secrets, some cherished, some buried.

Her gaze swept over the group with an assessing warmth, lingering on Leigh just long enough for her to feel as if she'd been seen in a way she couldn't quite explain. There was a weight to Evelyn's presence, as if she carried the history of the vineyard in her very bones, and when she smiled, it was slow, knowing, almost as if she had already anticipated every conversation they were about to have.

Introduced alongside Evelyn were Will and Pamela, a couple from New Orleans who seemed as mismatched as they were perfectly balanced. Will had a booming laugh that echoed across the vineyards, his voice rolling over them like the Louisiana bayou itself, thick, warm, and full of life. Will's hearty laughter rolled through the group as they exchanged introductions. He had the air of a man who could make a stranger feel like an old friend within minutes, his voice rich and full of life. His hands never stopped moving when he spoke, punctuating his words as if he were sketching out the scene midair. Pamela, in contrast, was petite and a quiet energy, her observant eyes darting from person to person, as if cataloging every expression, every stray comment. Leigh noticed the way Pamela leaned in when someone spoke, as though absorbing every nuance, every pause. Leigh found herself instantly drawn to these two; their differences complemented each other, just as they each added a distinct flavor to the experience.

"Ah, so y'all are Sonoma first-timers?" Will boomed, a twinkle in his eye. "Well, let me tell you, you picked the right place. Pamela and I have been comin' out here for years, ever since we stumbled into the town on a whim. We fell in love—this place has a way of getting into your soul, doesn't it?" He took a sip of his wine, letting the moment breathe before adding, "Although let me tell you, there's nothin' quite like a New Orleans night to compare! The jazz, the food, the… well, let's just say we've got our own brand of ambiance down there, too!" He gave a wink, making everyone chuckle.

Pamela, quiet but attentive, chimed in softly, "It's true. A stroll through the French Quarter at midnight… there's magic in the air. I always tell people that New Orleans isn't just a city, it's an experience." Her voice softer, almost like she was letting them in on a well-kept secret.

Leigh exchanged a glance with her friends, excitement flickering between them. "It's funny," she said, tucking her hair behind her ear, "out of all of us, only Alice has ever been, and that was years ago when she was younger for a quick trip. The rest of us have never actually seen New Orleans." She shook her head, almost in disbelief. "I think we need to change that."

Will laughed, raising his glass to them. "Well then, ladies, here's to Sonoma now and maybe New Orleans next! And if y'all ever do make it down, let Pamela and me be your guides, we'll make sure you see the real New Orleans."

The vineyard tour began not with a formal announcement but with a quiet shift in the air, a subtle gathering of attention around Evelyn as she took the lead. She moved with an easy confidence, her steps unhurried yet purposeful, and the group gathered close, eager to catch every word. Evelyn's voice was rich, and each word held a depth that wrapped around them like the vines themselves, pulling them back to an era when the winery's history was fraught with struggle. "At the start of Prohibition in 1920, there were over 256 wineries across Sonoma," she said, gesturing to the lush vineyard surrounding them. "By the end of that bleak chapter in 1933, only fifty survived." She paused, fingers gently grazing the edge of a leaf, as if each vine held memories of those who had cared for it before. "We were one of the fortunate few. But it wasn't all luck… sometimes, we leaned on our connections. A bit of charm, a touch of defiance, and perhaps a few well-placed friends who looked the other way." A mischievous glint flickered in her eye as she let the words settle.

Kay raised an eyebrow, the glimmer of intrigue dancing in her eyes. "Defiance?" she echoed, her voice full of curiosity prompting Evelyn to go on.

Evelyn's laughter was soft but rich, like the smoothest aged Merlot. "Oh, yes. During those years, there were clandestine tastings. Guests would arrive under the cover of night, cloaked in shadows, slipping through secret doors in the cellar. Only those who knew the password or the right knock were granted entry." Evelyn leaned closer, her voice dropping to a conspiratorial whisper. "The Sinclair family may not have sold to everyone, but for those with a taste for the forbidden… well, our wines kept flowing, just for them." She winked, a playful, knowing gleam in her eye. "Certain influential friends made sure of that."

As they moved deeper into the vineyard, Leigh let her imagination take over. She could almost hear the low murmur of hushed conversations, the clinking of crystal against silver in the flickering candlelight. She pictured elegantly dressed guests stealing sips of contraband wine, their laughter a whispered defiance against the law. It was easy to get lost in the past here, to sense the weight of those who had come before them, lingering like ghosts in the vines.

Then Evelyn's tone shifted, tinged with something wistful. She began to tell the tale that had haunted her family for generations, the story of the missing Sinclair heirlooms. "The goblets," she began, her voice a touch softer, almost reverent, "are two antique silver cups, passed down through generations as a symbol of the Sinclair family's legacy. They were a wedding gift to my great-great-grandparents, cherished and used only for our most special guests." Her gaze softened as she described them, her words almost like a spell. "Intricately engraved with our family crest, encrusted with small rubies and sapphires… they're breathtaking. Or rather, they were." She exhaled, as if the loss still weighed heavily after all these years.

Marie's eyes widened. "So… they're lost?"
Evelyn nodded, her voice tinged with a wistful sadness. "During Prohibition, we hid them away, fearful they'd be

seized. And sometime in the 1930s, they simply vanished. Some believe a family member took them, hoping to sell them for a quick fortune. Others insist they're hidden somewhere on the estate, waiting to be uncovered." Her gaze drifted toward the vines, her fingers trailing absently across a leaf. "Finding them would solve so many of the family's current troubles. If they were to reappear, they could restore so much, our history, our legacy… perhaps even mend certain fractures in the family." Her voice was soft, but the emotion behind it was unmistakable. It wasn't just about the goblets. It was about what had been lost along with them.

Leigh shivered slightly, more from the tension that had suddenly thickened in the air than from the cooling breeze. She turned as newcomers arrived, Nicholas and Olivia, Evelyn's children, materializing as if summoned by the weight of the conversation. Nicholas, tall and sharply dressed, held himself with the kind of restraint that suggested a lifetime of guarding his emotions. His gaze flicked over the group with a cool assessment, his eyes sharp and unreadable. Olivia, poised and elegant, stood beside him, but there was something guarded about her expression. Leigh caught a flicker of something, resentment? Sadness?, as she glanced toward her mother. It passed quickly, but not quickly enough.

Then there was David Foster, a distant cousin and the estate manager, who had appeared so quietly behind them that Leigh startled slightly at his presence when he was introduced. He was lean, sharp-featured, his piercing eyes constantly moving, studying each of them with an intensity that felt almost calculating. He barely spoke, but his presence said plenty.

When Evelyn spoke of the goblets, Leigh saw David's jaw tighten almost imperceptibly, his eyes narrowing as though guarding a secret. The strained atmosphere in the

Sinclair family was palpable, the way each one seemed to brace themselves as Evelyn told more of her story, as if those missing goblets were a wound that refused to heal. Beside her, Marie caught Leigh's eye and raised an eyebrow in a silent question, as if to say, Did you feel that, too?

The conversation lingered in Leigh's mind as they walked, the weight of the story settling in her chest. There was an unspoken tension in the Sinclair family, a crack beneath the polished surface of their legacy. The missing goblets seemed to be more than just lost treasures; they were a symbol of something deeper, something unresolved. And though Leigh wasn't sure what that was yet, she had the nagging feeling that much of that story was far from over.

As the group prepared to part ways with Evelyn and the other guests, Will and Pamela, they exchanged warm farewells, lingering a little longer in the dimming golden hour light that softened the edges of the vineyard. Evelyn's sharp, knowing smile held a hint of affection as she wished them well, her fingers brushing Leigh's arm in a parting gesture that felt oddly intimate, as though imparting something unseen. "Enjoy your evening, ladies," she said, her tone both inviting and elusive, as if she herself knew the story wasn't quite finished.

Leigh turned, catching Pamela's playful wink, a silent acknowledgment of the day's strange charm and lingering questions. As they walked away, the vineyard stretched behind them, golden light spilling over the rows of vines, making them look almost endless. It was easy to imagine that secrets lay nestled deep among the twisting leaves, waiting, perhaps, to be unearthed.

Once back in her room, Leigh sank into a cushioned chair by the open window, the cool breeze carrying the faint scent of lavender and distant grapes. She reached for her phone and dialed Tom's number, knowing he'd pick up quickly. Sure enough, the call barely had a chance to ring before his warm, familiar voice greeted her.

"Hey there! How's the winery?" His tone, though miles away, wrapped around her like a favorite sweater, grounding her in a way that reminded her why she cherished these trips as much as she did coming home to him.

"Oh, Tom," she sighed, smiling as she looked out over the sprawling vineyards bathed in the soft light of early evening. "It's beautiful here. It's like I've stepped into another world. The estate is magnificent, rows of vines as far as the eye can see, winding pathways that seem to have stories hidden in every corner. And there's Evelyn… she's the owner, this fascinating woman who carries herself like she's walked straight out of a classic novel. She's part of the Sinclair family, generations of winemakers, and there's something almost regal about her, like she belongs to another era."

She paused, picturing Evelyn's knowing smile as she told them about the past. "She shared the most incredible stories about how her family survived Prohibition. They weren't just lucky, they were clever. Imagine secret tastings, guests slipping through hidden doors in the cellar, only the ones who knew the right knock or password getting inside." Leigh laughed softly. "And then there's this whole mystery surrounding these lost Sinclair heirlooms—antique silver goblets encrusted with rubies and sapphires. They vanished sometime in the 1930s, and no one knows whether they were stolen, sold, or just hidden too well. Evelyn made it sound like a legend, but I could tell… she believes they're still out there somewhere."

Tom chuckled, a soft rumble over the line. "Leave it to you to find another mystery when you are supposed to just be admiring the vineyards. You're going to come back as an amateur sleuth again, aren't you?"

Leigh laughed, sensing the warmth of his teasing. "Only if the case involves wine and gorgeous scenery," she shot back, already imagining the stories she'd tell him when she returned. Tom's voice was soft with genuine happiness for her, and it seemed like he was right there with her, sharing in her little adventure.

After they hung up, Leigh set her phone aside and stretched, feeling the sense of excitement for the evening ahead. They had dinner plans, an elegant little restaurant in town that she had read about, the kind of place where dressing up felt like part of the experience. It wasn't just a meal; it was a chance to step out of the everyday, to indulge in good food, good company, and maybe even a little of the magic that seemed to linger in the air here.

She rummaged through her suitcase, her fingers brushing over familiar fabrics until she found the outfit Marie had insisted she buy on a recent shopping trip. At the time, she'd doubted it was her style, but now it appeared perfect for the night. She slipped on the stylish blouse, a deep, rich mauve color with delicate lace details at the sleeves, paired it with dark, fitted jeans and a pair of heeled boots that made her feel unexpectedly elegant. She caught her reflection and smiled, surprised by how polished and put-together she appeared—yet still herself. Marie had been right after all and Leigh was grateful she had encouraged her out of her usual loose jeans and t-shirt.

Later, as they arrived at The Girl & The Fig, the warm ambiance enveloped them, the antique bar gleaming beneath soft lights and the garden patio twinkling with fairy lights. Fragrant herbs rosemary, and lavender, filled the air, mingling with laughter and the faint noises of the other diners. Leigh noticed a sense of calm settle over her, a reprieve from the shadows of what appeared to be tension lingering at the vineyard.

They each took their time exploring the menu, enchanted by the French-inspired dishes and imaginative cocktails. They started with a cheese and fruit platter, each piece meticulously arranged, a feast for the eyes as much as the palate. The colors were vibrant: the deep purple of fresh figs, ruby-red strawberries, and creamy slices of blue cheese that practically melted at the touch. A drizzle of honey and a scattering of candied walnuts added a hint of sweetness, rounding out the flavors in perfect harmony.

For drinks, Kay opted for a Sonoma Sour, the rich plum color glowing in the dim light, a slice of blood orange floating lazily on top. Leigh went with a classic French 75, its delicate bubbles carrying the crisp tang of lemon with every sip. Marie selected a spiced apple gin fizz, the frothy top dusted with a hint of cinnamon, while Alice's choice, the Watermelon Sugar Spice-y, was a bright pink concoction garnished with a thin jalapeño slice. Her eyes lit up at the first sip. "Oh wow," she said, grinning. "This could be dangerous in the best way."

When their entrées arrived, the choices seemed to reflect each of them. Leigh's wild flounder meunière, bathed in a lemon-caper sauce, was refreshing and balanced, and she savored each tender bite. Kay, embracing indulgence, selected the steak au poivre, each bite melting in her mouth as she sighed with satisfaction. Marie, craving something comforting, went for the quiche Lorraine, rich and buttery, while Alice, her mind still dwelling on Evelyn's story, twirled her fork absently in bucatini with clams, her gaze occasionally drifting as if lost in thought.

As they chatted between bites, Leigh finally voiced what had been nagging at her. "I can't shake this weird sensation about the tour," she admitted, tracing the rim of her glass with her fingertip. "There was something… off about the way the Sinclairs reacted when Evelyn brought up those missing goblets."

Marie nodded, her voice thoughtful. "Did anyone else notice how tense they got? Especially David, he looked almost offended."

Leigh exhaled, swirling the last of her drink. "It seemed as if he didn't want the story to be told. Or who knows," she added with a flippant grin, "it's possible they planned the whole thing for our benefit. A little theatrics to add an air of mystery."

She thought back to the moment Evelyn started talking about the old stories and the history of the winery. How Nicholas had stared off toward the vineyard like he'd rather be anywhere else, bored and completely disconnected. And Olivia, while saying all the right things, had a flicker of something sharper behind her polished smile, a flash of irritation that vanished as quickly as it came.

Alice chuckled, though there was an edge of nervousness in her voice. "Between him and the talk of ghosts, I think I'll need another drink just to keep my nerves in check."

Kay grinned, raising her glass. "You know, I bet that ghost tour earlier got us all seeing shadows in every corner. Pretty soon, we'll be expecting apparitions to join us for dessert!" Her light-hearted comment broke the tension, and they laughed, grateful for the chance to unwind.

Yet, despite the warmth of their laughter and the delightful meal, Leigh couldn't quite rid herself of that quiet sense of unease. There was a definite allure to the mystery of the Sinclair estate, a pull she sensed they each experienced, even if unspoken. Still, as they finished their meal, she tried to shake off the feeling, convincing herself that tonight, they were just a group of friends enjoying a wonderful evening in Sonoma.

When they stepped out into the night, the cool breeze carried a faint scent of roses from the nearby gardens, and they experienced an almost deceptive calm wrap around them, a momentary lull in a place woven with secrets. Leigh looked up at the twinkling stars overhead, reassuring herself that whatever mysteries did or did not lay hidden in the vineyard's shadows, tonight they were simply onlookers, four friends enjoying a beautiful evening in Sonoma, enjoying the beauty around them.

# 5 WHISPERS ON THE HAUNTED WALK

Continuing out into the cool Sonoma evening, leaving behind the warmth and lively chatter of The Girl & The Fig, the night seemed charged with an unspoken energy, like the air shortly before a storm. A shiver of anticipation ran through Leigh, not only from the cool breeze, but from the thrill of the night's next adventure. The Sonoma Plaza Ghost Walk Tour promised eerie tales and restless spirits, and she couldn't help but wonder what they might uncover.

Sonoma Plaza stretched before them, bathed in the golden glow of streetlights that flickered slightly, casting long, wavering shadows across the cobblestone paths. The square, with its historic buildings, carried an undeniable weight of the past. The scent of aged oak and distant wood smoke drifted through the air, mingling with the soft murmur of the few late-night wanderers still lingering nearby. Leigh's pulse quickened. Whether it was from excitement or unease, she wasn't entirely sure.

Their guide, a tall, gaunt man who introduced himself as Elias, appeared from the darkness, his dark trench coat and flickering lantern adding a touch of old-world mystery to the scene. His presence was both commanding and oddly ethereal, as if he belonged to another time. He wore an old-fashioned hat tilted slightly, casting a shadow over his face that left only the glint of his sharp eyes visible. His voice, smooth and deep, slipped through the quiet evening air like a whisper. "Welcome, brave souls, to the Sonoma Plaza Ghost Walk Tour," he intoned. His voice was calm, but carried an undertone of mystery that drew the ladies in right away.

"Tonight," Elias continued, his gaze sweeping over each of them, "you'll hear tales that stretch beyond the veil of the living, stories of those who linger, restless, woven into the very stones of this town." With a slight bow of his head, he gestured for them to follow, leading them deeper into the heart of the plaza. The lantern's glow wavered against the buildings, distorting their outlines just enough to make them appear like something was moving in the shadows.

Leigh glanced at her friends. Alice, usually quite fearless, seemed a little hesitant tonight. Her arms were wrapped around herself, fingers gripping the collar of her jacket, her eyes darting toward every flicker and sound. Marie, on the other hand, looked intrigued, though there was a small crease between her brows as if she, too, could sense something strange in the air. She stayed close, her expression a blend of curiosity and caution, her fingers tapping thoughtfully against her purse, as if processing every word Elias had spoken.

And then there was Kay, completely absorbed in her photography as if she existed in a world of her own. While Elias spun his eerie tales, Kay barely seemed to register them, her focus locked on her camera as she captured everything around them. Leigh watched as her friend snapped shot after shot, her lens lingering on the lamplit alleys, the cracked and weathered bricks, and even on Elias himself, his face slipping in and out of the shadows like something out of an old noir film. Kay had an eye for the unusual, always spotting details no one else noticed. One second she was capturing the broad, sweeping eeriness of the empty plaza, and the next, zooming in on something tiny but telling, a flickering lantern, a lopsided gravestone, the glint of something in a window that hadn't been there a second before.

Leigh nudged Marie and said, "You know, this is exactly how it started last time, right?"

Alice groaned dramatically. "Let's all agree now, if we stumble across a dead body again, we turn around and go to the spa instead."

Kay lowered her camera long enough to smirk at them. "But then, who would document and solve all the eerie clues for posterity?"

Leigh shook her head, laughing. "I swear, if you find a hidden message in one of your photos, I'm sitting this one out."

Still chuckling, they followed Elias as he led them through winding alleyways, stopping in front of the Old Sonoma Hotel. The building stood solemnly against the night, its pale walls almost glowing under the dim streetlights. Elias turned, his lantern casting long shadows as he began his next story.

"This hotel once hosted a guest who, as the legend goes, never truly checked out," he said, lowering his voice to a near-whisper. "A man who died suddenly, his last act unfinished—he had written a letter to the love he lost, but he never had the chance to send it. Some say he still roams these halls, searching… waiting for someone to deliver his message."

Leigh shivered slightly, not entirely from the cool night air. There was something about unfinished business that unsettled her in a way she hadn't expected. She glanced at Alice, who had pulled her jacket tighter around herself, her eyes flicking toward the darkened windows of the hotel.

Marie, sensing the tension, nudged Alice and said with a grin, "Well, at least he's not looking for a new girlfriend. Imagine the awkward ghost-date situation."

Alice let out a breathy laugh, shaking her head. "I'd rather not, thanks."

The mood lightened, and Kay took that as her cue to lift her camera again, angling for a dramatic shot of the towering hotel. She crouched slightly, tilting the lens to make the building appear even more ominous, catching the warped glass panes and peeling shutters. "In case our ghost friend wants a new headshot," she murmured.

They moved on, winding through quiet alleyways that seemed to close in around them, the shadows pressing down like secrets shared only with the night. Elias wove history into ghost stories, his voice rising and falling with practiced suspense, but for the women, the night had taken on more of a fun, spooky-adventure vibe rather than full-on terror. Alice still clutched Leigh's arm a little tighter than usual, though, especially when they paused in front of a centuries-old church.

"They say," Elias whispered, his voice barely carrying over the wind, "that figures appear in these windows late at night, standing silently, watching… waiting." Leigh felt the hairs on her arms rise as she stared at the dark, empty windows. Alice, biting her lip, squinted as if willing herself to see something lurking in the shadows.

Kay, ever the opportunist, took a step backwards and grinned mischievously. "Okay, huddle up. We need a group shot."

Leigh narrowed her eyes. "Why?"

Kay raised her brows. "Because, my dear friends, possibly we'll catch something looking back at us."

Marie rolled her eyes but moved in, and Alice

hesitated before finally cracking a smile and squeezing in too. "If something shows up behind us, I swear I'm throwing your camera into the fountain," she muttered.

Kay snapped the picture, then studied the screen with exaggerated seriousness. "Hmm. Hard to tell. Might have to lighten the shadows… perhaps zoom in a little…"

Leigh groaned. "Just don't call me at three in the morning when you convince yourself there's a ghostly hand on Alice's shoulder."

They laughed, the eerie tension of the night shifting back into their usual rhythm, half curiosity, half mischief.

Halfway through the tour, Elias stopped the group outside a stately, weather-worn inn with heavy shutters and ivy creeping up its walls. "This inn," he began, pausing dramatically, "is said to be haunted by a widow who waits and stands by the window each night, longing for her husband's return—a man who, some say, never left the battlefield." Right then, as if the story itself had summoned a response, a sharp gust of wind rushed through the narrow street, swirling fallen leaves around their ankles. The women instinctively huddled closer, pulling their coats tighter as the chill found its way under their collars. Leigh let out a breath, exchanging amused glances with her friends. There was something about ghost stories in the right setting that made even the most skeptical person feel a tiny thrill. It wasn't fear exactly, more of a nervous, buzzing energy, like the anticipation before the drop on a rollercoaster.

Marie broke the tension first, crossing her arms as if she was ready to take on the spirit herself. "If she's been waiting that long," she whispered loud enough for everyone to hear, "she ought to consider moving on, or at least getting a nice comfy chair." The group erupted into laughter, each of them a little louder, voices echoing in the quiet street as the nervous edge softened into genuine amusement.

"Oh, come on, Marie," Kay chided with a grin, "you'd haunt us for a lot less." She raised her phone as if she were preparing to snap a picture. "Besides, you'd make a fabulous ghost. Can't you almost see her, ladies?" Kay imitated Marie's dramatic pose, arm outstretched and lips pursed, making everyone burst out laughing again. Even Elias, ever the enigmatic guide, couldn't hold back a small, amused smile.

After their laughter faded, Elias took a step closer, lantern held high as he leaned in, his voice low and conspiratorial. "I have to say, it's good to see such fearless company tonight. I hope your time in Sonoma has been just as lively as this evening." His eyes glinted under the streetlight as he then asked, "So, where are you ladies staying?"

Marie, still grinning from Kay's antics, tucked her hands into her coat pockets. "Oh, a wonderful place called the Sinclair Winery," she replied, tossing a glance toward her friends with a wink. "It's been lovely, beautiful views, endless wine, and not a ghost in sight. Yet, anyway," she added, her smirk turning mischievous.

Elias raised an eyebrow, his expression slipping into something almost dreamy. "Ah, the Sinclair Estate," he murmured, his tone darker. "A beautiful choice. But I wouldn't be so sure about that ghost-free guarantee. You see, even the Sinclair Winery has its fair share of... peculiar occurrences."

The women exchanged curious glances and leaned in closer. Elias moved closer as well, his voice hushed. "They say that when the vineyard is quiet, lights drift through the vines at night, not flashlights, but something stranger. Orbs of cold fire, flickering between the rows, moving like they have a purpose. Some claim they're the spirits of the vineyard's original workers, still watching over the fields. Still tending to their vines." He let the words settle before adding, "Or perhaps just waiting."

A shiver ran down Leigh's spine as she remembered the vast, echoing cellar at the winery, the shadowy corners piled high with cobweb-covered barrels. The whole place had felt steeped in history, and in the dim light, she could almost picture those mysterious lights drifting through the fields, illuminating ghostly faces. She imagined the workers Elias spoke of, toiling away under the night sky, their figures fading into mist as they disappeared into the vines.

Leigh swallowed and glanced at Marie, who nudged her, eyes gleaming with excitement. "Think we'll see any wandering lights tonight?" Kay whispered, barely containing her anticipation.

Leigh smirked. "I wonder if we can ask for a taste of their ghostly gatherings if we do." She stifled a giggle, and Kay elbowed her playfully, rolling her eyes. Alice snorted beside them, quickly covering her mouth as if trying to keep her own laughter from escaping.

"Oh, and I'll be sure to get it all on camera," Kay promised, holding up her phone like a ghost-hunting tool. "And you," she pointed to Alice, "are definitely going first if we see anything."

"Why me?" Alice laughed, eyes wide. "I'm not volunteering to be ghost bait! That's Marie's job, she's the bravest."

Marie shrugged, smirking. "Fine, but if I get possessed, you all owe me your wine."

The group dissolved into laughter again, teasing and nudging each other over who would make the best ghost-hunting partner. It was comforting, this lighthearted banter, grounding them back in the present, away from the eerie stories Elias had woven so well.

As the tour wrapped up, Elias took a step back and

gave a deep, theatrical bow. "Ladies, it has been a pleasure guiding such brave souls tonight. May your stay in Sonoma be as rich in mystery as it is in wine." His eyes twinkled as he straightened, the lantern swinging gently at his side.

The women gave him a round of applause, their voices bright against the hushed quiet of the dimly lit streets. As they turned to leave, a shared sense of adventure hummed between them, a thrilling mix of laughter, lingering stories, and the undeniable possibility that maybe, just maybe, they weren't as alone as they thought.

In silent unison, they decided to end the night on a lighter note, strolling over to Sweet Scoops Homemade Ice Cream. The shop was a bright spot in the dim plaza, bustling with locals and tourists alike. The chalkboard menu boasted an array of unique flavors, and the smell of fresh waffle cones and sugary sweetness filled the air, lifting their spirits.

Leigh scanned the menu, her mouth watering as she landed on the balsamic raspberry. She took a bite, the tartness of the fruit melding with the cream, and couldn't help but close her eyes to savor the burst of flavor. Alice, still looking a bit shaken, found comfort in the rich salted caramel Oreo, her face visibly relaxing with each spoonful. Kay, always drawn to something bold, chose a mango-raspberry sorbet, a scoop as vibrant as her personality, while Marie took her first bite of A Lota Choco Lata, she proclaimed it "chocolate therapy in a cone" with a sigh of pure delight.

They took their treats outside, huddling around a small table under the shop's glowing awning. As they recounted the evening's ghost stories, their voices rose and fell with laughter, mixing with the faint sounds of the plaza and the whispering night, the warmth of friendship enveloping them as they recounted the night's stories, each retelling getting more dramatic than the last. The ghostly tales, once chilling, had now become part of the night's adventure, woven into a collection of shared moments.

When they returned to the Sinclair Estate, the night had closed in around them, wrapping them in a thick silence that seemed filled with anticipation due to Elias's ghost stories still fresh in their minds. Shadows hung heavy among the sprawling oaks, their twisted branches looming against the deep blue of the night sky, casting a dark beauty over the grand estate. The air was cool, carrying with it the faint scent of earth and distant vineyards. As they approached the mansion, Evelyn stood at the door, her elegant frame backlit by the soft glow of the chandelier behind her.

"Hello, ladies!" she greeted them with a knowing smile. "I trust you enjoyed your first evening in Sonoma?" Her tone was warm, but there was something else there too, an unspoken invitation, a promise that there was more to discover.

Leigh caught the subtle glint in Evelyn's eye, a flicker of something unspoken. It wasn't a warning, nor was it foreboding, just a hint of mystery left dangling in the air, like a story waiting to be told.

Evelyn continued, "Tomorrow morning, I'll share a bit about the estate's history. There's plenty to tell." Her voice carried the same ease as before, but enough was left unsaid, a deliberate pause that invited curiosity.

As she began to bid them goodnight, Kay stopped her and flipped through her phone, showing Evelyn the photos she'd captured throughout the day. "You've got an eye for beauty," Evelyn said. Her gaze softened as she leaned in, examining the images of the vineyards bathed in sunset and shadowed corners of the estate that seemed to hold secrets of their own. "I'd love to see how you capture my winery over the rest of your stay," Evelyn added, her tone filled with a warmth that matched the admiration in her gaze. Kay beamed, her enthusiasm bubbling over as she promised to send Evelyn all the best shots.

Their conversation drifted to the evening's tour, and Kay mentioned the ghost stories they'd heard about Sinclair. Evelyn nodded knowingly, a smile playing on her lips. "Oh, they're quite true," she said, with a faint glimmer in her eye. "Many of the staff, and more than a few guests, have had their fair share of strange encounters over the years." Her words had a weight to them, as though she herself had seen things she couldn't quite explain, and the subtle shiver in her voice made Leigh's skin prickle with anticipation. She found herself studying Evelyn in a new light, admiring her quiet authority over the estate and the way she balanced warmth with intrigue. Leigh couldn't help but sense a growing fondness for her.

Back in their guesthouse, the cozy rooms, comforting and warm, also felt alive with an unsettling energy. Leigh heard a faint tap against the window, a branch in the wind most likely, but her imagination conjured shadowy figures pressing close, just beyond the glass. The floorboards groaned underfoot, each creak echoing in the silence. Alice sat on the couch, eyes darting around as she murmured, "It's happening again, isn't it? We're getting drawn into another mystery." Her voice carried a mix of amusement and wariness as she glanced at Leigh. "Did those Savannah ghosts follow us all the way to California?"

Leigh laughed, though a spark of unease flickered in her voice. "Alice, I think Sonoma is just giving us a friendly welcome. Savannah's ghosts wouldn't cross state lines just to haunt us," she teased, nudging Alice playfully. Yet, the memory of Savannah seemed to hover close, as if their last adventure wasn't quite finished with them. Alice gave a half-smile, muttering about how she wasn't entirely sure she was ready for another round of ghostly intrigue. But Leigh noticed the familiar glint of excitement in her friend's eyes, a flicker of curiosity that hinted at her love for history and mysteries. Leigh had seen it before, back in Savannah, in libraries and dimly lit corridors, where Alice's love for uncovering secrets shone brightest. And now, despite her reluctance, it was there again, peeking through her apprehension like light through a cracked door.

Leigh knew this side of Alice well, the way her eyes would spark to life at the prospect of uncovering a secret, of piecing together fragments of the past. Even now, Alice's face softened, and she mused aloud, "Usually, I'd be all in for diving into the history and untangling the stories of a place. But..." she trailed off, her gaze flickering as if weighing her own reluctance. Leigh chuckled to herself, sensing that despite her friend's protests, Alice couldn't resist the pull of a good mystery. Perhaps a tiny adventure was exactly what Alice needed to reignite her spirit.

Leigh arched a brow, an amused smirk tugging at her lips. "You say that now," she said, nudging Alice again. "But give it a day. You won't be able to help yourself."

Alice groaned, flopping back against the cushions, but she didn't argue. They both knew she was already hooked.

Marie leaned back thoughtfully, her fingers tracing delicate patterns on the armrest of the couch as her voice dropped to a near whisper. "Do you ever wonder if these places keep memories of their own? Like little fragments of the people who lived and loved here, left behind to echo through the years?" Leigh let the thought sink in, her mind conjuring up the ghosts of the past—not the kind that rattled chains in the dark, but the kind that lingered in a small laugh, a fading perfume, the faintest imprint of a hand on a railing. She imagined the lives that had passed through the estate, the joy, the heartbreak, the whispered promises exchanged beneath the glow of candlelight. How many moments had these walls witnessed? And did the house, in some small way, remember them all?

She smiled, shaking off the slight eeriness. "Or possibly it's just these old places playing tricks on us," she offered, her voice light, though she wasn't entirely convinced.

They each turned in for the night, retreating to the solace of their rooms, but as Leigh lay beneath the soft weight of her blankets, the stillness of the house pressed in around her. She closed her eyes, willing sleep to come, but just as she teetered on the edge of slumber, a sound pricked at the edge of her consciousness. A faint shuffle. A whisper-soft murmur. The kind of noise that could have been the wind… or something else entirely.

Her pulse quickened, but she forced herself to take a steady breath. It was nothing. Just her mind playing tricks on her.

And yet, as she drifted into sleep, her dreams swirled with pieces of past and present, of laughter and loss, of stories waiting to be uncovered. Who knows, maybe they hadn't left all the mystery behind in Savannah after all.

# 6 A TRAGIC ACCIDENT

The morning dawned in a soft haze, casting a gentle light through the guesthouse windows, illuminating the worn wooden beams and colorful, hand-painted tiles that gave the kitchen a timeless charm. Leigh and her friends moved around the small space in an unspoken, easy rhythm. Each friend reached for mugs, stirred creamer, and quietly poured coffee with that kind of graceful ease only close friends could share. There was a sense of peace in the air, something familiar, not just from the morning sun filtering through the curtains, but from the comfort of being together in a space that seemed like a sanctuary.

As they settled around the table, Kay was the first to break the silence, picking up her mug and letting out a sigh that seemed to carry months of weariness with it. "I can't remember the last time I slept this well," she admitted, her voice carrying both surprise and relief, bringing gentle and understanding smiles to the others. "Maybe... being here, away from everything, will finally let me unwind." She paused, her expression shifting thoughtfully. "I don't know what it is lately that has me so worked up. It's like there's something I've been chasing. I have this pull for something more, something I can't quite name." Her fingers tapped absently on the mug as she looked away, searching for words. "I've just felt so… restless. It's this gnawing feeling, like I need something to shake me out of this routine, but I haven't figured out what that something is."

Leigh listened, her gaze softening with understanding as she nodded, recognizing the familiar ache her friend described. There was something about hearing Kay's restlessness laid bare that struck a chord, stirring up Leigh's own half-buried feelings about purpose and change. How many times had she herself wanted to push against the confines of daily life, to reach for something she couldn't quite define? This place, with its quiet beauty and stillness, felt like the perfect backdrop to reflect on those feelings. Perhaps Kay wasn't the only one ready for more self reflection.

The moment stretched between them, quiet and thoughtful, until Alice's phone vibrated against the wooden table, shattering the stillness. The sudden noise made Alice's fingers twitch toward it, her gaze flickering over the screen with a hesitation that didn't go unnoticed. Usually, Alice was the one who barely glanced at her phone, the kind to toss it into the depths of her bag and forget about it for hours.

Leigh raised an eyebrow, smiling with a gentle nudge, as if to ask, What's going on?

Alice only gave her a small, absent smile before glancing down at her screen again. She seemed torn, almost distracted in a way that Leigh was unable to place. Then, as another message came through, she got up, muttering something about taking a quick call, and slipped quietly out to the far end of the porch. Leigh watched her go, noting how unusual it was to see Alice so tense. It added a subtle ripple to the morning, an undercurrent of distraction amid the peaceful setting.

Inside, the room settled once more into a peaceful

quiet, each of the women lost in their own thoughts, savoring the warmth of their coffee and the shared stillness of the morning. It was one of those rare, fleeting moments where time seemed to slow, where the world outside could wait just a little longer.

Marie's gaze drifted toward the window, her eyes softened as they followed the morning light filtering through the trees and spreading across the dewy lawn. "This morning seems so peaceful, doesn't it?" she murmured. "Almost like the world's holding its breath." The others murmured their agreement, each lost in the stillness that wrapped around them. The morning mist clung to the edges of the garden, veiling the roses and climbing ivy in a dreamy haze, and the soft chirping of birds was the only sound punctuating the silence.

Leigh took a deep breath, savoring the earthy, familiar scent of fresh coffee. Her friends' quiet chatter blended with the natural sounds outside. But as they let themselves sink into the peaceful rhythm of the morning, a sudden burst of movement and noise near the main house shattered the illusion. The flurry of activity disrupted the quiet as staff members rushed toward the entrance, their hurried footsteps crunching on the gravel path. More unfamiliar faces appeared, their urgent movements and hushed, clipped voices entirely out of place in the otherwise serene estate.

Their coffee forgotten, Leigh and her friends shared a tense look before pushing back their chairs and gathering their belongings. Heartbeats quickened as they made their way out of the comfort of the guesthouse and across the lawn, the chill of the morning air sharper now. Curiosity and a creeping unease gnawed at them as they approached the growing crowd, a strange feeling of dread settling over them like a weight.

When the terrible news reached them, it came in

broken whispers and murmured fragments, pieces of a puzzle that refused to fit together. Snippets of conversation drifted through the crowd, the cellar... the stairs... no one heard anything... The words made little sense at first, a collection of scattered thoughts until one detail landed like a stone in Leigh's chest.

Evelyn Sinclair, the warm and vibrant hostess who had welcomed them so graciously, had been found dead at the bottom of the cellar stairs.

The authorities were declaring it to be a tragic accident, a simple misstep, but the words seemed hollow, wrong somehow, as though they didn't belong to the woman Leigh remembered so vividly from just a day before. Evelyn had seemed ageless, full of energy and poise, her laughter ringing out across the estate as she shared stories with pride and an almost mystical allure. Leigh couldn't shake the image of Evelyn's bright eyes and the confident way she moved through her world. How could someone like her simply stumble?

More fragments of the story trickled in from the hushed conversations around them. A staff member had gone looking for Evelyn that morning after she hadn't shown up for breakfast. The cellar door had been ajar, its heavy iron handle smeared with something dark, maybe dirt, maybe something else. And at the bottom of the worn stone steps, Evelyn had lain crumpled in a heap, her dress twisted around her, a single shoe resting several steps above her body. A fall, they said. But something about it felt... off.

Leigh felt a shiver run down her spine, a mix of disbelief and sorrow that left her unsteady. As the reality of the news settled around them, Officer James McBride approached them. He was a tall man, his calm, sturdy presence offering a brief sense of reassurance amidst the chaos. His navy-blue uniform lent him an air of authority, but it was his gentle, steady gaze that helped ease the tension. After ushering them into a quiet corner in the house, he asked the ladies about their evening, their movements, if they'd seen or heard anything unusual.

Leigh and her friends did their best to answer, each recalling how they had returned late from the day's adventures, Evelyn's voice still echoing in their minds as she had made small talk with them and then bid them goodnight with that same enchanting warmth they admired. Her words had been casual, her goodbye nothing more than a promise to see them in the morning. The broken promise now left an eerie emptiness. Leigh glanced around at her friends, seeing the same troubled expressions on their faces. Something just wasn't right.

In the midst of the chaos and questioning, they crossed paths with Will and Pamela, the couple they had met on the winery tour the previous day. Pamela's hand trembled as she gripped Will's arm, her face pale, her eyes red-rimmed with disbelief. "Evelyn was so... so radiant yesterday. I can't believe it," she murmured, her voice cracking. Will's expression was tight, his gaze unfocused as he looked toward the main part of the house. "Doesn't make sense," he muttered under his breath, casting a wary glance around. "She was too full of life." Leigh felt a swell of sadness at their words, the unspoken questions lingering between them like a fog. How could someone so vibrant simply be gone?

David Foster, the estate manager, was also questioned, but his demeanor was starkly different from anyone else. While others seemed shaken, David's expression was oddly distant. His gaze flickered, never quite meeting anyone's eyes, and when he spoke, his responses were clipped, as though he were choosing each word with precision, his voice carrying an edge of something she couldn't quite place, was it grief, or was it something else?

"It's just… an unfortunate accident," he muttered, the words barely above a whisper.

Kay leaned in, her voice hushed. "Poor man. He must be devastated."

Marie nodded, though her brow remained furrowed. "He's probably in shock." Still, her eyes lingered on David, as if something about him didn't quite sit right.

Once the authorities had gathered what they needed from the rest of staff and guests, Nicholas Sinclair himself entered the room, his presence casting a shadow over the already somber gathering. Leigh noticed a stiffness in his movements, the way his shoulders were drawn, his face etched with lines of grief and tension she hadn't seen before. There was a heavy sense of duty that now seemed to weigh on him as he approached them.

"I wanted to see how you're holding up," he said quietly, his voice rough with emotion.

Leigh stepped forward, offering a comforting hand on his arm, filled with sadness for the man who had lost so much. "We're so sorry for your loss, Nicholas. Evelyn made such a beautiful impression on us. We'll never forget her kindness," she said softly, hoping to offer him even a sliver of comfort in the face of so much pain.

Nicholas nodded, a flicker of gratitude crossing his face, though his gaze remained distant, as if he were somewhere else entirely. "Thank you. The authorities believe it was just a tragic accident. I suppose… things like this happen," he said, his voice trailing off, leaving an uncomfortable silence in its wake. As he turned away to leave, Leigh caught a fleeting expression on his face—a bit of something dark crossing his expression. Not just grief. Not just loss.

Something else.

Guilt? Regret?

She couldn't be sure, but a chill crept up her spine. Her intuition stirred, quiet but insistent.

After Nicholas left, silence hung heavy over the friends as they exchanged uneasy glances. Leigh could see the same troubled thoughts reflected in their eyes, the creeping sense that something was profoundly amiss. Kay, usually the first one to brush off negativity, was the first to voice it, her expression torn. "I wanted a break from the ordinary, but not like this," she murmured, her tone hushed as though afraid the walls might overhear her discomfort. Leigh could tell that Kay was grappling with her own unease, caught between the thrill of adventure she had craved and the grim reality they now faced.

Leigh nodded slowly, her mind spinning in circles. Her thoughts twisted like dry autumn leaves caught in a gust of wind, scattering in all directions. "Evelyn didn't seem like someone who would just… fall or be careless," she said, her words trailing off as the image of Evelyn's vibrant smile from the day before flashed before her eyes. Evelyn had been so full of life, with a strength and grace that seemed unshakable. How could someone like that be brought down by something as simple as a stumble? It didn't sit right with Leigh.

Marie, the most rational one among them, tried to inject some reason, her voice soft but steady. "Accidents happen," she offered, though her gaze betrayed a flicker of doubt. "It's probably just one of those awful occurrences. We shouldn't turn this into something it's not." She looked around at each of them, as if trying to reassure not only her friends but herself. Marie's words hung in the air, but Leigh could tell by the tightness in her shoulders, the way she crossed her arms, that she herself wasn't entirely buying into the idea of an accident.

Alice shifted in her seat, her usually composed face

pale. "What if it wasn't an accident?" she whispered skeptically, her voice slicing through the room's thick tension. Leigh turned to Alice, caught off guard by the fear in her friend's eyes. "Last night, after we got back from the tour, I heard… something," Alice began, her tone low, almost a confession. "My room faces the main house, and I could hear whispers, footsteps, too. It was close to the cellar, but just faint enough that I started doubting myself. I told myself it was just the house settling, or maybe the wind. But this morning, when I was on the porch, I thought I saw someone lurking by the cellar door. I couldn't make out who it was from that distance, but…" she trailed off, her voice dropping lower. "It didn't feel right."

The friends fell silent, Alice's revelation settling heavily over them. She'd already mentioned her suspicions to the authorities, but with no clear details to share, and having only just arrived at the winery, she couldn't be certain it meant anything. The police had assured her she'd likely seen the early morning commotion as Evelyn was discovered, but Leigh sensed Alice wasn't convinced. And neither was she.

A noise pulled them from their thoughts, and they looked up to see Nicholas standing there once more, his face drawn. He forced a polite smile, though his eyes looked distant, shadowed with something that seemed more than just grief. "I know this is all a shock," he said, his voice thick, "but if you need anything, please don't hesitate to ask. I hope you're able to find some way to enjoy the rest of your stay."

Leigh thanked him, her words sincere, but as he turned to go, she saw the odd change in his expression once again. Dread settled in her chest, creeping up her spine and leaving a heaviness that was hard to shake. Once he left, the friends shared a silent look, an unspoken understanding passing between them. They all noticed something odd, even if they were unable to put it into words.

David Foster's behavior gnawed at Leigh as well. As the last person known to see Evelyn, his distant, clipped responses lingered in her mind. The way he seemed so detached, almost too composed, it unsettled her. It was Kay who almost, though not quite, defended him, suggesting, "He seemed close to her, didn't he? Possibly he's just… upset." But Leigh noticed the doubt in her friend's voice, the subtle hesitation that told her Kay wasn't entirely convinced, either.

Alice broke the silence again, her voice trembling slightly. "Do you think… Evelyn's death might have something to do with those missing goblets?" she asked, her question landing like a stone. Evelyn had talked about them during the tour, her eyes gleaming with a hint of something unspoken, like there had been more to the story than she was willing, or able, to share.

Leigh experienced a chill as her thoughts seemed to edge towards a shadowy image. Marie crossed her arms, her jaw set as she tried to make sense of it all. "We promised no more mysteries on this trip, but… it's all so odd."

Kay sighed, shaking her head with a rueful smile. "Here we go again…" They exchanged a knowing look, tinged with the thrill of curiosity but weighed down by the reality of their situation.

Despite the tension twisting in her stomach, Leigh was unable to shake the sense of worry that now clung to her. She had worked so hard recently to learn to ground herself, to push aside that always present sense of unease when it threatened to overwhelm her. She knew she was capable of letting herself get swept up in worry about things that were not always as troubling as they seemed.

She hated that feeling, the sinking heaviness of it, and yet it was a sensation that had grown familiar in her life. She'd learned to manage it, to distract herself, but it was always so hard to brush off. She told herself to breathe, to focus on the present, to enjoy the moment and not let the unease grow into something bigger.

This getaway was supposed to be their escape, a time to reconnect, to recharge, to leave their everyday lives behind and enjoy a few carefree days. But, of course, they had always been the type to dive deeper, to probe at the unknown instead of taking things at face value. Their shared love for solving mysteries ran deep, an unspoken bond that had formed over countless movie nights, true-crime documentaries, and the stacks of books they had swapped back and forth. It had always been more than a hobby, it was their way of finding meaning, of seeking the "why" in every shadowed corner.

In a way, that curiosity was what had made their friendship so strong. They shared this need to understand, to see beyond the surface, and it added a certain spark to their lives. They'd always laughed about it, joked that their skills would put the pros to shame. But now, faced with a real tragedy that seemed mysterious, Leigh found herself wondering if they were in over their heads. Was this truly a terrible accident, a horrible twist of fate? Or were they glimpsing questions where none truly existed?

Seeking some escape from the weight of the moment, they gathered their things and slipped out of the guesthouse. Each step toward the car felt like a small effort to shake off the sense of sadness and unease wrapping itself around them. The usual lightness of their companionship was absent now, replaced by a quiet heaviness that seemed to cling to the air. They moved in silence, each of them lost in their own thoughts, the tension from the morning now hanging over them.

# 7 WINE, SUSPICIONS, AND SHADOWS

The drive to Buena Vista Winery felt like a welcome escape, a chance to shake off the lingering weight of the morning. The tragedy at Sinclair Estate still clung to them, a shadow that refused to lift, but the shifting scenery outside the car offered a contrast, rolling hills bathed in warm sunlight, vineyards stretching in neat, endless rows, and ancient oaks that arched over the road, filtering the golden light through their branches. It was the kind of peaceful landscape that normally left Leigh breathless, but today, the beauty of it barely registered. The air in the car was thick with an uneasy silence, each of them lost in their own thoughts, still processing everything they had seen and heard at the estate.

From her seat in the back, Leigh watched the shifting landscape as well as her friends' faces. Alice, usually the first to rattle off little-known facts about the places they visited, was uncharacteristically quiet in the front passenger seat. Her arms were crossed, jaw set, her gaze locked on the road ahead as if she were trying to will herself to focus on anything but the nagging thoughts in her mind. Next to Leigh, Marie was doing her best to lift the mood, making small talk about the scenery, the winery, anything to keep the conversation from circling back to the uneasy questions still hanging in the air. But Alice seemed locked into her thoughts, her voice finally breaking through Marie's light remarks.

"I'm telling you," Alice said, her tone steady, but with a hint of agitation beneath it. "David Foster's behavior has been off ever since we got here. There's something going on with him, I have a feeling about it."

From the driver's seat, Kay sighed, her fingers tightening slightly around the wheel. "Alice…" she started, her voice softer than usual, careful. "Not everything has to be a conspiracy. It was a terrible accident. Sometimes bad things just… happen." She paused before adding, "And David has been nothing but kind."

The subtle shift in Kay's tone didn't go unnoticed by Leigh, not irritated, exactly, but more defensive than usual. Kay wasn't the type to blindly defend someone, but there was something in the way she spoke, a quiet protectiveness, as if she had the need to shield David from suspicion. Perhaps it was because he had been especially attentive to their group, lingering just enough to be noticed, particularly around Kay. He never overstepped, never drew too much attention to himself, but his presence was always sensed, a quiet undercurrent, steady and watchful.

Leigh leaned back, mulling it over. David Foster wasn't outwardly suspicious, but there was something about him that didn't quite add up. He didn't have the effortless charm of Nicholas Sinclair, nor the easy warmth of Evelyn. He carried himself with a certain intensity, a quiet observance, as though he was constantly absorbing everything around him, weighing it all. What stood out the most, though, was where his focus seemed to lie. He was deeply concerned about the winery's future, he had made that clear, but strangely, there was little to no interaction with Evelyn's children, Nicholas and Olivia. Wouldn't they be just as integral to the estate's legacy? Shouldn't they be the ones he was concerned with? That small inconsistency lodged itself in the back of Leigh's mind, a piece of a puzzle she hadn't yet put together.

As they neared the winery, the tension in the car didn't quite dissolve, but the sight of the sprawling vineyards ahead provided a welcome distraction. The grand stone entrance of Buena Vista came into view, its historic charm standing in stark contrast to the unease that still lingered between them. Leigh exhaled, watching the golden fields stretch out in perfect rows, trying, just for a moment, to let the beauty of the place settle over her. The whole place had an unbelievable picturesque beauty to it.

The air was filled with the scent of the sweetness of ripening grapes. Leigh took a deep breath, letting it settle around her, grounding her in the present even as her thoughts flickered back to Evelyn's accident. She forced herself to take in the details of the scene, almost as a silent plea for distraction. It was serene, almost too perfect, but even this beauty couldn't completely erase the sadness simmering beneath the surface.

Inside the tasting room, it was all charm and rustic elegance, the kind of place that made you want to linger. Old oak barrels lined one wall, their surfaces polished smooth by years of use, their rich, oaky scent blending with the fruity notes of fermenting wine. The wooden walls were a deep, comforting brown, their knots and grain giving the space a lived-in feel. Overhead, beams stretched across the ceiling, their dark wood aged to perfection, adding to the cozy intimacy of the room. Leigh glanced at her friends, taking in the way Marie tilted her head back slightly as she breathed in the scent of wine, the way Kay ran her fingers along the edge of the tasting menu, and how Alice stood with her arms folded, eyes scanning the room as if taking in every detail at once. Candles flickered on every available surface, their golden glow casting shifting shadows across the space, making it seem almost otherworldly. Leigh was enchanted, captivated by the quiet opulence of it all.

As she took a long sip of her Chardonnay, the velvety wine running down her throat, she muttered to herself, "Are we going to get sucked into some mystery every time we go somewhere?"

Hearing the words aloud made her chuckle, the thought striking her as almost absurd. This was the type of thing that would happen in an old detective show, where the protagonist always stumbled into trouble no matter where they went, almost like something straight out of Murder, She Wrote or Psych. But as ridiculous as it seemed, she had to admit that a little distance from the initial shock of Evelyn's accident had helped. The tension that had gripped them so tightly was finally loosening, the sharp edges softening into something more manageable. It didn't seem quite so extreme anymore, just another chapter in their ever-growing collection of strange experiences.

Marie leaned in, nudging her with a smile. "You're not wrong. We're like moths to a flame with this stuff," she admitted with a small laugh, glancing around the dimly lit room. After a moment, her expression softened, and she let out a quiet breath. "But honestly? Aside from poor Evelyn's accident, this trip has been a welcome break from the chaos back home. I love my job, getting to travel, see new places, meet interesting people, but sometimes it's like a juggling act that never stops." She paused, swirling her wine slowly in her glass, watching the liquid catch the candlelight. "It's hard to be fully present with my family when I'm constantly being pulled in a dozen different directions. The boys are in high school now, and it feels like every time I blink, they're closer to graduating. I keep trying to hold on to the time we have, but it always seems like it's slipping right through my fingers."

Leigh studied her friend, her heart tightening with understanding. She knew Marie's job had always been a delicate balance between adventure and sacrifice, between feeding her own sense of wanderlust and the ache of leaving pieces of herself behind at home. And wasn't that what they were all trying to do in their own way? Balancing, adapting, chasing experiences while also desperately clinging to the moments that seemed to vanish the second they were fully realized. It was a strange sensation, wanting time to slow down, yet sensing the relentless pull of the future barreling toward them.

Their guide from the winery beckoned them toward a narrow, winding stairway, disappearing into shadow. With each step downward, the world above grew farther away, the hum of conversation and warmth of candlelight fading into an eerie quiet. The air thickened around them, damp and cool, wrapping itself around Leigh's shoulders as she descended, a chill that had nothing to do with the actual temperature. One by one, they stepped into the underground tunnels, their footsteps echoing softly in the stillness. The walls, rough and ancient, bore the weight of time itself, their jagged crevices and faint traces of moss hinting at years of secrets locked within the stone.

Sconces flickered along the walls, their weak glow doing little to banish the shadows that stretched and shifted unnervingly. The space didn't need theatrics to feel haunted, there was something naturally unsettling about it. She felt shivers crawl up her spine. This place felt as if it held memories in its very structure, memories that resided in the stones and seeped into anyone who dared tread here.

The deeper they walked, the softer their voices became, an unspoken agreement settling between them. Even their guide's tone changed, dropping into something quieter, almost reverent, as if the cellar itself demanded respect. "This winery," he began, pausing as his eyes flicked over each of them, "has its own share of strange happenings." His words hung in the air, weighty and deliberate, before sinking into the darkness. He turned slightly, casting a cautious glance over his shoulder, his expression one of practiced wariness. "Over the years, there have been… incidents. Footsteps echoing through these halls, though no one is there to make them. Bottles shifting on their own, as if nudged by an unseen hand. And some even say they've seen the ghost of a former winemaker, still lost in his work, long after his last breath."

The guide's words made Leigh's heart quicken, but her curiosity grew too, pulling her closer. She felt Marie sidle closer, her warmth a slight contrast to the cold air that seemed to seep from the walls themselves. Leigh felt her lean close, her whisper against her ear, just loud enough to pierce the quiet. "Why do we keep picking haunted places to vacation again?"

Leigh barely stifled a laugh, giving her a playful nudge. "Because we're idiots. Or maybe we're just hopelessly drawn to mystery and the unknown," she whispered back, rolling her eyes at their shared mischief. A grin passed between them, a knowing one, acknowledging the shared thrill that could become a signature of their trips. Somehow, when planning each getaway, all four of them always agreed on one rule before they ever picked a destination: if it was rumored to be haunted, it went to the top of their list.

Yet not everyone was amused. Alice's gaze remained fixed on the shadows, her face tense, as if she expected some phantom figure to step out of the darkness at any moment. She leaned in closer to the group, her voice just a notch above a whisper. "I swear, this place has the same feeling as Sinclair," she murmured, casting a wary glance around. "There's something spooky here, too." She hesitated, glancing at Kay before continuing, "And I'm serious, David, he knows more than he's letting on. Especially since he was the last one to see Evelyn".

Kay let out a soft sigh, her expression fond but slightly incredulous. "Alice, come on. David?" Her voice held a gentle, reassuring tone. "Do you really think he had anything to do with Evelyn's accident?" She shook her head with a wry smile. "He's been nothing but helpful to Nicholas and his family. Besides, he's intense, yes, but that doesn't make him suspicious." She met Alice's gaze warmly, friendship shining through as if to gently pull her back from the edge of her worries.

Leigh tilted her head thoughtfully, taking in Kay's words but unable to fully silence the nagging doubt in her mind. "Helpful, sure," she mused, choosing her words carefully. "But he does seem… invested in the estate's future. Possibly even a bit too dependent on it." She let her voice trail off, her unease subtle but undeniable. "I mean, who's to say that kind of pressure couldn't push someone to reconsider their priorities?" She shrugged, not wanting to come off as accusatory, but the suspicion lingered, casting its own quiet shadow.

Then, as if the house itself had been listening, a loud pop echoed through the cellar, shattering the silence. The sudden noise made them all jump. A cork had burst free from a bottle on the shelf, and the bottle itself tipped over, tumbling forward and clattering to the ground with a hollow thud, finally rolling to a stop just inches from their feet.

Alice let out a small gasp, clutching Leigh's arm, her eyes wide with shock. But then, realizing how tightly she was holding on, she broke into a shaky laugh, releasing her grip. "Oh my," she muttered, pressing a hand to her forehead. "I'm wound so tight, I'm jumping at bottles now! Someone pour me another glass before I have a heart attack." She shook her head at herself, her chuckle growing more genuine, the tension in her shoulders slowly ebbing away.

The guide, clearly enjoying their reactions, grinned and let out an easy chuckle. He waved a hand in the air as if brushing away the tension. "Ah, yes, our famous ghost at work!" he said with a wink. "Or maybe just a bottle that's had a little too much time to itself down here." He paused, eyeing the bottle with mock severity. "Or even better, perhaps it's the winery's not-so-subtle way of reminding everyone to buy another round before they leave."

The moment hung in the air, and then Kay burst out laughing, a light, contagious sound that quickly spread to the others. The sheer ridiculousness of it all, the way they had all collectively jumped at something so small, the way the bottle had rolled so perfectly toward them, as if it had been guided by unseen hands, was too much to ignore. The laughter spread like wildfire, first a few chuckles, then full-blown, stomach-clutching amusement. Leigh laughed so hard she felt tears prick at her eyes. The cool, dark cellar, once filled with uncertainty and hushed voices, now rang with the warmth of their laughter, pushing back the lingering unease.

"Maybe we should stick to wine tastings and leave the searching for mysteries and sleuthing to the professionals," Leigh quipped, holding up her glass with a smirk.

The others lifted theirs as well, and their glasses clinked together, the sound ringing out in the cellar. In that moment, the unease slipped away, melting into the laughter, leaving only the shared joy of friendship and the comfort of the present. They let themselves savor the warmth and lightness, their voices and laughter mingling as they leaned into the moment, letting the mystery and shadows wait for now.

# 8 GLEN ELLEN'S CHARM

With a final laugh and a warm wave to the Buena Vista Winery guide, the ladies stepped out of the cool embrace of the cellar and into the golden light of midday. Leigh blinked against the brightness, the warmth of the sun instantly wrapping around her. The weight of history and mystery they'd just left behind seemed to lift, dissolving into the crisp Sonoma air, replaced by a fresh energy that thrummed beneath her skin.

She caught sight of their convertible, parked gleaming under the morning sun, its red paint almost glinting as though it had been waiting for their return. This was exactly the kind of day she had imagined when they first planned the trip, adventure, laughter, and a little bit of the unexpected. She turned to her friends, a mischievous glint in her eyes.

"What do you think, ladies?" she asked, resting a hand on the smooth metal of the car. "Let's take this day top-down. Fresh air, sunshine… the best remedy for everything." She let the words linger, her voice light, but a deeper truth curled beneath them. Sometimes, the simplest things, wind in your hair, laughter with friends, a road stretching out before you, became exactly what a heart needed.

The others didn't need a moment of convincing. They piled into the car, their movements full of easy joy. Marie slid into the driver's seat, adjusting her sunglasses with a confident smirk before reaching for the ignition. As she eased the car onto the winding road, a gust of wind rushed in, playfully tugging at their hair, carrying with it the scent of sun-warmed earth, crushed leaves, and the faint sweetness of ripening grapes.

Leigh leaned back into her seat, letting the wind whip past her face, carrying away the tension she hadn't even realized she'd been holding. This, this feeling of endless possibility, was why she loved moments like these. The vineyards stretched out on either side of the road like rolling green and gold waves, each row of vines standing in perfect harmony with the land. Sunlight danced across the leaves, casting shifting patterns of light and shadow, as if the land itself were alive and breathing beneath the California sky.

She watched the scenery slip past, her heart swelling with something she couldn't quite name, gratitude, maybe, or possibly the sheer wonder of being here, in this moment, with these people. But then, a thought settled over her, Evelyn.

The horrible accident that had happened to the woman who had once called this place home lingered in her mind. Leigh knew she and her friends were all feeling the quiet weight of that tragedy. But now, as the hills stretched before them in perfect, sun-kissed serenity, she wondered if Evelyn herself was somehow guiding them, showing them the beauty of her home, her pride, her legacy. The thought sent a small shiver down her spine, not of fear, but of something deeper, connection, perhaps. A reminder that stories, both the joyful and the heartbreaking, lived on in the places they left behind.

By the time they reached the quaint, tucked-away town of Glen Ellen, Leigh sensed the tension from earlier in the day melt away, replaced by a more peaceful, carefree energy. She hoped the charm of the town would work its magic on all of them. Glen Ellen seemed to be holding its own quiet story, welcoming them with a rustic charm that seemed timeless, like they had stumbled into a piece of the past. Leigh breathed in, grateful for the slower pace. (She hoped the same would happen for her friends, especially after the hectic morning.)

They stepped out of the car for a quick stretch, eager to move their legs after the drive. The moment her feet hit the ground, Leigh took a deep breath, absorbing the sights around her. Cozy little shops lined the streets, each more inviting than the previous one. Flower boxes overflowed with vibrant bursts of color, soft pinks, fiery reds, deep purples, all against the warm, earthy stone of the buildings. Sunlight filtered through the trees, casting soft patches of light and shadow that seemed to dance as they walked.

Leigh took it all in, her gaze bouncing from one detail to the next. The cheerful awnings, faded just enough to make them feel like part of the place, stretched out over shop doors, as if inviting them in for a taste of what lay beyond. She noticed the locals sitting at little iron-wrought tables outside cozy cafes, sipping coffee and chatting in low tones, adding to the gentle hum of the town. A few tourists meandered by, holding hands or leaning close to whisper something to each other, lost in the peaceful charm of it all. The whole town seemed to breathe slower here, almost like it was telling her to breathe deeper, take her time, and linger a little longer.

As she glanced over at her friends, Leigh felt a surge of happiness. Their captivation mirrored hers. Kay had her camera out, snapping photos of everything, every cobblestone, every handcrafted sign, every little nook and cranny that captured her eye. Alice was practically bouncing out of the car, already scanning the boutiques with a look of excitement. Leigh could hear her murmur about the souvenirs she hoped to find. Sure enough, Alice would probably leave with something, she always did. Then there was Marie, nudging Leigh every few moments, her eyes twinkling with excitement. She had that playful gleam, the one that made it clear she was already imagining the fun they were going to have in the next store.

After wandering through a few shops, they found themselves chatting in the streets, taking in the sights, poking through antique stores and quirky boutiques. They weren't on a tight schedule, just enjoying the charm of the place. Leigh glanced at her watch and decided it was time to keep things moving.

"Alright, ladies," she called with a mischievous smile. "Time to hit the road again. I've got something even better lined up."

Her friends looked at her, intrigued, brows raised. "Better than this?" Kay asked, her camera dangling from her neck.

Leigh grinned. "Trust me! And no, it's not another shopping trip." She winked at them, loving the curious looks they exchanged.

Alice was the first to speak up, her voice teasing. "You're always full of surprises. Lead on, Leigh. We're with you!"

Marie clapped her hands together, clearly excited for whatever Leigh had up her sleeve. "Okay, I'm curious now. Let's go!"

Leigh chuckled to herself, watching them with fondness. They trusted her to take them somewhere worth their time, even if they didn't know exactly where they were going. That was the beauty of exploring new places, sometimes the best adventures came from letting go and seeing where the road led. With a wink, she started toward the car, leading the way with a playful, secretive air.

When they pulled into Jack London State Historic Park, Leigh could barely contain her excitement. She was eager to see her friends' faces when they realized what she had planned. As they parked, Leigh pulled the brochure she'd tucked in her purse earlier, a little grin playing on her lips. She handed it over, and she watched as their expressions morphed from confusion to shock, and finally pure, unfiltered delight.

Marie's jaw dropped as she read the brochure. "A horseback tour? Through vineyards and redwoods?" she gasped, her voice brimming with surprise.

"That's right!" Leigh said, enjoying the thrill of her successful surprise. She reached into the back seat, her smile widening as she retrieved a stack of wide-brimmed hats she'd picked out for them. Each hat suited its new owner perfectly, carefully chosen to reflect each friend's personality. Marie's was adorned with a cheerful, colorful ribbon, bright and full of life. Alice's had a charming polka dot band, quirky and a touch playful. Kay's was understated yet elegant, a simple beauty. And Leigh's own had a vintage flair, complete with a sprig of faux wildflowers tucked into the band, a nod to the romance of the countryside. She handed them out with a flourish, and they all laughed as they adjusted their new headgear, tilting the brims and striking poses that made Leigh laugh until her sides hurt.

They made their way toward the stables, and Leigh caught Kay sneaking glances at the horses, her expression a blend of awe and nervousness. She couldn't resist teasing, leaning close and whispering, "You know, Kay, I thought you were supposed to be the fearless one here!"

Kay shot her a look, half amusement and half genuine anxiety, but Leigh gave her shoulder a reassuring squeeze. "Trust me," she said, "If I can do it, you've got this."

It was a tiny bit of a lie, Leigh thought. She was definitely out of her comfort zone too, but seeing her friends there, ready to dive into this adventure with her, made her doubts disappear.

Their guides, Liam and Tessa, greeted them with warm smiles, immediately putting them at ease. They introduced each horse with such care, as though each one was a friend they couldn't wait to share with the ladies. Alice was paired with Luna, a gentle gray mare with soulful, wise eyes that seemed to study Alice just as much as she studied her. Marie's horse, Bella, was a sleek bay with a hint of mischief, playfully nudging her arm as if asking her to join in on the fun. Kay's match was Gus, a solid, dependable brown gelding with a calm presence that suited her. And finally, Leigh was introduced to Copper, a spirited chestnut whose fiery coat matched the energy she sensed bubbling inside her.

They all took turns posing for photos, standing next to their horses, at first hesitant, then laughing as each horse leaned in for a quick nuzzle or nudged them gently, as if they were part of the fun too.

Marie, who had never been this close to a horse before, was wide-eyed as she reached out to tentatively pet Bella's nose. "It's like I'm in one of those old Westerns! Only, you know, less rugged and more… adorable," she said with a laugh, her awe evident.

The guides patiently helped them into their saddles, making sure each one felt comfortable and secure, explaining the basics of handling a horse with reassuring clarity. Soon, they were on their way, winding through the path that stretched before them, a blend of wild beauty and serenity. They rode past rows of vineyards, the vines thick and green, their grapes glistening in clusters, catching flecks of sunlight that peeked through the canopy. Then, as they entered the redwoods, a hush fell over the group, the sheer height and majesty of the trees casting an almost reverent quiet around them.

Leigh glanced back at her friends, soaking in the sight of them, each one lost in the experience. Alice's eyes were wide with wonder, her usual quiet demeanor replaced by awe as she took in everything around her. Marie was beaming, her energy infectious, and for a moment, Leigh didn't recognize her, he was so caught up in the thrill of something new and freeing. And then there was Kay, who was gripping the reins just a little tighter than needed but still managing to snap photos of the landscape, her horse, and even some candid shots of the others. Leigh couldn't help but admire how Kay's determination to capture every moment seemed to push past her nerves.

The trail twisted and turned, offering breathtaking views with each bend, a hillside covered in golden vines, then a thicket of redwoods. The sunlight filtered through the towering branches, dappling the ground in a warm, honeyed glow that Leigh found herself savoring. It was as if time had slowed, each step of the horses marking a moment to be savored, every sound of nature merging into a soft, calming symphony.

When they reached a quiet stretch of the trail, Kay let out a nervous laugh, holding onto her reins as though they were her lifeline. "Leigh, if I get thrown off, I'm blaming you!" she called, her voice a mixture of laughter and nerves.

Leigh couldn't help but chuckle, calling back over her shoulder, "Just hold on tight! And remember, you're the one who was begging for new adventures, right?" They shared a laugh, and Leigh could see the tension melting from Kay's shoulders, even if just a little.

After a few more turns, they paused for a break, letting the horses rest as the group shared stories of the ride so far. Alice, always observant, pointed to an old carving on one of the redwoods. "Look at this," she said, tracing her fingers over the faded date carved into the bark. "It's like a little piece of history, just hidden out here."

The ride eventually wound down, and they arrived at VJB Cellars, their destination. They slid off their horses, laughing and chatting, cheeks flushed from the excitement and sunshine. Some were still brushing away bits of imagined dust, but the memories of the ride were already settling in as treasured ones. The group quickly settled into a comfortable lounge area for a wine tasting, their laughter blending with the clink of glasses.

"Alright, who loved the ride?" Leigh asked, as they each took their first sip of wine.

"I do think I could get used to horseback riding," Marie said, grinning. "And those redwoods? They were magical."

Kay raised her glass, looking quite proud of herself for sticking with it. "I'm just glad I survived without being thrown off."

"I'll drink to that," Alice added with a smile.

Just when they thought the surprises were over, Leigh had one last secret up her sleeve. As they pulled away from VJB Cellars, laughing and talking about the ride, she slid into the passenger seat beside Marie. Her grin was nearly impossible to hide, the glint in her eyes telling Marie that something was coming.

"Alright, Marie, just drive," Leigh said with a grin that was full of mischief. Her voice dropped a little, playful authority in her tone. "And no guessing. I mean it." She crossed her arms, giving her friend a look that said, I'm serious, though deep down, she knew Marie's curiosity was already on fire.

Marie's gaze flicked over to her, and though she didn't say anything, her raised eyebrow said it all. She was dying to know.

As they wound their way through the quiet, sun-dappled roads toward Santa Rosa, Leigh sensed her own excitement building. Every twist and turn through the peaceful countryside seemed to add a layer of suspense. The countryside, with its rolling hills and vineyards, seemed to wrap them in a peaceful kind of quiet. But for Leigh, her mind was full of memories, especially from those past conversations with Marie. She had remembered those little clues Marie had dropped over the years—the love of Peanuts that had followed her since childhood, the Snoopy graphics on her Apple Watch, the way her face softened at even the slightest mention of Charles Schulz.

Finally, after what seemed like hours of anticipation, they pulled into a parking lot. Leigh stole a glance at Marie, who was still focused on the road. The moment the giant statues appeared ahead, Leigh's heart did a little flip as she saw Marie's eyes widen in surprise. Across the lot, larger-than-life Peanuts characters greeted them with open arms: Snoopy, Charlie Brown, Lucy. Marie's hand flew to her mouth, and her jaw dropped, a gasp escaping her that seemed filled with both shock and pure, unfiltered joy. She was nearly trembling, her eyes glossy as she took in the statues as if she'd stumbled upon a piece of her own history, magically brought to life.

"Leigh," Marie whispered, her voice breaking with laughter and something deeper, something almost reverent. "Are you kidding me?" Her gaze shifted from the statues back to Leigh, a glimmer of childhood wonder flashing across her face. "This… this is amazing. I grew up on Peanuts! Look at Snoopy!" Her excitement was palpable, her joy infectious.

Marie's face softened with gratitude, a mix of shock and joy that was completely infectious. "This... this is perfect," she whispered, as she took it all in. "Thank you, Leigh. Seriously."

As they stepped into the Charles Schulz Museum, it was like stepping into a time machine, one that transported them straight to the heart of childhood memories and pure nostalgia. The walls were alive with original Peanuts artwork, the kind that seemed like they were catching glimpses of the very soul of Charles Schulz. Comic strips framed in vintage wood hung like priceless relics, each one telling a story that was both timeless and deeply personal. Marie moved from exhibit to exhibit with visible joy, her fingers lightly grazing the edges of each frame as if touching them might make the memories tangible. She shared stories about her favorite comic strips, her voice soft with fondness, recounting moments she'd read and reread as a child.

In one particular gallery, Marie's excitement peaked when she spotted a rare first-edition Peanuts book behind glass. Her eyes sparkled as she leaned in close, a smile lighting up her entire face. "I can't believe I'm actually seeing this!" she whispered, almost as if speaking too loudly would shatter the magic of finding it. Leigh experienced a wave of warmth, seeing her friend so immersed in a world that clearly held a place in her heart.

At one point, they came across a life-sized Lucy's psychiatric help stand, a bright yellow booth with the iconic "The Doctor is In" sign. Alice seized the opportunity, playfully jumping behind it, insisting on "diagnosing" each of them with mock seriousness. When Leigh stepped up, Alice leaned forward with a feigned air of professionalism, tapping her chin in exaggerated thought. "Hmm... an addiction to surprises, Leigh? I think we've finally figured you out," she teased, making them all laugh until tears glistened in the corners of their eyes. Leigh played along, protesting her "diagnosis" with a dramatic eye roll, but inside, she felt a joy that words couldn't capture.

Leaving the museum, they were in high spirits, all of them laughing as they walked through the doors into the fading sunlight. Leigh took a moment to watch her friends' faces, flush with excitement, their eyes sparkling with the joy of the day. There was something about seeing them like this, so free, so happy, with that childlike wonder still glowing in their faces, that made Leigh's heart swell with gratitude. Today had started with a somber reminder of life's fleeting nature, but in this moment, it was like they had all gained a quiet recognition of the preciousness of time, the beauty of living in the moment, and how important it was to enjoy every bit of it, no matter how big or small.

As they walked toward the car, Leigh glanced at the sunset, casting long, inviting shadows across the parking lot. It seemed like the world itself was giving them one last embrace for the day. Tomorrow would bring more adventures, more memories to make, but for now, Leigh let herself stay in the moment, capturing every smile, every laugh, every glimmer of joy, holding onto them like treasures, etched as deeply as the shadows of the redwoods they had left behind.

# 9 A SHOWDOWN WITH DAVID

The drive back to the estate offered an easy quiet, the kind that only existed between people who didn't need to fill the silence. Each of them settled into their seats, their thoughts lingering somewhere between the events of the day and the warm promise of an evening unwinding. The gentle hum of the tires against the road, the rhythmic sway of the car, it was all so soothing. Leigh let her mind drift, experiencing that familiar, happy exhaustion that came after a full day of exploring with friends.

They talked in the way close friends do, their conversation meandering, easy. Souvenirs became their latest topic, each trinket they'd picked up a little anchor to a memory. Marie held up a delicate glass ornament, shaped like a tiny wine bottle, the light catching in its curves, making it sparkle. "Isn't it perfect?" she said. "This Christmas, it's going front and center on my tree." Leigh pictured it nestled between twinkling lights, bringing Marie right back to this trip every time she saw it.

Kay carefully cradled a bottle of locally made olive oil, turning it over in her hands as if she could already taste it drizzled over a fresh salad. "I'm sending this to my sister," she said, tucking it back into the bag. "She's going to love it."

Alice unwrapped a hand-painted ceramic bowl, her fingers tracing the delicate bluebirds circling the rim. "This is for my aunt," she said, smiling. Leigh knew she was already picturing it in her aunt's kitchen, filled with fresh fruit in the summer or possibly holding a steaming bowl of stew in the winter. A little piece of this trip, of this beautiful place, finding its way into her home.

As the conversation shifted to the Charles Schulz Museum, their energy lifted again—laughter spilling easily as they relived the nostalgia of the visit. Kay pulled out her phone, scrolling through their photos, each one a frozen piece of the joy they'd shared.

"Look at this one," she said, angling the screen toward them. It was a shot of an iconic Peanuts strip that had sent them into fits of laughter earlier, and seeing it again was enough to make them crack up all over. Another picture showed them grinning beside a giant Snoopy statue, and one of Leigh and Alice peeking dramatically around the edges of an oversized comic panel, as if they were eavesdropping on Charlie Brown and the gang.

"We should've been cast in the strip," Marie joked, flipping her hair over her shoulder with exaggerated flair.

The museum's gift shop had worked its magic on all of them. Alice pulled out a Snoopy keychain, dangling it from her fingers with a smirk. "For my husband," she announced. "I mean, let's be honest, mostly for me. But technically, for him."

Leigh laughed, knowing full well that Alice would probably claim it for herself before the week ended. She, too, had indulged in a small keepsake, a picture book of Schulz's art, capturing those timeless moments she knew she'd flip through again back home when she needed a smile.

Leigh's fingers absently traced the edge of the other paper bag in her lap, where a tea towel lay tucked inside her souvenir from the Glen Ellen shops. Adorned with clusters of delicate wine grapes, it would hang in her kitchen, a small reminder of this corner of the world and this wonderful trip.

But as she thought of heading back to the Sinclair winery, reality began to settle in—a gentle yet poignant reminder that Evelyn wouldn't be there to greet them. She had seemed so alive, so woven into the very fabric of the estate, that it was hard to believe she was now gone. Leigh still heard her warm laughter, remembered the way her face had lit up when she'd talked about the vineyard. How was it that they had known her for only a day, yet she had seemed like an old friend? She only hoped that Evelyn's legacy would live on in the vineyard, that her family would keep its heart and warmth alive.

Her thoughts shifted to David, the distant cousin who always seemed to linger right outside the circle of conversation, like a shadow on the edge of their curiosity. And Evelyn's children, Olivia, who held herself so tightly closed it was impossible to know what she really thought, and Nicholas, with that effortless charm that somehow seemed a little too polished, too well-rehearsed. They were all mysteries in their own way, drawing Leigh's attention whether she wanted them to or not. She knew it wasn't really their place to wonder, but the questions hung in the air, unspoken yet impossible to ignore.

Marie's voice cut through the hum of the car, her tone playful, but with that unmistakable glint of determination. "Alright, am I the only one dying to ask a few questions around the winery?" She tilted her head, eyes flicking between them. "Because I swear, if I get even the tiniest opening, I'm going for it."

Alice snorted. "Oh, we know. Subtlety has never been

your strong suit."

Kay laughed, shaking her head. "And yet, somehow, you always manage to get people to spill their guts."

Marie grinned. "It's a gift."

Leigh smiled, listening to the easy banter. She loved this about Marie, her fearless way of moving through the world, her refusal to tiptoe around things the way Leigh so often did. It wasn't that Marie was reckless; she was direct, unafraid to ask the questions everyone else only danced around. Where Leigh would hesitate, weighing the pros and cons, Marie would dive right in, arms wide open, ready for whatever came next. It was something Leigh had always admired, something she sometimes wished she had a little more of.

As they turned into the long driveway leading up to the estate, the laughter quieted, fading into the hush of the approaching evening. The late-day sun stretched their shadows long across the gravel, and for the first time, the vineyard didn't seem as inviting as it had before. The rolling hills, once so golden and warm in the afternoon light, seemed darker now, the vines shifting in the breeze like something restless. The house itself stood against the sky, just as beautiful as before, but there was a stillness to it now, something right beneath the surface that made Leigh's stomach tighten.

She glanced at her friends. No one said anything, but she could tell they felt it too, that subtle shift in the air, the weight of something just out of reach. Perhaps it was nothing. Possibly it was just the exhaustion of the day settling over them. Or maybe, just maybe, the secrets of this place weren't quite ready to stay buried.

The gravel crunched softly beneath their feet as they made their way toward the main house, the easy laughter from the car ride now a fading memory. Leigh adjusted the strap of her bag on her shoulder, glancing up at the grand estate before them.

Near the entrance of the tasting room, David stood with a rigid posture, his eyes on them as they approached. He was waiting, but his smile from their first meeting was gone. His face was unreadable, his gaze sharp, almost wary. Leigh studied him, trying to decipher the emotions hidden behind his expression. What was it? His stance, shoulders squared, gave him a guarded air, like he was bracing himself for something that hadn't yet been said.

Marie didn't hesitate. She had never been one to tiptoe around the truth, and tonight was no different. "David, we want to talk about Evelyn." Her voice was steady, firm, but not unkind. There was something in her tone, an understanding, quiet patience that made it clear she wasn't there to accuse, just to listen.

Leigh stole a glance at her friends, catching their surprised expressions. They had expected this conversation, but not so soon, and not with such directness. Still, none of them looked away. They had all felt it, that undercurrent of something unsaid, waiting to break free.

David's jaw tightened, his fingers twitching before he crossed his arms over his chest. He shifted his weight, looked down, then back up, his mouth a thin line. For a moment, Leigh thought he might walk away, shut them out completely. But then, there it was. A crack. A hesitation. A flicker of something in his eyes, like he was standing on the edge of a confession he wasn't sure he could make.

"There's nothing to discuss," he replied, his voice rougher than before. "If it's about this morning… it was an accident." His words hung in the air, defensive, adding weight to the silence that followed. Leigh could sense the tension thickening, like a storm cloud ready to burst. David's response seemed too quick, too rehearsed, and it left an unsettling feeling in her chest.

Kay stood a few steps back, arms folded tightly across her chest, her gaze watchful but uncertain. Leigh noticed the furrow between Kay's brows, the small sign that her confidence in David's innocence was beginning to falter. Earlier, Kay had been the first to defend him, convinced of his sincerity. But now... now, there was doubt in her eyes. Subtle, but there. The way she shifted her weight, her fingers pressed into the fabric of her sleeves, she was questioning things in real time, the foundation of her certainty cracking just a little.

Leigh turned back to David, watching the way his fists clenched at his sides, the knuckles turning white. There was definitely something off, his reaction seemed wrong, not just grief, but a kind of tension that seemed to vibrate through him, a nervous energy that hinted at something he was hiding. Leigh's natural instinct was to stand back, to observe, but the importance of the moment compelled her forward. Summoning a sliver of Marie's boldness, she felt the words slip out before she could second-guess herself.

"You're deeply involved in the estate," she said carefully, measuring each word, "and you seem... almost angry at something. Is it just the unfairness of it all?" She hesitated for just a beat, watching his face. "It's just that... Evelyn was last seen with you before her accident. Is there something else troubling you?"

David's eyes darkened. Subtlety, but Leigh saw it, the way his gaze sharpened, how his jaw went rigid, as if she'd just hit a nerve.

"I'm not sure what you mean by that," he replied, his voice low and sharp, defensive in a way that made the hairs on Leigh's arms rise. "I've done nothing but help this family. Don't accuse me of things you know nothing about." There was a bite to his words, a bitterness that clashed with the calm persona he had shown before.

Leigh's eyes widened slightly. She hadn't expected such a sharp bite to his words. She had thought he'd be sad, possibly frustrated, but this? This was something else. A wall slamming down.

"I wasn't accusing you of anything," she said, softer now, wishing she had just stayed silent. "I just meant …"

"You meant what?" he cut in, his voice taut, his shoulders squared.

Leigh hesitated. The way he was looking at her now sent a shiver of unease through her. This wasn't grief speaking. This was something else entirely.

Before the tension could escalate further, Nicholas appeared, his entrance almost too perfectly timed, like he had been waiting just out of sight, ready to intervene the moment things got out of hand. His sharp eyes flicked over the group, catching the tail end of the exchange. Leigh saw his polished smile falter for a fraction of a second, a tiny crack in his otherwise impenetrable demeanor.

With a smoothness that appeared both practiced and impersonal, he stepped between them, his hand resting briefly on David's shoulder, not a comforting touch, but a silent command, a quiet force meant to keep him in check. The moment was subtle, but Leigh didn't miss the way David tensed beneath it, his jaw still tight, his hands still curled into fists at his sides.

Nicholas's gaze was piercing, though he masked it quickly. In the next breath, his smile reappeared, but it held no warmth, just a surface-level civility that seemed as artificial as the too-perfect rows of vines stretching behind them.

"Let's go," he said, his tone clipped, laced with a barely concealed frustration. "We have some important things to discuss."

There was no room for argument. Without waiting for a response, he grabbed David's arm, not aggressively, but firmly, like he was corralling a situation before it spiraled. With a glance toward the group, he threw out a parting remark, his voice light but insincere.

"Lovely seeing you ladies. Enjoy your evening."

It was the kind of polite dismissal that left no room for further conversation, no opening for follow-up questions. Leigh, Kay, and Marie were left standing there as Nicholas steered David away, the two men disappearing into the estate, their retreating figures stiff with tension.

Leigh let out a slow breath she hadn't realized she'd been holding. The entire interaction had left a strange, unsettled feeling in her chest. Beside her, Kay's arms remained folded, her posture locked in a stance that looked more like self-protection than confidence. She looked as though she wanted to say something but held back, her lips pressing into a thin line. Leigh saw the exact moment doubt started to creep into her expression.

Kay had been so sure of David earlier, defending him with the certainty of someone who truly believed they understood another person's character. But now? Now there was hesitation in the way her fingers gripped her forearms, in the way her weight shifted from foot to foot. The conflict showed plainly on her face. Leigh experienced a pang of empathy, knowing how hard it was for her friend to reconcile the positive impression she had of David with the unsettling reactions they had witnessed.

The four of them stood there in silence, the echoes of the conversation still lingering in the air, heavy and unresolved. They turned to look out at the sprawling rows of vines stretching into the distance, their long shadows casting jagged patterns against the dirt paths.

As they turned and made their way through the main house, it seemed as if each step peeled back layers of history embedded in the very walls. Leigh could now understand why Evelyn spoke of this place with such pride, why she held onto its legacy. This wasn't only a house, it was a testament to generations of love, loss, and resilience.

Each room seemed to have its own presence, its own atmosphere that shifted as they moved through the corridors. There was an undeniable elegance to it all, a beauty that had softened with time but never faded. The mahogany floors creaked underfoot, their polished surfaces worn smooth by decades of footsteps. The wallpaper, though faded, still held traces of its former grandeur, its dusky golds and muted greens casting a quiet, timeless glow.

Family portraits lined the walls, their gilded frames catching the dim light. The faces in them frozen in time, some smiling with childhood innocence, others bearing the weight of responsibility. Leigh found herself lingering on certain ones, drawn to the unspoken stories behind their eyes. A solemn-looking man with sharp features and piercing eyes seemed to watch her as she passed, his expression unreadable. A woman beside him, likely his wife, had a softer presence, her gaze filled with something almost wistful.

In one room, a grand fireplace commanded attention, its stone facade intricately carved with symbols she didn't recognize. The mantle served as a shrine to the family's past, adorned with silver candlesticks, antique clocks, and an assortment of trinkets that seemed carefully curated over generations. Leigh's gaze lingered on a small porcelain figurine, slightly chipped at the base but clearly cherished. She imagined a child's hands holding it for comfort during a stormy night or a woman polishing it, bringing it back to life each time.

Alice, trailing behind, caught up with a burst of excitement. Her eyes sparkled as they entered a cozy corner filled with books and information about the estate's long history. "Look at this!" Alice called out, her voice breaking the stillness. She had found an album filled with old photographs, maps, and handwritten notes, telling the story of the winery's origins and the family tree, laid out with names, dates, and faded sketches of people long gone. Alice traced the lines on the page, connecting names and relationships with the enthusiasm of someone discovering a hidden treasure. Marie joined her, bending over the materials, silently reading names and dates, piecing together the family tree. Together, they wove a tapestry of lives that had built and sustained the estate through generations.

Nearby, Leigh and Kay found a pair of overstuffed armchairs near a large bay window that overlooked the vineyard. The chairs seemed made for moments like these, comfortable, inviting, perfect for quiet reflection. Leigh sank into the chair, letting it envelop her as she gazed out at the vineyard beneath the dimming sky. Rows of vines stretched endlessly, their leaves swaying in the breeze. The soft rustle of leaves mingled with the murmur of her friends' voices. She breathed in deeply, savoring the scent of aged wood and lavender that filled the air, enjoying the sense of peace that settled over her. Yet, beneath this serenity, a spark of unease lingered, a subtle reminder that there was more to discover here than met the eye.

Alice's voice broke through Leigh's reverie, pulling her attention back to the group. Her eyes shone with that familiar gleam of excitement she always got when reading about history. Leigh knew Alice must have found something intriguing.

"Listen to this," Alice said, breathless, gripping a fragile sheet of paper as if it held a secret meant only for them. "Apparently, there had been a scandal involving Evelyn's grandparents. Her grandmother, Beatrice, accused her brother, Edward, of stealing the family's prized silver goblets after a major fallout over the estate. He vanished without a trace shortly after that, the goblets, too."

Marie's eyes widened, drawn in by the story. "Do you think he's the ghost they say haunts the estate? Trying to set the story straight?" she asked, her voice dipping into a hushed tone, making the room seem smaller and more intimate. Leigh chuckled softly, but the eerie thought planted itself in her mind. She could almost imagine Edward's ghost wandering the halls, searching for lost trinkets and fragments of a life taken too soon.

The light began to shift, casting long shadows on the walls as the sun dipped lower. Leigh glanced around, sensing an energy in the quiet spaces between their words. Each shadow seemed to hold a mystery, each flicker of light a reminder of a story half-told. There was something strange about this place, a palpable energy, as if the echoes of that long-lost dispute between Beatrice and Edward were still alive, in the air like an unfinished song caught on the wind.

The weight of the past followed them back to their guesthouse, their conversation a mix of playful speculation and genuine curiosity. Even as they laughed and teased one another about ghosts and hidden treasure, the energy surrounding them remained unspoken but undeniable.

Once inside, they kicked off their shoes and collapsed onto the couches, the evening's events settling over them like a warm, heavy blanket. The guesthouse, cozy and inviting, like a haven after a long day of exploration.

"Alright, ghost hunters," Kay teased, stretching her arms. "Are we solving family feuds tonight, or are we actually getting some sleep?"

Alice nodded but declared, "Fine. But if a ghost shows up, I'm waking all of you up."

"Deal," Marie yawned.

Leigh lingered, staring out the window at the moonlit vineyard. She inhaled deeply, grounding herself in the present, even as her thoughts wandered to the past.

Eventually, exhaustion won out, and they each retreated to their rooms. The laughter faded, and silence filled the house. As Leigh lay in the cool sheets, the night pressing in around her, she wondered what else this place had in store. This story held more, she sensed it.

And something told her they were only just getting started.

# 10 UNCORKING CLUES AT JACUZZI VINEYARDS

The next morning, Leigh stirred awake to the quiet hum of a hairdryer coming from the bathroom, and from the adjoining room, muffled voices and bursts of laughter hinted that the others were already up and getting ready. With a contented sigh, she swung her legs over the edge of the bed. Her reflection showed the lingering remnants of sleep, slightly puffy eyes and creases from the pillow, but there was also a glow, the kind that came from late-night stories, good wine, and the promise of another perfect day.

They took their time dressing, teasing each other about bedhead and debating which sundresses would look best in photos. Eventually, they squeezed back into the tiny convertible, its vibrant blue paint gleaming in the morning light. Adjusting their sunglasses and tying scarves over their hair to combat the inevitable wind, they settled in. Just as Marie turned the key in the ignition, one of the winery staff jogged over, phone in hand, his broad grin infectious. "Hang on! I've got to get a picture of you ladies, seeing friends make the most of a vacation is a wonderful treat." His voice held a warmth that only deepened their joy, and as they huddled together in the backseat, arms tangled and laughter bubbling over, Leigh's heart swelled. She took a mental snapshot, too, of Kay's radiant grin, Alice's playful wink, and Marie's easy laugh. In that instant, a bit of nostalgia crept into Leigh's chest, as though these memories were already precious gems she'd revisit on quieter days.

The drive up to Jacuzzi Family Vineyards shifted the mood subtly, the laughter quieting to silent appreciation as the landscape opened up before them. A dramatic scene unfolded, with rows upon rows of grapevines tracing the hillside. The winery itself was nestled atop the hill, a grand estate with Tuscan-style architecture that looked as though it had been plucked from an Italian postcard and dropped into California. An expanse of olive groves sprawled toward the horizon, their silvery-green leaves shimmering in the breeze. The trees stood like silent sentinels, their presence grounding and ancient. Between them, bursts of lavender added a pop of color, their scent mingling with the salt-tinged breeze drifting in from the San Pablo Bay. Leigh caught sight of a few scattered fig trees, their branches heavy with ripening fruit, and the occasional flutter of birds darting through the branches, their calls a melodic contrast to the hush of the open land.

The scent here was something entirely its own, earthy and rich, with hints of sun-warmed wood, crushed herbs, and the faintest trace of citrus from the nearby lemon trees. Every so often, the wind carried the distant laughter of other visitors, blending into the rustling leaves, creating a peaceful soundscape.

Leigh took it all in, a wonderful calm settling over her, but something tugged at her attention. Alice, usually the one lost in nature, fully immersed in each moment, seemed distracted. Leigh watched as her friend pulled out her phone, glancing down every few minutes with a faintly troubled expression. Alice's brow creased just slightly, her fingers tapping the edge of her phone case as though debating whether to check a message or tuck it away. There was a shift in her usual energy, a slight hunch to her shoulders, a distant look that seemed out of place here, amidst so much beauty. Leigh had an instinctive pang of worry, but rather than a probe, she simply tucked the moment into her mind, a gentle reminder that everyone carries unseen worries. She only hoped that when Alice was ready, she'd let them in.

For now, she would let the tranquility of Jacuzzi Vineyards try to work its magic.

After wandering the winery's stunning grounds, Leigh and her friends decided they couldn't resist the idea of a picnic. The winery's kitchen offered an enticing selection of artisanal bites, and within minutes, they'd gathered an impressive spread. Armed with their feast, they meandered through the vineyard paths, the golden sunlight warming their shoulders as they searched for the perfect spot.

They found it under the sprawling branches of an ancient olive tree, spreading out a borrowed woven blanket in shades of earthy reds and deep blues that brightened the green grass below. Sunlight dappled through the leaves, casting soft, moving shadows that danced across their faces as they settled in, voices falling to a warm murmur as they took in their surroundings. Leigh ran her fingers over the blanket, savoring the sensation of fabric against her skin, the cool grass beneath, and the quiet calm that settled around them in the shaded nook.

Marie laid out their picnic, and when she was finished, the display looked like something straight out of a high-end food magazine. There was a wooden charcuterie board filled with creamy brie that oozed at the edges, slices of nutty Asiago, and wedges of sharp pecorino that melted into each bite. Leigh's mouth watered at the sight of dried apricots, one of her absolute favorite snacks, their vivid orange skin gleaming in the sunlight, alongside golden almonds and a little pot of local honey that glistened like liquid amber. Beside the cheeses lay delicate rolls of prosciutto and salami, and crusty, perfectly round slices of baguette. She spread a dollop of fig jam on the bread, layered it with peppery arugula and a slice of prosciutto, savoring the delicate balance of sweetness and spice.

The sandwiches were art in themselves, fresh mozzarella stacked high, nestled between roasted red peppers, with fragrant basil leaves peeking out. The smells, sights and tastes made Leigh feel like she had been transported to Italy. She poured herself a glass from a bottle of Pinot Noir, marveling at the deep ruby color, then took a sip, letting the wine roll over her tongue. It was smooth yet bold, each sip revealing layers of dark cherry, plum, and an almost smoky finish that lingered, complementing the richness of their meal.

Between bites, they began sampling a couple of the wines, passing glasses around and trying to mimic the wine-tasting gestures they'd seen earlier. Leigh smiled as she watched Kay swirl her glass with all the elegance of a wine connoisseur, then dramatically raised her eyebrows as she brought it to her lips. "I detect…hints of…lavender?" she announced, her voice as serious as if she were on a tasting panel. Her friends burst out laughing, with Alice rolling her eyes.

"Lavender? Really?" Alice teased, shaking her head and lifting her glass. "More like hints of 'you're making this up,'" she added with a wink, taking a sip herself and trying her best not to laugh as she squinted, pretending to ponder the flavors. Leigh had to laugh at her friends, their animated expressions and exaggerated gestures only adding to the joy of the moment.

The picnic seemed timeless, as though they'd stepped into an afternoon that stretched on forever, free from any of life's usual interruptions. For Leigh, this was what she had been craving the most from this vacation, the easy, unfiltered joy of friendship, the freedom of an afternoon that belonged to no one but them.

Their laughter rang out through the shaded olive grove, mingling with the distant hum of the vineyard's daily bustle. Between teasing each other and reaching for another slice of cheese, the conversation ebbed and flowed, dipping into memories from past trips, funny stories from home, and the occasional deep thought about life, love, and everything in between. It was like a moment suspended outside of time. But just as she reached for another sip of wine, a hushed murmur from a nearby table caught her attention. She wasn't fully listening until one name, clear as day, drifted toward her through the warm afternoon air.

Evelyn Sinclair.

Only a few feet away, a gruff groundskeeper with a face weathered by sun and hard work spoke in a low, conspiratorial tone with two winery staff members the ladies had met earlier, Rick and Laura. Rick leaned in, nodding knowingly as he spoke, and Laura glanced around cautiously, as if she'd been pulled into something forbidden. Her friends noticed the curious conversation as well. The ladies fell silent, pretending to be absorbed in their glasses, but Leigh sensed the shift, she knew her friends well, and there was no mistaking the gleam in their eyes as they caught bits of the hushed conversation drifting their way.

"She was asking all kinds of questions about those

goblets," Rick murmured, lowering his voice, but not enough to evade their ears. "Even had a huge blowout with David about it before…well, you know. Before she fell."

The four friends exchanged glances, each of their expressions reflecting a spark of curiosity. Alice's raised eyebrow, Kay's small, knowing smile, Marie's widening eyes. Leigh sensed her pulse quicken as her eyes darted between them. She sensed the air crackling, each of them silently agreeing that eavesdropping on this wasn't something they should simply brush off. She leaned closer, barely breathing, soaking in the whispered words.

"Think she really found something?" Laura asked, her voice tinged with disbelief and curiosity.

The groundskeeper scratched his head, glancing at his companions with a grin that seemed almost sly. "Old Evelyn sure believed it. Found some letters and papers, she said. She was close, too close, possibly. Right before, well, you know the story." He let his words trail off, his smirk shifting into something more somber.

Leigh saw Marie's eyes light up, her face barely containing the thrill building inside her. She knew that look; Marie was hooked, and honestly, so was Leigh. Before she stopped herself, she felt her legs rising beneath her, as if propelled by some invisible force. "Excuse us," she began, taking a step toward the trio with an apologetic smile. "Sorry to interrupt, but we couldn't help but overhear the mention of the Sinclair Winery. We're guests there and couldn't resist asking, what's all this about goblets and… accidents?"

Laura straightened, a smile spreading across her face as if she'd just been waiting for someone to show interest. "Oh, I'd be more than happy to tell you a bit," she said warmly. "I love telling visitors about the old stories of all the wonderful wineries around here! Evelyn Sinclair, well, she was convinced there were these goblets, special ones, hidden somewhere on the estate. She spent years digging through old family records, reading up on anything she could find. Supposedly, they're priceless. Perhaps even tied to some kind of secret within the family. She wouldn't let it go, even though David and others told her countless times to drop it."

Rick nodded, crossing his arms and chuckling. "David had a temper on him. I'll tell you that much. He was her estate manager, supposed to keep things in line. But Evelyn? She'd be out there with maps, letters, anything she thought might be a clue. She swore those goblets weren't just valuable, but that they meant something. Like she was piecing together some grand puzzle no one else could see. And David? He was constantly frustrated by her obsession, always trying to reel her in."

The ladies exchanged glances, their eyes sparkling as though each of them sensed a magnetic pull toward the mystery. Leigh couldn't help but feel her heart beat faster, the thrill of something hidden, something yet to be unearthed. It was that same tingling sensation she'd get from reading a suspense novel, only now she was the one living in the pages.

"Then she had her accident," the groundskeeper added quietly, his face clouding as he shook his head. "One day, she's right on the verge of some breakthrough, and the next, well…let's just say plenty of folks around here believe it was no accident at all."

The words hung in the air, thick with implication, and Leigh felt the weight of them settle around her and her friends. She glanced over at Kay, whose brows knitted together as she swirled her glass thoughtfully, her face full of skepticism and intrigue. "Okay, I'll admit it. Something's not right here," Kay murmured, her eyes narrowing with that familiar spark Leigh knew all too well.

Leigh turned back toward Rick, Laura, and the groundskeeper, offering a warm smile. "Thanks for the stories, and, of course, the wine," she said, keeping her tone light, though her mind still buzzed with unanswered questions.

"Oh, anytime," Laura replied with a grin. "And hey, if you find those goblets, you owe me a glass of whatever they were meant for."

Rick chuckled, tipping his hat toward them. "Enjoy your stay at the Sinclair. Just, uh... watch your step on those staircases."

Marie gave a dramatic shiver as they walked away, linking her arm with Leigh's. "Well, that wasn't ominous at all."

The group sat silently for a moment, each absorbed in the implications of what they'd heard. They gathered their belongings, clearing the remnants of their picnic, but their thoughts weren't on the meal or the views anymore. Leigh noticed the slight breeze that had picked up, sending a soft rustle through the nearby grapevines, as if the vines themselves were whispering secrets.

As they made their way back toward the main path, Alice was the first to break the silence with a grin. "Who else feels like we've stumbled straight into an episode of a new show called The Wine Detectives or something?"

Marie giggled, shaking her head, her eyes gleaming with excitement. "I can see it now, four middle-aged women, cracking the case wide open by eavesdropping on winery gossip. Solving mysteries with a bottle of Chardonnay in one hand and a cheese board in the other."

Leigh laughed, a genuine, heart-deep laugh that filled her with joy. "Here we are, just trying to sip wine and eat cheese, and suddenly we're in the middle of family secrets and heirlooms gone missing," she said, her voice carrying an incredulous edge that mirrored her friends' expressions.

Kay raised her glass, her smirk knowing. "To the four wine detectives! May our questions never go unanswered, and may we never run out of Pinot Noir."

They clinked glasses, each face alight with laughter, but beneath the jokes, Leigh sensed the spark of something real, a shared sense of adventure that brought them together. This new information had them all intrigued, a challenge of a mystery that united them beyond the comfortable routines of their lives. For now, they were the ones inside the story, living the kind of adventure they would read about or see on screen. And with her friends beside her, each of them ready for whatever lay ahead, Leigh was more excited about the unknown than she had been in a long time.

# 11 UNSETTLING BEHAVIOR

They walked through the grounds of Jacuzzi Family Vineyards, the gentle afternoon sun settling over them. The air was sweet, tinged with the scent of ripening grapes and something else, a hint of rosemary blooming somewhere nearby. With her eyes closed, Leigh could almost believe she was in the heart of Italy, far away from the demands of everyday life.

As they approached the courtyard, Alice let out a soft gasp, her pace quickening. Leigh followed her gaze and had the same spark of admiration. The courtyard was breathtaking. Stone walls worn smooth, timber beams above them catching patches of sunlight, and beautiful flowers draped along the edges of the veranda. It was as if every detail had been placed with intention, a love letter to the past.

Alice turned to them with an excited glint in her eyes. "You know, I was reading about this place earlier," she said, gesturing around them. "Valeriano Jacuzzi, Fred Cline's grandfather, was one of the seven Jacuzzi brothers who immigrated from Italy. They originally started out making airplane propellers, of all things, and later, they invented the Jacuzzi spa."

Marie raised an eyebrow. "Wait, the Jacuzzi Jacuzzi?"

Alice grinned. "Yep! But before all that, Valeriano was passionate about farming. That's why this vineyard exists today. It's a kind of tribute to his roots, blending his Italian heritage with the California wine country." She glanced around, her expression softening. "It's not only a business, it's a family's history brought to life."

Leigh smiled, taking in all the details. The winery wasn't merely a nod to its founder's family, it was a lovingly crafted tribute. Each archway and alcove seemed to hold whispers of family and shared dreams, each detail a reminder of Valeriano's vision. Leigh sensed a quiet awe, recognizing the deep respect woven into every stone, beam, and vine.

They wandered into the piazza, the heart of the winery, and Leigh marveled at the Italian charm. This wasn't some rushed replication but rather a deeply personal, true-to-life rendition of an Italian farmhouse, rustic and beautiful in its simplicity. She almost heard the echoes of long-ago gatherings, Italian voices carrying through the air, clinking glasses, stories told over full glasses of Barbera or Sangiovese, the warmth of family coming from the stone walls.

As they moved on, the ladies found themselves in the Jacuzzi Family Vineyards marketplace, drawn by the vibrant colors and enticing smells. The shelves were lined with jewel-toned jars, each one filled with something delicious. Fig spreads, citrus marmalades, tapenades made with olives plucked from the surrounding groves. Leigh's gaze landed on a display of Taste of Tuscany gift sets, the carefully arranged jars of artichoke hearts, roasted red peppers, and olive tapenades making her mouth water. She pictured them on her kitchen counter back home, the flavors instantly transporting her back to this wonderful afternoon.

Alice picked up a hardcover about the Jacuzzi family history, her fingers tracing the embossed gold lettering with something close to reverence. "They built all of this," she murmured, half to herself, clearly captivated. Leigh knew Alice well enough to see the spark in her friend's look; she was already lost in the story, drawn into the legacy behind the vineyard.

Meanwhile, Marie was at a tasting station, practically glowing over a spread she had sampled. "Lemon basil… roasted garlic…" she murmured, lifting her cracker to Leigh in a mock toast. "I would eat this on everything!" Her delight was obvious, and Leigh smiled, shaking her head as Marie happily reached for a second cracker.

A few steps away, Kay had found a bottle of balsamic vinegar with hints of blackberry and dark chocolate. She turned to them, grinning as she tilted the bottle in the light. "I've found the perfect addition to every salad I'll ever make, and possibly a few bowls of vanilla ice cream," she said with a wink. Her love of sweets was well known among the friends and Leigh knew it would be far more likely to be used on the bowls of ice cream than the salads.

Leigh selected a jar of sun-dried tomato and olive tapenade, imagining how good it would taste with a nice crusty baguette. The food, the laughter, the easy friendship, it seemed so right. Something about exploring a new place, tasting unfamiliar flavors, and sharing those small discoveries with friends always managed to pull her a step away from the routines of everyday life. It was like pressing pause on all the tasks and worries, letting her see the bigger picture of how full and beautiful her life really was.

They lingered a little longer, reluctant to leave the courtyard and its stories. The place had a magic of its own, making each of them feel part of something bigger.

As they finalized their purchases in the cozy marketplace, Leigh's face lit up when she spotted Will and Pamela, the charming couple they'd met at the Sinclair Winery. With their easy laughter and infectious energy, Will and Pamela were the type of people you'd want on any wine tour. Enthusiastic, kind-hearted, and quick to appreciate life's small pleasures. When the couple suggested joining them for an olive oil tour, Leigh glanced at her friends, who nodded eagerly. It seemed like the perfect spontaneous addition to the day.

While they waited for the tour to begin, the conversation naturally drifted to Evelyn. They had learned so much about her today, about her absolute devotion to the vineyard and her almost obsessive determination to find the lost goblets. Leigh caught the look of concern in Pamela's eyes as she spoke about Evelyn's quiet nature and how she had spoken briefly of the struggles of owning the winery. Alice shook her head, her lips pressing into a tight line. "It's always surprising how much people hide behind a smile," she murmured, almost to herself.

Leigh turned to her, recognizing once again the distant expression in her friend's eyes. Alice wasn't only talking about Evelyn. Whatever the thought was, whatever memory or thought had surfaced, she tucked it away just as quickly. Leigh felt sympathy, not just for Evelyn but for Alice too, for all the things people carried that no one else could see.

Will crossed his arms, thoughtful. "You know, I would think Nicholas and Olivia should be just as interested in finding those goblets as Evelyn was," he said.

Pamela nodded. "They are funny, though, their dynamic is a little... off, isn't it? Nicholas seems to be the one in charge, always the more forceful one in public, but…" She hesitated, exchanging a glance with Will before continuing. "Every time Olivia talks to him privately, she has this way about her, almost like she's scolding him."

Leigh considered their observations. Her curiosity piqued. It was subtle, the way siblings could have power struggles no one else quite understood. She hadn't paid much attention to the way Nicholas and Olivia interacted before, but now, thinking back, she understood what Pamela was talking about.

Their guide soon waved them over, leading them toward the olive oil mill. The aroma hit them first, an earthy fragrance that clung to the air and seemed to envelop them as they entered. Leigh took a deep breath, enjoying the richness of the scent. She loved olive oil, not only for the flavor, but for the way it transformed a dish with just a drizzle, elevating something as simple as crusty bread or roasted vegetables into something indulgent.

Their guide, a wiry man with an expressive face, began explaining the stages of pressing, his voice alive with passion as he pointed out the machinery and shared stories of the region's olive oil traditions.

"And here we have the real magic," he said, his voice lifting with excitement as he poured a small puddle of olive oil into tasting cups. The ladies each took a small sip. This first one was a Tuscan blend, grassy and peppery, bursting with an intensity that prickled the back of Leigh's throat. She blinked as her eyes watered a bit. Across from her, Marie gave a startled cough and a small snort.

"Oh wow," Marie gasped, clearing her throat. "That one's got a kick!"

That was all it took to send them into laughter, the kind that bubbled up uncontrollably when one person's reaction set off the rest. Leigh tried to stifle hers as she swallowed, but Kay had already dissolved into giggles, shaking her head at Marie's dramatic expression.

They moved on to a California blend, smoother, milder. Leigh closed her eyes as she sampled it, letting the flavor settle, noticing the way it seemed to grow stronger. Kay raised her cup with a grin. "This one tastes like spring in a bottle," she declared.

The guide, amused by their reactions, launched into stories of the intricate olive-growing process, describing the subtle art of balancing flavor profiles. His enthusiasm was catching, and soon they were discussing the nuances in olive oil with surprising seriousness, as if they were seasoned experts. Will joined in, humorously recounting a tasting mishap from a past trip that had them all roaring with laughter.

"One time," he began, grinning mischievously, "Pamela and I were at this tiny farm in Italy, and the host, gestured for us to take a 'shot' of this really special olive oil. Now, me, thinking I'm some kind of connoisseur, I go for it. Full gulp."

Leigh winced in secondhand embarrassment as Pamela grinned.

"He nearly choked to death," Pamela chimed in. "The poor man thought he had killed a tourist."

"I did not choke to death," Will protested. "I merely… reevaluated my life choices in real time."

"You turned so red I thought we were going to have to find an ER in the middle of Italy," Pamela teased. Their group burst into laughter.

Encouraged, Pamela added her own story. "Oh, and then there was the time my cousin mistook a bottle of garlic-infused olive oil for honey and poured it over her breakfast toast."

Leigh cringed and laughed at the same time. "Please tell me she didn't actually eat it."

"Oh, she did," Pamela said, smirking. "And then spent the next two hours wondering why her cinnamon toast had such a funny flavor."

The conversation continued to flow freely, each story weaving into the next as they sampled their way through the different oils.

As they all left the tour and strolled back through the vineyard, the late afternoon sun bathed everything in a rich, golden light. Shadows from the grapevines stretched across the ground, making the world around Leigh appear like a painting come to life.

She looked at her friends, hesitating for a moment before asking, "So, are you all still enjoying my itinerary?" Her voice came out softer than she intended, with an annoying touch of shyness creeping in.

Marie was the first to respond. "Are you kidding? We're obsessed with it! Leigh, you've done a fabulous job." Her eyes sparkled as she looked around, taking in the vineyards, the rolling hills, the beauty of it all. "It's so nice just to be here, soaking it all in, not working, not rushing, just…being."

Leigh smiled, her heart swelling with gratitude. She was aware of how hard Marie usually worked, always managing a dozen things at once. Seeing her so relaxed, so present, reminded Leigh of why she'd chosen each stop so carefully.

Kay was nodding emphatically. "Every place has been amazing, and they all seem like such hidden gems!" She let out a happy sigh, almost like a child seeing something for the first time. "I love how every stop has been something new, something I'd never think of finding. I don't get to travel much, this whole thing has been eye-opening."

Alice chimed in, a peaceful smile on her face. "For me, it's the break I needed. Just stepping away from the usual, the to-do lists, the everyday noise. This trip is a breath of fresh air."

Leigh couldn't help the warm surge of pride that filled her chest. What had started as a little passion, organizing trips, hunting down unique spots, sharing itineraries with friends, had blossomed into something that seemed like part of her soul. Planning these trips was like storytelling, like crafting a journey to be lived and remembered. She loved the thrill of researching, of finding places others overlooked, of imagining her friends' and others' reactions. Even the marketing, the social media strategies, the engagement with fellow travelers, the effort to keep things fresh and exciting, didn't seem like work. It was an art, a kind of puzzle she adored piecing together, and each trip taught her something new.

And yet, there was always that small voice in the back of her mind, whispering doubts. What if someone didn't love an itinerary? What if they left a bad review or felt let down by an experience she had carefully curated? So far, she'd been lucky. Every trip had been met with enthusiasm, excitement, and glowing feedback. But that fear of disappointment lingered, a quiet hum beneath all the joy.

Pamela nudged her gently, bringing her back to the moment. "You're lucky, you know. To have work like this."

Leigh nodded, a soft smile spreading across her face. Lucky didn't even begin to cover it. She was blessed, marveling at how life had aligned to let her do what she loved, alongside family and friends who supported her unconditionally.

As they said their goodbyes to Will and Pamela, the ladies wandered toward the veranda to gather their things, their bags full of carefully chosen mementos. Leigh stifled a laugh as Kay turned to the group with mock seriousness. "Ladies, after all this wine and olive oil, I think it's time for a little hydration and possibly a snack."

Alice chuckled, patting her stomach. "Agreed. We've been living the high life all day, time to balance it out a little!"

They drove back to the Sinclair Winery, savoring the warmth of the afternoon as they talked about the day's highlights and looked forward to the evening ahead. The plan was to relax a bit, maybe freshen up, before heading out for dinner. Leigh had an overwhelming sense of happiness as they walked, a feeling that wrapped around her as warmly as the California sun.

They arrived back at the Sinclair estate just as the last light of the day was softening into evening, casting a warm, golden glow over the vineyard. The ladies gathered their things from the car, chatting about their favorite wines, the olive oil, and the many little souvenirs they'd picked up. Leigh was adjusting the bags over her shoulder when she noticed Alice pausing, her gaze sharp, eyes narrowing toward a spot near the back entrance of the estate.

"Look over there," Alice whispered, nodding in the direction of David, who was standing in a small alcove near the ivy-clad walls, his back tense, his posture rigid. He was speaking in low, hurried tones to Nicholas, whose face looked equally troubled. Leigh sensed a strange prickle of unease as she watched them. The serene charm of the winery seemed suddenly out of place next to the dark undercurrent of their conversation. Now, an invisible chill threaded through the air, as though the very spirit of Evelyn Sinclair had swept through, pressing them to listen, to pay attention.

"What do you think they're talking about?" Marie murmured, barely loud enough for them to hear.

Leigh strained to catch fragments of the conversation. Her heart quickened when words like "Evelyn's will" and "estate" drifted toward them, as ominous as the approaching night. She shared a quick, startled look with her friends. They all stood frozen, caught in the eerie moment, as if Evelyn herself had whispered in their ears, urging them closer, daring them to uncover the winery's secrets.

Without warning, Nicholas's voice rose, breaking through the tension. "This isn't over!" he snapped, his voice carrying an edge of fury that sent a chill through Leigh's spine. His face flushed red as he stormed off, leaving David standing alone, looking drained and grim. Just as he turned to head back inside, his gaze flickered in their direction.

Leigh's breath caught. Had he seen them? She quickly averted her eyes, her pulse pounding.

"Okay, what was that all about?" Kay whispered, her voice pitched with excitement, a glint in her eye.

Leigh exhaled, glancing around at her friends. "How do we always seem to be in the perfect place at the perfect time to keep our imaginations and curiosity just piqued enough to poke into mysteries that may or may not be real?" she muttered, half-amused, half-anxious. Her voice wavered between excitement and caution, and she knew the others felt it too, the thrill of being in the midst of something far bigger than they'd anticipated.

"Perhaps it's fate," Marie chimed in, a sly smile curling her lips. "Or we're just really nosy."

Alice chuckled, her eyes still trained on the spot where David had been standing. "Nosy? Try born detectives." She shook her head with a smirk. "I mean, who could resist? 'Evelyn's will'? 'Estate'? Those words don't just come up in casual conversation."

Kay nudged Leigh with a grin, her voice dropping

conspiratorially. "So… what do you say? Do we just let it go, or do we get involved?"

Leigh laughed, the sound bursting out unexpectedly, breaking some of the tension. "Oh, please, we're already involved! It's not like we haven't spent the whole day piecing together the mystery just to ignore it now." Her voice taking on a dramatic flair. "We may as well stop pretending and let it happen," she added.

They laughed, the sound warm and slightly wicked in the fading light. There was a shared exhilaration between them, a sense that they were bound together in this strange, unfolding story. And though they weren't sure what they'd stumbled into, they couldn't help but be drawn to it.

As they made their way toward the house to freshen up, Leigh's mind was already racing, piecing together what they'd overheard. She exchanged a look with Alice, who gave her a knowing nod. Whatever secrets the Sinclair estate held, they weren't about to let them stay buried without a little digging.

# 12 HAUNTED TALES AT THE DEPOT HOTEL

The late afternoon slipped into early evening as Leigh curled up on the couch in their charming rental house. The vineyard's quiet hum still echoed in her ears, and the soft, golden light filtering through the windows warmed her as she relaxed. She pulled her phone from her bag and smiled as she dialed home. The familiar anticipation bubbled up in her chest as she listened to the first ring, and the second, until Tom's voice, warm and familiar, filled her ear.

"Hey, Leigh! How's my favorite adventurer?" he greeted, his voice light, laced with the comforting sound of home.

Leigh chuckled. "Hey, yourself. It's been amazing so far. Sonoma is gorgeous, you'd love it here. How are things back at home?"

Tom exhaled a laugh. "Busy, as usual. I had lunch with Matthew, Alex, and Emma today. You should've seen them, Leigh. It's so interesting watching our kids piece together this whole 'adulting' thing in real time. Matthew's still stunned that gas costs what it does. He kept calculating it per mile, muttering, 'How do people afford to drive anywhere?'"

Leigh laughed, immediately picturing her oldest son with his ever-calculating mind, probably pulling out his phone to compare gas prices in real-time. "That sounds like Matthew. Over analyzing, but in the best way." She imagined the wheels turning in his head, already brainstorming ways to offset the cost—possibly an app that tracked the most fuel-efficient routes, or some elaborate side hustle to make extra money. While some people shied away from the effort of turning ideas into action, Matthew thrived on it. He loved learning, loved the challenge of making things work, and no doubt, by next week, he'd have a full-blown plan to solve the world's gas-price crisis.

"And Alex," Tom continued, amusement in his voice, "has been diving into insurance plans. He came to lunch with a whole spreadsheet. A spreadsheet, Leigh! He's officially the responsible one now."

Leigh smiled to herself. "Of course he did." Alex never made a decision lightly. He would have researched every angle, weighed every pro and con, and perhaps even made a color-coded chart to break it all down. He had a quiet, methodical way about him, always wanting to be absolutely sure of a choice before committing. No matter how tedious, he'd put in the time to get it right.

"And Emma?" Leigh asked, already knowing the answer. "Let me guess, she's taking it all in stride?"

Tom's tone softened with affection. "Naturally. She's the calm one, reminding her brothers it's all a part of growing up. But even she had a moment when the topic of her recent grocery bill came up. She said she just stared at the receipt and thought, 'How is cereal this expensive?' Leigh, I barely kept a straight face."

Leigh smiled, picturing her daughter rolling her eyes at the absurdity of it all. Emma had this wonderful way of acknowledging life's annoyances without letting them get to her. She was able to vent about something for five minutes, then shrug it off and move on to the next thing that made her happy. It was a quality Leigh admired, one she wished she had more of herself.

Her laughter filled the room as she leaned back against the cushions. "It's funny, isn't it? Watching them stumble into these little moments of adulthood. You think you've prepared them, but then they hit something so obvious to us, yet completely new to them, and their faces just…" She shook her head. "It's priceless."

"Priceless," Tom agreed, "and humbling. Honestly, it seems like I'm learning from them almost as much as they're learning from us. They're figuring out how to adapt, to navigate change. It reminds me to stay open to life's curveballs."

Leigh's smile softened as she traced the stitching on the couch cushion absentmindedly. "Me too. They're so resilient. It makes me proud, and a little nostalgic. They're not little kids anymore, but once in a while, I catch a glimpse of those wonderful traits they have had since they were tiny. Matthew explaining something in way too much detail, Alex double-checking everything, Emma rolling her eyes at anything serious." She swallowed the lump in her throat. "I love those moments."

"I do too," Tom said warmly. "I'm glad they still act like kids sometimes, even if they're growing into these amazing adults."

A slight ache settled in Leigh's chest, that bittersweet mix of love, pride, and the relentless passage of time. "I miss you all," she murmured.

"We miss you too," Tom replied, his voice quiet but full of emotion. "But you soak up every minute of that trip. Make the most of it, Leigh."

She closed her eyes for a moment, letting his words

settle in. "I will," she promised.

They lingered on the phone for a moment longer, swapping stories, exchanging updates and laughter, before Leigh hung up.

Leigh sank further into the plush couch, the soft fabric a welcome relief after a long day of exploring and sipping wine. The room was filled with the warm camaraderie of her closest friends. Marie, Kay, and Alice were sprawled around the room comfortably, their voices blending with the soft clink of glasses and the hum of faint music playing in the background.

Marie had her legs tucked beneath her, a glass of red wine in hand, gesturing animatedly as she shared a story about her twins. Kay sat cross-legged on the armchair, swirling her drink absentmindedly. Alice lounged on the chaise, her posture relaxed, though Leigh noticed her fingers fidgeting slightly around her stemless glass.

Leigh plopped down closer to them, letting out a deep, contented sigh. As much as she loved this trip, her thoughts kept drifting back to her kids. She had dreaded this phase of life for so long, worrying that once they were grown, she'd be lost, like a part of her identity had disappeared along with their childhood. But instead, watching them step into adulthood had been... incredible. She had expected heartache, but instead, she was in awe. Even the mundane moments, Matthew obsessing over gas prices, Alex tackling insurance with the intensity of a research analyst, Emma in disbelief at overpriced cereal, were like milestones. She loved seeing them experience life for the first time in ways they had never considered before. It was funny how they had once relied on her for everything, and now, here they were, figuring it all out. She was still their mother, but now she was also a spectator, watching them build lives of their own. And surprisingly, she was okay with that.

"How's Tom?" Kay asked, her voice light but genuinely curious.

Leigh grinned, leaning back into the cushions. "Good. He had lunch with the kids today. Apparently, they're all getting their first real taste of adulthood. You know, the fun stuff, gas prices, insurance, groceries…" She shook her head. "Matthew called it 'a scam.'"

The group erupted into laughter, Marie nearly spilling her wine as she leaned forward.

"Oh, I remember that feeling. It was definitely a rude awakening," Marie chimed in, brushing a strand of hair from her face. "Meanwhile, John's been on twin duty with Hunter and Riley. Between school, sports, and their social lives, he's convinced they've cloned themselves. The man swears he's seen each of them in two places at once."

Alice snorted. "Poor John. Keeping up with two teenagers sounds like a full-time job and then some."

Marie shrugged, a playful grin on her face. "He'll survive. He knows the real boss will be back soon to straighten things out."

Kay laughed, taking a sip of her drink before chiming in. "I'm sure John cannot wait for you to be back to help! As for me, my school family practically runs my life right now. Kindergartners are adorable, but boring they are not! And let's not even talk about Kay's Zoo, cats, dogs, a guinea pig. Total chaos. One of my coworkers volunteered to keep an eye on the house this week, and she calls it Kay's Wild Kingdom. Honestly, it might be easier to completely abandon control to the animals and students.

Alice smirked, her voice filled with amusement. "Chaos sounds about right. I'm so grateful Zach is holding down the fort back home. Between his work and the kids, and…" Her words faltered slightly, her smile dimming for a moment before she quickly added, "But he's got it. He's used to our brand of madness."

Leigh caught the subtle flicker of hesitation in Alice's voice and the way her smile didn't quite reach her eyes. She tucked that observation away for later. This was their time to unwind, and if Alice wanted to talk, she'd find the right moment.

Instead, Leigh clapped her hands together, breaking the reflective mood. "Alright, ladies," she said, standing up with a burst of energy, "it's time to get ready for dinner. Sonoma glamour awaits!"

A chorus of groans and laughter followed as they all reluctantly pulled themselves up from their cozy spots. The night was young, and so was their adventure.

The room instantly came alive with movement and chatter. They migrated upstairs, various conversations echoing down the hallway as they rifled through suitcases and garment bags. Leigh pulled out her favorite navy sundress, but found herself trying on Kay's chunky gold and blue necklace after her friend insisted it would bring out her eyes. Marie was draped in a lightweight shawl that Alice swore added an air of elegance, while Kay, after much convincing, tried on one of Marie's lipsticks, a bold red that made her laugh and blush at the same time.

"Stop staring," Kay said, swatting at Leigh playfully.

"I'm not staring," Leigh teased. "I'm admiring. You look stunning, Kay."

Alice raised her glass in a mock toast. "To stolen accessories and Marie's surprisingly good taste in lipstick!"

The four of them dissolved into giggles, their earlier conversations slipping into the background as they prepared to leave and finally drove off for an evening of good food, good wine, and, hopefully, a few less ghostly surprises.

Upon arriving at The Depot Hotel's charm wrapped around them the moment they stepped through its heavy wooden doors. Leigh had to pause and take it all in. The space seemed alive with history, every detail whispering stories of its past life as an 1870 train depot. Exposed brick walls, weathered with time, framed the room, while antique lanterns cast a soft light. Wooden beams stretched across the ceiling. Everything was a reminder of the countless travelers who had once passed through this space. The air was filled with the comforting aroma of freshly baked bread mingling with notes of basil, garlic, and a hint of wine. Leigh could almost hear the echoes of distant train whistles in the quiet hum of conversation of the space.

As they settled into their table near a crackling stone fireplace, Leigh caught sight of an old black-and-white photograph mounted on the wall. It depicted The Depot in its original glory, trains lined up against the platform, passengers bustling about. She imagined the space bustling with life, the sound of wheels screeching to a halt, porters shouting, and travelers sharing hurried goodbyes. There was something beautiful about how this place had transformed, its purpose shifting over time. Once a station of departures and reunions, now a gathering space where people still connected, still made memories—only with wine and pasta instead of ticket stubs and travel trunks.

Their server, Carla, approached with a wide smile that instantly put them at ease. She had the air of someone who genuinely loved her job, moving with a confidence that suggested she'd been here long enough to know every guest's story by the end of the night. But there was something else in her eyes, a playful mischief that hinted at more than simple recommendations for the night's specials.

After introducing herself warmly and setting down their menus, she leaned in slightly, lowering her voice in a way that instantly made them all do the same.

"You ladies picked quite the spot," Carla said, her tone playful. "The Depot isn't only famous for its Italian cuisine, you know. It has a bit of… otherworldly history, too."

Leigh raised an eyebrow, her curiosity instantly piqued. The others leaned in, mirroring Carla's mischievous posture.

Carla gestured subtly to the surrounding walls. "This building has seen it all, travelers, romance, heartbreak, and some say a few of those souls never quite left."

Marie, mid-sip of her water, paused, her eyes widening slightly.

"There's an old story about a stationmaster," Carla continued, her voice dipping lower. "One night, after missing the last train home, he stayed late, finishing paperwork. He swore he heard the laughter of children echoing through the empty station. At first, he thought it was his mind playing tricks on him, but the sound didn't stop. It was playful, giggly, like kids chasing each other. The next morning, when he opened up for the first train, he found tiny, muddy footprints leading from the door all the way to the old ticket counter."

The women exchanged wide-eyed glances, a ripple of excitement running through them.

Carla's expression turned even more mischievous. "And then there's the lady in blue."

She gave a pointed glance toward the kitchen and back at them.

"She's been seen standing right outside the kitchen doorway, always in the same spot, looking out toward where the tracks used to be. Staff members say she never moves, never turns, never walks, only stands there, waiting. Some believe she was meeting a lover at the station, someone who never arrived. Others say she's a mother, waiting for a child she lost."

Alice shifted in her chair, clearly invested now. "Has anyone ever… spoken to her?"

Carla shook her head. "No one's gotten that close. If you look directly at her, she disappears. Just like that." She snapped her fingers for emphasis and grinned. "But sometimes, people say they catch a glimpse of blue out of the corner of their eye when they pass that doorway."

Marie shivered slightly, clutching her glass of water. "Okay, that's spooky."

Before they could press for more, Carla shifted gears with a smile. "Now, where are you ladies staying during your visit?"

Leigh hesitated for a moment, and answered, "The Sinclair Winery."

Carla's eyes lit up, and she leaned in even closer. Her voice dropped to an almost theatrical whisper. "Oh, that place has a story too. Did you know about Edward Sinclair?"

Marie nodded. "We heard a few stories about him and some stolen goblets, but we would love to learn more."

Carla's expression turned serious, her voice carrying a tone that made Leigh's spine tingle. She was a perfect storyteller. "Edward Sinclair, Beatrice Sinclair's younger brother, was accused of stealing a priceless set of goblets, family heirlooms. He denied it, of course, but the truth came out when he returned to the winery one stormy night to retrieve them. It was said he'd hidden them in the cliffs behind the estate, thinking no one would ever find them. But fate had other plans. People say he simply disappeared, but there are others who swear he was seen trying to climb down the cliffs and he slipped and fell to his death. They say his ghost haunts the property, endlessly searching for the goblets he'll never recover."

Alice frowned skeptically. "And people have actually seen him?"

"Oh, yes," Carla replied, nodding emphatically. "Guests have reported hearing whispers all around the property, and some say they've seen a shadowy figure roaming the vineyards. On quiet nights, you might even hear the faint clinking of goblets as if Edward's still trying to carry them away."

Kay laughed nervously, her grip tightening around her wine glass. "Well, that's one way to make sure I don't wander off alone tonight."

Leigh's mind raced with the eerie imagery that Carla's stories had created. She pictured Edward's ghost, a shadowy figure moving through the vines, his face etched with regret and desperation, his spirit tethered to the winery where his life had possibly ended so abruptly.

Carla broke the tension with a wide grin. "But enough ghost stories, let me tell you about tonight's specials. I promise they're far less haunting!"

The ladies eagerly listened as Carla described the butternut squash soup, the crispy margherita pizza, and the decadent pear and gorgonzola pizza. By the time she mentioned the tortini di chocolate for dessert, their earlier thoughts of ghosts had melted away into mouth watering anticipation.

They made a unanimous decision to share the specials, leaning into their usual dynamic of sampling a little of everything. They added a bruschetta platter to the order, and Kay suggested a Caesar salad to balance out the richness. Alice insisted they shouldn't leave without trying the burrata, while Marie, with a sly smile, waved the dessert menu. "We'll need to save room for a second dessert," she declared, as if it were a solemn vow.

While they waited for their feast, the conversation

naturally turned to the earlier odd conversation at the Sinclair Winery between David and Nicholas. David's odd behavior had clearly left an impression, sparking a flurry of theories, except for Kay, who sat uncharacteristically quiet, tracing the rim of her glass with her finger. Leigh tilted her head, sensing the weight of unspoken thoughts.

"What's on your mind, Kay?" she asked gently, her voice soft but laced with curiosity.

Kay hesitated, her gaze flitting to each of her friends before she sighed. "I don't think David is the one behind all of this," she admitted. "Perhaps... something supernatural really is at play here. Evelyn's death seems off, but I can't imagine anyone we have met doing anything terrible to her."

Alice raised an eyebrow, obviously skeptical. "Supernatural? Like ghosts?"

Kay nodded slowly. "I know it sounds ridiculous, but I really don't think anyone would hurt her... when I went on that walk before dinner, I got lost and David found me. He didn't have to, but he did, and he was genuinely kind. We talked for a while, and I didn't sense anything... sinister. He seemed sincere, like someone stuck in the middle of a mess he didn't create. I can't shake the feeling that Evelyn's death wasn't what it seems. He seems more lost without her than anything else. Perhaps something startled her, like she saw or felt something. A terrible accident, like the authorities said."

Leigh mulled over Kay's words, her brow furrowed. On one hand, Kay might be right. She had always been the optimist of their group, the type to see the good in everyone, to believe in second chances. Possibly the rest of them were too quick to leap to suspicion. But Leigh also couldn't ignore the eerie energy at the winery, the tension that clung to the air like fog. How it seemed odd that an accident would happen right when Evelyn was telling so many people that she was confident she had found out where the goblets were. It was hard to reconcile Kay's perspective with the mounting suspicions surrounding David, as well as Evelyn's children, mostly Nicholas.

Marie crossed her arms, her voice tinged with doubt. "So, you're saying a ghost scared Evelyn to death? That's… quite the theory."

Kay shrugged, her expression conflicted. "That does sound far-fetched, I know. Possibly I'm just absorbing too many of these ghost stories. I'm just saying it doesn't seem right to point fingers at David when we don't have all the facts. And with everything we've learned about the Sinclair family and that estate… can we really dismiss the idea of something otherworldly?"

Before they could debate further, the food arrived in a parade of tantalizing aromas and vivid colors. Carla set the dishes down with a flourish, and the group's collective murmurs of approval turned the focus to their meal.

The butternut squash soup was velvety and rich, with just the right hint of nutmeg. The margherita pizza arrived next, its thin crust bubbling with melted mozzarella and fresh basil. The pear and gorgonzola pizza was a masterpiece, sweet, savory, and tangy all at once. The bruschetta platter dazzled with fresh tomatoes, garlic, and ribbons of basil atop crunchy slices of bread. As they passed plates and shared bites, their earlier concerns and questions melted into the joy of good food and familiar company.

By the time they returned to the Sinclair estate, the darkness outside to Leigh seemed thicker, pressing against the windows like an unwelcome guest. Their little house loomed ahead, nestled in the shadowy night. No one mentioned the ghosts as they hurried inside, but Leigh felt the unspoken unease that connected them all. She couldn't shake the thought that the past still lingered here, woven into the vines and the walls of the old estate. Perhaps it was just her overactive imagination, fueled by too much wine and too many eerie stories. Or maybe some places truly held onto the echoes of those who had come before. She even swore she could see movements in the fields and bits of light. Fireflies, she told herself. Or possibly just the reflection of headlights from the main house.

Once indoors, the tension began to lift. The warmth of the house, the familiar comfort of their little group, made the unease seem almost silly. The laughter started small, Marie teasing Alice for ordering a "ghost-approved" Chardonnay at dinner, but soon, the conversation turned into an animated discussion about spirits and the strange occurrences they'd experienced so far.

Marie leaned back into the sofa, her grin mischievous. "Alright, who wants to bet that Edward Sinclair himself will come knocking on our door tonight, looking for his goblets?"

Kay chuckled, though her earlier thoughts lingered in her eyes. "If he does, I'll let him have my wine glass. It's close enough to a goblet, right?"

Alice grimaced. "You're braver than me. If I hear anything creaking tonight, I'm diving under the covers and pretending I didn't."

Leigh laughed, shaking her head at them, but even as she joined in the lighthearted banter, a heaviness remained in her chest. The air in this place seemed charged, like something unseen was watching, waiting. The stories of Edward's ghost, the strange way David had acted, Evelyn's sudden death, it all swirled together in her mind, forming a cloud that just wouldn't clear.

She thought about Evelyn, about the life she had built here. Could a person's energy really linger after they were gone? Leigh wasn't sure she believed in ghosts the way horror movies portrayed them, but she did believe in something, an imprint, possibly, left behind by people who had loved a place too much to truly leave it. And if anyone would still be here, it was Evelyn. This was her winery, her legacy. Maybe she was still protecting it, watching over it from beyond.

Marie stretched her legs out, her tone shifting to something softer. "You know, we've got enough ghost stories here to fuel our nightmares for a month. Perhaps it's time to shift focus and make sure to enjoy the vacation with some lighter activities. Sonoma's too beautiful to waste on fear."

Leigh nodded, grateful for the reminder. They had come here for an escape, for adventure, for wine and laughter and moments that would turn into stories of their own. Still, as they sipped their drinks and let their conversation drift to lighter topics, Leigh couldn't shake the sense that this wouldn't be the end of their discussions of The Sinclair Winery and its secrets.

Evelyn's death. David's odd behavior. The whispers of Edward Sinclair's ghost.

The mystery of it all hung in the air, waiting. A storm that hadn't yet broken.

# 13 NICHOLAS'S SECRETS

The next morning Leigh stretched beneath the soft covers, letting herself slowly awaken to the morning sunlight. The lace curtains swayed gently in the breeze, revealing glimpses of the seemingly endless vineyards beyond the Sinclair main house. The quiet here seemed unearthly; no traffic, no modern noises. Only the soft rustling of leaves and the chirping of birds greeted her ears. She breathed deeply, the calming scent of lavender mingling with the cool, earthy undertones of the grapevines. It was the kind of morning that invited lingering, encouraging her to stay wrapped up in this rare stillness. But as tempting as it was to sink back into sleep, the promise of another day exploring Sonoma with her friends was even stronger.

She rolled out of bed, pulling on a pair of soft jeans and a lightweight sweater, comfortable, but still put-together enough for a day of wineries and wandering. Something about the Sinclair estate made her feel like she should at least attempt to match its quiet elegance, plus she knew Marie would show up looking effortlessly chic no matter what. With a quick brush of her hair and a swipe of lip gloss, she padded barefoot downstairs, following the scent of freshly brewed coffee.

As she stepped into the dining area, her breath caught for a moment. The breakfast spread waiting for them looked like something out of a magazine. A crisp white linen cloth covered the table, fluttering slightly in the morning breeze coming in the windows. The porcelain plates, delicate with intricate blue patterns, perfectly aligned, and the silver flatware gleamed as if it had been polished moments ago. A tall vase of freshly picked wildflowers sat in the center, their vibrant colors adding a soft touch of charm. So understated but beautiful, simple in the best way.

Marie and Alice stood by the table, both grinning like kids on Christmas morning. Marie gestured grandly at the spread. "Can you believe this?" she said, shaking her head in disbelief. "When we opened the door, there it appeared, like something from a fairy tale. The staff from the main house must have brought it over before we even woke up."

Alice nodded, still looking a little dazed. "I thought perhaps I was dreaming. I mean, who has this level of breakfast appear on their doorstep?" She picked up a flaky croissant, turning it in her hands like she needed proof it was real. "If this is how they do mornings here, I might never leave."

Leigh sat down, wrapping her hands around a steaming cup of coffee. The first sip tasted wonderful, warming her from the inside out as she gazed at the mist lingering outside. It clung to the leaves, softening the landscape into something out of a dream. Cool air held the gentle warmth of the rising sun, combined with the appealing scent of buttery croissants and ripe berries.

Alice sat beside her, and leaned back with a contented sigh, her short pixie cut slightly mussed from sleep, not that she cared. She spread a dollop of raspberry jam onto her croissant, taking a slow, thoughtful bite. "This might be the best jam I've ever had," she murmured, savoring the delicious flavor.

Marie, already on her second cup of coffee, hummed softly under her breath. It was a tune Leigh couldn't place, both cheerful and soothing all at once. She was the early riser of the group, always the first to greet the day with an energy Leigh never quite matched. She watched her pour a third cup with amusement, wondering how much caffeine it actually took to maintain that level of morning optimism.

Kay, who had been quietly flipping through a local guidebook, finally looked up. "Did you know this estate's vineyard is one of the oldest in the region?" she said, tapping a page with interest. "They've been growing grapes here for over a century."

Leigh was about to comment when a loud commotion broke the tranquility of the morning. Her head snapped toward the open windows facing the vineyard, where Olivia and Nicholas stood a short distance away, their voices raised in heated argument. Though the words were too muffled to make out, the sharp, clipped tones told the story well enough. Olivia's hands moved with urgency, her face flushed with frustration, while Nicholas stood firm, his arms crossed in stubborn defiance.

"Do you think they are aware we're watching?" Alice whispered, her croissant forgotten as she tilted her head for a better view.

Leigh caught a flicker of something in Olivia's expression, frustration, possibly even embarrassment, as she glanced briefly in their direction before turning back to Nicholas. "They definitely do now," Leigh murmured, her own coffee forgotten as she tried to make sense of the scene.

"It's strange, isn't it?" Marie mused, her tone quieter

now. She absentmindedly buttered her toast, though she didn't take a bite. "We haven't really seen much of Olivia since we arrived. She had been polite when we met, but honestly, it seems like she's been avoiding us."

Kay, who had finally put her guidebook down, nodded in agreement. "Same with Nicholas. Aside from that brief chat we had with him, he hasn't exactly gone out of his way to talk to us. You'd think, as hosts who insisted their guests stay, they'd be a little more present, especially given everything that's happened."

Leigh watched as Olivia took a step closer to her brother, her words coming faster now, her voice edged with something that almost sounded like desperation. Nicholas remained unmoved, shaking his head with an air of finality.

"They did recently lose their mother," Leigh offered, though even as she said it, she wasn't sure if that was enough to explain the tension between them. "Perhaps they're simply grieving in their own ways."

Marie exhaled, leaning back in her chair. "That's true, but grief doesn't usually look like an all-out argument in the middle of a vineyard."

Leigh had to admit she had a point. Was this about something mundane, some squabble over the daily operations of the estate, or possibly something deeper? A crack in the polished Sinclair image, revealing tensions simmering right below the surface?

"Should we... I don't know, go out there and pretend we had a question for them?" Alice suggested, only half-joking.

Kay shook her head, reaching for another sip of coffee. "Nope. If they want to fight in full view of their guests, that's their choice. I, for one, am staying right here with my breakfast."

That settled it. Whatever was going on between Olivia

and Nicholas would stay their business, at least for now. Leigh resolved to focus on the beauty of the morning, on the laughter and cheerful company of her friends. This trip was supposed to be about unwinding, not playing amateur detectives in a family drama.

Still, as they returned to their breakfast, Olivia's tight expression and Nicholas's rigid stance lingered in Leigh's mind, an image she couldn't quite shake.

After their breakfast feast they decided they should walk through the vineyards a bit to stretch their legs. The sun warmed Leigh's shoulders as she strolled alongside her friends through the winery's meandering pathways. It was filled with quiet beauty, the grapevines stretching into the horizon like a sea of green, their leaves shimmering with dew. Sunlight filtered through the canopy above, painting the ground with shifting patterns of light and shadow. The faint scent of ripening grapes mingled with the earthy smell of the soil, and the occasional trill of birdsong broke the silence. Leigh trailed her fingers along the rough wood of a trellis as they walked, enjoying the hum of life around her.

Kay pulled out her phone and took a picture of the rolling hills in the distance. "Okay, this scenery is ridiculous," she said with a grin. "How is every single view around here postcard-perfect?"

Marie chuckled, adjusting her sunglasses. "Right? I feel like I should be dramatically swirling a glass of wine and contemplating life's mysteries."

Alice, walking a few paces ahead, turned and flashed them a teasing smile. "I mean, if we're contemplating mysteries, we don't have to look far."

Leigh shot her a knowing glance, but said nothing. Instead, she let the warm sun sink into her skin and focused on the simple pleasure of wandering a vineyard with her best friends. She couldn't help but feel appreciation for this moment, a reprieve from the tension that seemed to shadow the Sinclair estate.

But that shadow grew darker when Olivia appeared, coming from a narrow path that cut through the vines. Her hurried steps disturbed the stillness, and the sight of her pale face made Leigh's heart tighten with sympathy. Olivia looked utterly drained, her eyes red-rimmed, her movements unsteady. She hesitated, standing only a few feet away, as though debating whether to approach.

Marie, always the first to bridge an awkward silence, spoke up, her voice gentle but direct. "You look upset, Olivia. Is everything okay?"

Olivia's lips trembled, and for a moment, Leigh thought she might turn and walk away. Instead, she lowered herself onto a nearby stone bench, her posture collapsing under the weight of whatever burden she carried. Leigh exchanged a quick, uncertain glance with Alice and Kay before stepping closer, the curiosity and unease swirling inside her like a storm.

"Nicholas is pushing to sell the winery," Olivia began, her voice thin and frayed. She spoke as though the words themselves were a betrayal. "He's always been like this, always cared more about the money than the history or what this place means to our family." She paused, her gaze fixed on the ground. "And now... after what happened to my mother, I can't help but wonder if he possibly was involved in it."

The accusation landed like a thunderclap, and Leigh's breath caught in shock. She felt the weight of Olivia's words and her mind raced to piece together what little she knew about the Sinclair siblings. She thought back to the argument they'd overheard that morning, Nicholas's tense stance, Olivia's fiery gestures. Could the man be so desperate to sell that he'd harm his own mother? Leigh's pulse quickened, a sense of wariness creeping in.

Alice broke the silence first, her brow furrowed. "That's a serious thing to suggest, Olivia," she said gently but firmly. "Do you have any reason to think he would…?"

Olivia's head dropped, her hands fidgeting in her lap. "No proof. Nothing concrete. Only this worry I can't shake. My mother was so adamant about keeping this place in the family. It meant everything to her. And Nicholas never cared. He's always looked at this estate and saw dollar signs." Her voice softened, but there was an edge to it now, faint but there. "Sometimes I used to joke that she'd rather lose anything else than let the winery go. Nicholas never stood a chance of being heard. Neither did I, really."

Kay stepped closer, her voice measured and calm. "But why now? If he wanted to sell so badly, why not push for it while she was still alive? It doesn't make sense."

Olivia let out a shaky breath, her frustration palpable. "I'm not sure. I've been asking myself the same thing. All I know is that my mother would've fought him every step of the way. And now that she's gone…" Her voice cracked, and she quickly brushed at her eyes. "I'm sorry. I shouldn't be burdening you all with this. You're here to enjoy the weekend."

"No, don't apologize," Marie said, stepping forward to squeeze Olivia's hand. Her tone was warm and steady. "This is your home, your family. Of course it's overwhelming. We'd feel the same way in your shoes."

Leigh watched as Olivia's expression softened, but the sadness in her eyes remained. No, sadness, and something else. Something Leigh couldn't quite put her finger on. It hovered just beneath Olivia's words, in the way her gaze drifted past the vines without seeing them, or how her tone hardened when she mentioned the winery, almost like the place itself had taken something from her too.

It was a rare, vulnerable moment, but part of her couldn't shake the thought that there was more to Olivia's confession than just grief.

Why was she telling them this?

Was it just raw emotion spilling over, or was Olivia hoping they'd believe her, that they'd see Nicholas the way she did? And if so… how much of her story could they trust?

"Thank you for listening," Olivia said finally, her voice barely above a whisper. She stood, her movements slow and deliberate, and gave them a small, weary smile before turning and retreating toward the estate.

As Olivia's retreating figure disappeared behind the rows of grapevines, Leigh exhaled a breath she hadn't realized she was holding. She turned back to her friends, reading the same mix of curiosity and unease in their expressions. The silence between them now wasn't the peaceful kind. It was weighted, filled with unspoken questions that none of them quite knew how to voice.

"Well," Alice said finally, breaking the hush with a dry, wry tone. "So much for a quiet morning."

Marie huffed out a breath, shaking her head. "I mean… what just happened?" She glanced over her shoulder as if expecting Olivia to reappear. "Did she really just suggest…"

"That her own brother might have had something to do with their mother's death?" Kay finished, her brows lifting. "Yep. She sure did."

Leigh crossed her arms, shifting her weight. "It just came out of nowhere," she murmured. "I mean, I get why she's upset, but throwing out something like that?"

Alice let out a low whistle. "Right? Like, I was ready to sip wine and take a thousand pictures for my scrapbook, not walk into a family scandal."

Kay smirked. "You're not complaining, though."

Alice held up a finger. "I never said that."

The lighthearted comment worked to loosen the tension, and Leigh smiled despite herself. It was bizarre, no doubt, but there was something about the way Olivia had spoken—like she needed to tell someone, to release the burden she'd been carrying. Whether there was truth in it, that was another question entirely.

They began walking again, moving deeper into the vineyard, their steps gradually growing lighter, the earlier weight lifting like the mist slowly burning away under the morning sun. The cicadas hummed in a steady rhythm, filling the spaces between their thoughts, while butterflies drifted lazily past, their wings catching the light in flashes of color.

Leigh trailed slightly behind, her fingers brushing absently against the leaves as she walked. The surrounding stillness seemed different now, not empty, but expansive, like she had room to breathe. A couple years ago, she wouldn't have been able to do this. To let go of the unease, to stand in a place she'd never been and just be. Back then, her nerves would've taken over, twisting every unfamiliar experience into something daunting. Even the simple things, meeting new people, stepping into the unknown, had felt like obstacles rather than opportunities.

But today, even with the lingering shadow of Evelyn Sinclair's tragedy and the strange conversation with Olivia, she felt herself choosing something different. The unease was still there, sure, but it wasn't running the show. She wasn't shutting down, wasn't letting the what-ifs steal the moment. And that surprised her.

She inhaled deeply, letting the scent of the vineyard settle into her senses, and for the very first time in a long time, she felt like she wasn't just passing through life, she was actually living it.

Alice came to a stop ahead, her posture relaxed yet thoughtful. She placed her hands on her hips and tilted her face toward the sun, closing her eyes for a moment as if soaking it all in. When she finally spoke, her voice was quiet, almost a whisper. "Honestly," she said, "just being here has helped me regroup. There's something about the peace of this place that makes me feel like I can think straight again." She let out a small, contented sigh and added, "It's so nice not having to make any real decisions for once. No pressure… just this."

Leigh watched her friend closely, noting how the lines of tension in Alice's face had softened. Lately, Alice had seemed braced for something, like she was waiting for the next thing life would throw at her. Seeing her let go, even for a moment, filled Leigh with a quiet kind of happiness.

Marie let out a long, contented sigh. She glanced toward the horizon, the sun catching the lighter tones in her dark hair. "It's the first time in ages I've felt like I could really breathe," she admitted, her voice tinged with a quiet vulnerability. "Life gets so loud, you know? This, this is quiet in the best way."

Leigh nodded, understanding exactly what Marie meant. Back home, life never truly quieted down. Even in the happiest moments, family gatherings, work victories, little everyday joys, there was always an undercurrent of responsibility humming beneath it all. A to-do list that never fully disappeared. Here, though, it was as if someone had hit the mute button on all of that. No one needed anything from them. No one was expecting an answer, a decision, a solution. They just got to be.

Kay adjusted the strap of her bag and scanned the

vineyard with the sharp eye of someone always searching for the perfect shot. "It's moments like this," she mused, lifting her phone, "that remind me why everyone needs a trip like this. Sometimes, you just have to step away to see things clearly." She snapped a picture of the sunlight spilling across the vines, angling the shot just right, before glancing at the screen with a satisfied smile.

Leigh experienced a swell of affection for her friends, a deep, abiding appreciation that they were here, together, in this perfect moment. The beauty of the scenery seemed amplified by their presence, as if the landscape itself was conspiring to give them the solace they needed.

"I'm so glad we're here," Leigh said softly, her voice carrying just enough to reach them.

Marie turned, grinning. "Me too. I mean, I could've used a spa day, but this is a solid second choice."

Alice snorted. "Please. You'd have been bored at a spa within twenty minutes."

Marie gasped, placing a hand over her heart. "How dare you? I am perfectly capable of lying on a massage table in total relaxation…"

"For five minutes," Kay interjected. "Then you'd start talking about how they should use a different essential oil blend."

Marie huffed, but her smile lingered, and just like that, the mood was light again.

As they continued walking, Leigh let the serenity of the vineyard wash over her, taking it all in. The sounds of life around them, the sun on her skin, the easy companionship of her friends. She didn't know what the rest of their trip would bring, what twists or surprises were waiting just around the corner. But right now, she wasn't worrying about any of that.

Right now, this was enough. The sunlight on her skin,

the laughter of her friends, the easy comfort of simply being here. And for once, she wasn't questioning it, wasn't waiting for the next worry to creep in. She just let herself have it.

# 14 RUMORS IN THE VINEYARD CAVES

Later that morning, as they left Sinclair Winery behind, the tension of the morning faded with each passing mile, replaced by the hum of the road and the promise of a fresh start at the next stop. The drive to Gundlach Bundschu Winery was peaceful, the kind of ride that should've let Leigh's mind settle. But her thoughts were a jumbled mess of questions and incomplete theories, like a shuffled deck of cards. She tried to put them in order to make sense of the tangled mess, but she knew better. Overthinking had never once led her to a clear answer. If anything, it only made things worse.

With a deep breath, she forced herself to let it go. Whatever needed to be figured out would come in its own time. For now, she had a glass of wine waiting for her at what was supposed to be one of the best stops on their trip. That was enough.

As they pulled up to the winery, Leigh enjoyed the magical scene around them. The morning had settled into that perfect late-morning glow, where everything seemed a little more vibrant, a little more alive. The rows of vines stretched endlessly under the bright sky, their lush green leaves whispering in the breeze. There was something almost transportive about places like this. The way the architecture, the landscaping, even the way the light hit the buildings made it seem like they had stepped into another world. Some wineries resembled Tuscany, others appeared like the rolling hills of France or the countryside of Spain. Each one had its own charm, its own personality, and Gundlach Bundschu was no exception.

Kay let out a sigh as she took in their surroundings. "Okay, tell me this doesn't seem like we just walked onto a movie set," she said, grinning as she turned in a slow circle. "Every place we go, it's like a new scene from some old-world European film." She gestured toward the rustic, ivy-covered buildings with their welcoming courtyards and arched doorways. "They don't only make wine, they build entire moods."

Leigh laughed and nodded. "I was thinking the same thing. It's like they design these places to make you forget where you actually are."

"Exactly!" Kay said. "We could be anywhere right now, some hidden vineyard in Italy, a tucked-away French chateau. But no, we're only a couple of hours from a Target."

That earned a chuckle from the group as they strolled into the shaded courtyard. The quiet hum of conversation mixed with the rustling of vines, a peaceful backdrop that made it easy to relax. It was clear that everyone here had come for the same reasons, good wine, good company, and a break from the noise of everyday life.

Alice suddenly pointed toward a nearby field where a small herd of sheep grazed lazily in the sunshine. "Did you know they actually use those guys for vineyard maintenance?" she said, tucking a loose strand of hair behind her ear. "I read that they help keep the land healthy, trimming the grass and naturally fertilizing the soil."

Kay arched an eyebrow. "So, you're telling me those sheep are basically eating to earn their keep?"

Alice smirked. "Exactly. Add in wine breaks and that seems like the perfect career to me!"

As they wandered further into the grounds, their excitement grew about exploring the winery's famous caves. None of them had ever been inside a wine cave before, and the idea of stepping into the cool, stone-walled tunnels where barrels aged in the dark seemed like the type of adventure that fit perfectly into their trip.

Leigh glanced back at Alice, who had drifted a few steps away from the group, her gaze unfocused. It wasn't anything obvious, only a slight shift, the kind of thing only a close friend would notice. She wasn't frowning, exactly, but there was a certain weight in her expression, like she was lost in thought.

Leigh hoped the tour would be just what Alice needed, a light, fun distraction. If something was really wrong, she would've said something by now. At least, Leigh thought she would. But she also knew that not every problem was a big, life-changing crisis. Sometimes, the smallest things, the uncertainties, the worries that didn't have clear answers, might steal sleep and linger in the back of your mind for days. She hoped Alice was aware she didn't have to figure it all out alone.

Kay's voice pulled her back. "Alright, I'm officially ready to move on from this morning's drama." She spread her arms wide, taking in the sprawling vineyard with a dramatic sigh. "New winery, new energy. No weird vibes, no nonsense. Just wine, caves, and me being my usual delightful self."

Leigh grinned. "I like that plan."

Marie nudged Kay. "You say 'no nonsense,' but let's

be real, you are the nonsense."

Kay gasped, hand to her chest. "How dare you? I am a pillar of sophistication."

Alice, snapping out of whatever thought had pulled her away, rolled her eyes. "Kay, you once fell off a barstool trying to 'cheers' too enthusiastically."

"Okay, that was one time," Kay said, holding up a finger. "And I still maintain that barstool was wobbly."

With laughter still bubbling between them, they followed the path toward the entrance of the winery caves, ready to see what new experience awaited them inside.

Their guide, Marco, appeared at that moment, waving at them from the caves where they would begin their tour. His wide grin and dramatic flourish immediately set the tone for the adventure ahead. He looked like a man who truly enjoyed his job, who couldn't, standing amidst this beauty? "Welcome, ladies!" he called, his voice rich and resonant, echoing off the walls behind him. "You've chosen the perfect day for an adventure beneath the vines. Prepare yourselves for an underground journey into the history, heart, and occasional scandal of California winemaking!"

Whatever lingering tension remained from the morning at Sinclair was quickly fading in Marco's lively presence. He was one of those people you instantly liked. Charismatic, animated, with a glint of mischief in his eyes that made it clear he had stories waiting for the right audience.

Marie, ready to dive into any new experiences with both feet, spoke up, her voice rising in playful anticipation. "Scandal, you say? You've got our attention now!"

Marco laughed heartily, clearly enjoying the banter. "Oh, just wait. You'll hear plenty about that as we go along. But first, let's descend into the caves and we can see what secrets they have to share."

Leigh felt a grin tug at her lips as she followed him, her friends trailing close behind. The cave entrance loomed ahead, cool and shadowy, a stark contrast to the golden light above. A little thrill of anticipation flickered in her chest. There was something about stepping underground that seemed like crossing into another world. Wineries always had a way of transporting you, often designed to make it seem as though you'd wandered into a different country. But caves? Caves held secrets.

As they walked into the dimly lit interior, the temperature shifted instantly, dropping into the kind of coolness that clung to your skin. The air smelled damp and earthy, laced with the scent of aging oak barrels and the faintest hint of fermentation. The stone walls, rough and worn with time, made the space seem ancient, like it had existed long before them and would remain long after. The soft scuff of their footsteps echoed around them, making the cavernous space appear both vast and intimate all at once.

Marco paused in a cozy alcove lined with neatly stacked barrels, each one marked with a date and vintage. He reached for a bottle and poured them each a glass of golden Chardonnay. "Let's start with a sip," he said, holding up his own glass. "To good company, great wine, and the stories these walls could tell."

Marie smirked, raising her glass. "And to the fact that it's never too early for wine in wine country."

"Cheers!" the women chimed, their glasses meeting with a satisfying clink before each taking a sip. The wine tasted crisp and bright, cutting through the coolness of the cave with a burst of citrus and vanilla.

Marco led them deeper, spinning tales of the

Bundschu family. How they had persevered through California's wild history, their dedication to winemaking and sustainability. "This place has seen it all, earthquakes, wildfires, economic crashes. Yet, here it stands," he said, sweeping his arm dramatically. "That's dedication." He gestured toward the dim corners of the cave, where old oak barrels sat quietly, aging the wine that would eventually find its way into their glasses. "These caves, ladies," he said with a flourish, "provide the perfect environment for aging wine. Consistent temperature, humidity, nature's cellar, if you will."

Kay, always quick with a quip, leaned in, her eyes glinting. "Nature's cellar, huh? Maybe I'll build one in my backyard. You know, for my own wine stash, that wine that's been collecting dust in the cabinet for months."

The group burst into laughter at the thought, the sound echoing filling the space with warmth despite the coolness around them. Marco's eyes twinkled, clearly delighted by their easy camaraderie. "It might not be quite the same," he said, "but I'm sure you'd find a way to make it work."

Their laughter continued to echo through the cave behind them, bouncing off the stone walls. Leigh glanced at each of her friends: Marie, ever the life of the party with her direct and unfiltered humor; Kay, standing slightly apart, a constant observer with her camera, but no less a part of the group's heartbeat; Alice, who had a way of bringing calm with a soft smile, but who, Leigh had learned, was often more thoughtful and sharp-witted than she let on. Together, they were an inseparable unit, each one of them a thread in a tapestry of shared experiences that had only grown stronger with time. These were the women who had been with her through all the ups and downs of life, and now, here they were, in the heart of Sonoma, creating new memories.

As they continued through the caves. Leigh couldn't help but smile at the ease of their friendships. They'd been friends for years, yet each of these trips brought something new. New memories, new jokes, and new ways to appreciate one another.

The tour led them into the grand dining room carved into the cave's very bones. The moment they crossed the threshold, Leigh gasped. It was nothing short of breathtaking. Candlelight flickered across the vaulted ceiling, casting an ethereal glow on the grey walls, which seemed to pulse with life. Rows upon rows of wine barrels stood like soldiers, their polished wood gleaming in the amber light, each one holding stories untold. At the center of it all was a long table, its gleaming surface adorned with crystal glasses, each one filled with the deep red liquid that Marco had promised would change their lives.

"This," Marco said reverently, his hands sweeping out to encompass the room, "is our crown jewel. The Vintage Reserve Cabernet. A wine as rich and complex as the stories it inspires." He looked each of them in the eye, his voice low with a kind of pride that made the air in the room seem thick with respect.

Leigh took her seat at the table, filled with anticipation. She reached for her glass, the crystal cool in her hand. The first drink was like nothing she'd ever tried. The wine was bold and complex, each note unfolding like a symphony of deep, velvety flavors. The first sip was smooth and full, the kind of bold, velvety flavor that made her want to close her eyes for a second just to savor it. She didn't, though, she wanted to take it all in. The warm glow of the candles, the laughter drifting between friends, the way everything in this moment seemed easy and right.

Across the table, Alice held her glass to the light,

studying the deep red swirl before taking a slow sip. Her lips curved into a satisfied smile. "I think this might be my favorite wine tasting so far," she mused, setting her glass down with a content sigh.

Leigh nodded, tilting her own glass playfully. "Yeah, I could get used to this."

The peace of the moment, and the simplicity of good wine and good company, everything had come together perfectly.

But as the wine's rich flavors lingered, she could swear she saw something shift in their guide's mood. The air all around them seemed to grow still, the flickering candlelight casting long, twisting shadows across the walls. Marco's expression, which had been open and welcoming just moments before, darkened slightly with concern. He leaned in, his voice dropping, as if he were about to impart some kind of forbidden knowledge.

"You know," he began, his eyes darting between them, "everyone's been talking about the Sinclair Winery. People are saying it's doomed. There's been more than one heated argument between Nicholas Sinclair and David Foster, the estate manager. Public arguments, no less." He paused, letting the words hang in the air like a mystery waiting to be unraveled. "And with Evelyn gone… well, it's left everyone wondering what's next."

Leigh had a chill that had nothing to do with the temperature of the cave, as the implications of Marco's words sank in. The flicker of candlelight cast strange shadows on her friends' faces, making the cavernous room seem distorted and adding a certain extra spookiness to the conversation. Evelyn's death had always seemed like a puzzle with missing pieces, and now Marco's words were adding to that growing sense of disquiet. The more she learned, the less Evelyn's accident seemed like an accident at all. And it wasn't just idle gossip. The tension between Nicholas and David wasn't some whispered rumor confined to the estate. It appeared other wineries in the region were talking about it, too.

Kay was the first to break the silence, her voice sharp but with an edge of curiosity that Leigh recognized all too well. Kay's mind never stopped working, always analyzing, always calculating. It was the same instinct that made her a master at spotting discrepancies in a restaurant bill or remembering every detail of a conversation Leigh had long since forgotten.

"What kind of arguments?" Kay asked, not missing a beat, her voice steady, though the intensity in her eyes betrayed her intrigue. It was like watching a detective shift gears—no time for drama, just facts.

Marco took a slow sip of his wine, eyeing Kay warily before responding. "Money, mostly," he said, leaning in slightly, his voice dropping to a near whisper. "Nicholas wants to sell. David is loyal to the family's legacy. But there's more… Whispers about Evelyn searching for something in her last days. Goblets, I heard. And people are now saying her death wasn't entirely…" Marco paused, letting the implication hang in the air. It was as if saying it aloud might make it real.

Leigh's heart skipped a beat. Goblets again. Her mind immediately raced to the fleeting mention of them earlier, that strange sensation she'd had in the vineyard, and all the whispers they had pieced together since arriving at Sinclair Winery. It was like the last puzzle piece had been dropped, but it didn't fit. It wasn't even close to fitting.

Marie let out a small, incredulous laugh. "Is this one of those 'no one in the family gets along' situations? I swear, I've seen this movie a hundred times. Someone always wants to sell the vineyard, and someone else wants to protect the family's honor." She shook her head, swirling the wine in her glass. "Next thing you know, we'll find out someone's been sneaking around in the dead of night with a lantern and a shovel."

Leigh appreciated Marie's attempt to lighten the mood, but the humor didn't quite land. The unease was still there, filling the room with an invisible weight. She looked at Kay, who was swirling her wine as if it might somehow offer the answers they were looking for. Leigh knew that look. Kay was already piecing together the puzzle in her mind, pulling at the frayed edges of the mystery to see what unraveled.

Kay finally spoke again, her voice measured. "Do you think Evelyn found the goblets?"

There was something comforting in that, the way Kay always looked for the reason behind the chaos. But this was no ordinary puzzle, and Leigh wasn't sure if any amount of logic would make sense of it. The goblets, Evelyn's death, the arguments over money, it all seemed like too much to be a coincidence.

"Maybe she did," Kay continued, her voice soft but firm. "But even if she didn't, someone else might've been looking for them."

Leigh's mind raced. Was it possible Evelyn's search for the goblets have put her in danger? Had someone else been looking for them too? And if so…, were they still searching?

Alice, who had been quiet for far too long, let out a long, exaggerated sigh, her shoulders slumping in what Leigh thought was in response to the weight of the conversation. The more serious the topic, the more she tried to avoid it lately. It was a defense mechanism Leigh had used herself many times before.

"All I'm sure of is," Alice began, a wry smile tugging at her lips, "we should get hazard pay for all these mysteries." She raised her glass to her lips in mock surrender. It worked for a second.

Marie grinned, raising her glass to join Alice. "Here's to us, amateur detectives in the making. Let's just hope we're better at this than we are at directions," giving a pointed look at Leigh.

Leigh groaned, shaking her head as the memory resurfaced. Just that morning, she had confidently led them in the exact wrong direction while trying to navigate their way around the winery. She could still hear the chorus of laughter as they realized they had practically walked in a circle.

The laughter rang out, light and genuine, but beneath it, Leigh could sense the lingering uncertainty. The questions were only multiplying, and she could see it in each of their eyes. Kay's steady gaze. Marie's smile that didn't quite reach her eyes. Alice's forced cheerfulness. They all felt it. They all knew that the Sinclair Winery wasn't just hiding secrets. It was wrapped in them, like a veil that only grew thicker the closer they got.

And yet, as unsettling as it all was, there was an undeniable thrill to it, too. Leigh recognized the feeling, that rush of curiosity, the excitement of untangling a mystery alongside her best friends. They weren't just here for a relaxing wine tour anymore. They were wrapped up in something much bigger than they'd anticipated. And deep down, Leigh had a thought that whatever came next would be more than they bargained for.

Hopefully, it would just be intriguing. Not dangerous.

# 15 THE RED HERRING REVEALED

Bidding farewell to the Gundlach Bundschu Winery's stunning caves, hills, and sheep, the women set off to wander the delightful streets of downtown Sonoma. The town had a storybook charm, cobblestone paths wound between historic buildings, their facades a mix of elegant brickwork and rustic wooden signs. The crisp afternoon air carried the scent of fresh baked bread from a nearby bakery, mingling with the sweetness of jasmine vines draped over shopfronts. Conversation, laughter, and distant church bells added to the town's idyllic ambiance. Leigh took it all in and smiled.

Leading the way, Marie glanced between a shop window and her phone's map of their next destination. "We're definitely coming back to that shop later," she declared, pointing at a display of vintage handbags.

Alice, lagging behind, was lost in thought. Her forehead creased as she murmured something about missing clues, clearly still piecing together their last conversation at the winery. Leigh gave her a playful nudge. "Hey, Sherlock, take a break. Even Columbo had to eat, remember?"

Kay, trying to capture every moment, stopped

abruptly to snap a photo of a cascading flower display outside a café. The deep purple and pink blooms spilled from their planters in an effortless cascade. "Look at this!" she exclaimed, showing off her perfectly framed shot.

"I just love this place!" she said, her voice full of excitement. "Do you suppose they'll let us move in?"

"Only if you promise to pay rent in Instagram pictures," Marie teased, tossing a smirk over her shoulder.

The cozy warmth of Café La Haye welcomed them like an old friend. A charming space that featured rustic wooden beams, flickering candlelight, and large windows that framed the bustling street outside like a living postcard. Leigh had an immediate sense of ease as they were seated at a corner table.

As they perused the menu, Leigh couldn't help but notice how bits of everyone's personalities came through, even in something as simple as ordering lunch.

Kay's decision was made in an instant. "The buttermilk-brined chicken. Done. I mean, how could I not? The brine makes it juicy, the crispy skin makes it perfect, and I fully plan to document the whole experience." She gestured dramatically, as if already composing the perfect shot in her mind.

Marie tilted her head, studying the menu like it was a fine piece of art. "I'm going for the little gem salad. Light, crisp, and elegant, kind of like me." She arched an eyebrow at Kay, who let out an exaggerated sigh.

Alice tapped her fork absently against the menu, her eyes flicking back and forth between two options. "Risotto or pasta? Pasta or risotto? This seems unfair, like trying to pick the best novel ever written."

Leigh smirked and chimed in, "I'm getting the risotto, so if you choose pasta and regret your choice, hands off my plate."

Alice gave a thoughtful nod. "Regret? I don't believe in it. But I do believe in strategic sharing."

As their dishes arrived, each one plated like a masterpiece, the conversation turned to the morning's events. Between sips of rosé and the clink of silverware, they dissected every odd moment at the Sinclair winery, particularly the way the mystery of the goblets kept coming up.

Marie swirled her wine thoughtfully. "If Evelyn really knew about the goblets and where they were, why not just say so? It seems that would have saved her a lot of stress."

"Maybe she didn't trust anyone," Kay suggested, slicing into her chicken. "Or perhaps she worried someone close to her was searching too, but not to help the Sinclairs."

Alice leaned forward, her pasta momentarily forgotten. "Or she thought she could find them herself. Fix things on her own. I mean, I get that. Sometimes the simplest problems seem impossible to ask for help with, like needing someone to review your writing, or admitting you have no idea how to navigate the settings on your own phone." She gave a small, knowing smile. "It's ridiculous, but the little things are the hardest sometimes."

Leigh listened, her eyes drifting between her friends and the street outside. It seemed almost like they were discussing the latest cozy mystery novel rather than a real-life puzzle. The whole thing, an old estate, whispered secrets, a lost treasure, fit so perfectly into the kind of stories they loved. Possibly that was why it was so easy to talk about, like they weren't so much unraveling a real event but casually working their way through the plot of a novel over good wine and food.

After lunch, they explored several shops brimming with unique, handpicked items. They admired hand-painted ceramics, tested the scents of locally made candles, and debated the necessity of overpriced but irresistibly soft scarves.

Kay plucked a dramatic, wide-brimmed sunhat from a display and settled it onto her head, tilting it slightly. "Do I look more mysterious or more ridiculous?" she asked, striking a pose with mock seriousness.

Marie barely glanced up before deadpanning, "You look like a retired detective on her way to crack one last case."

"Perfect," Kay replied. "Angela Lansbury vibes achieved."

By mid-afternoon, they arrived at the Fairmont Sonoma Mission Inn & Spa, the kind of place that looked straight out of a luxury travel magazine. The drive up was lined with towering palms swaying in the gentle breeze, and as they stepped out, the soothing sound of water trickling from an ornate stone fountain filled the air. The entrance exuded an effortless elegance, with Spanish-style archways and warm terracotta tones that made it seem both grand and welcoming.

The moment they stepped inside, a wave of tranquility washed over them. The scent of lavender and eucalyptus was in the air, blending with the faint strains of soft spa music. Leigh felt herself exhale, as if her body knew it was about to be pampered.

Plush robes and soft slippers awaited them, and Marie, never one to miss an opportunity for theatrics, immediately slipped hers on and posed. "I have reached the height of glamour," she announced, twirling as though she were debuting a new high-fashion spa line.

They began their afternoon with a soak in the geothermal mineral pools, the naturally heated water enveloping them in velvety warmth. The steam curled into the air, swirling in soft, dreamy tendrils as they sank deeper into relaxation. Leigh let her head rest against the smooth edge of the pool, eyes drifting closed as the tension melted from her shoulders.

"This is what paradise should be like," Kay murmured, her eyes closed as she reclined against the pool's edge.

"Minus the mysterious accident investigations, hopefully," Alice added, cracking one eye open. The group burst into easy laughter, the sound carrying over the water.

Later, in the Roman bathhouse, the soothing hum of a waterfall mixed with the soft murmur of other guests. The air was rich with the scents of chamomile and sandalwood, and Leigh's mind quieted for the first time in days.

A guided meditation session, however, proved to be more entertaining than enlightening. Kay's attempt at deep breathing spiraled into exaggerated, theatrical exhales, sounding more like an amateur wind instrument than a peaceful yogi. Leigh bit down on her lip, trying to suppress her giggles, but the others weren't as successful. Marie had to turn away, shoulders shaking, while Alice clamped a hand over her mouth, eyes watering from the effort of stifling her laughter. The serene instructor pretended not to notice, but Leigh was pretty sure she saw a hint of amusement in her eyes.

Leigh glanced around at her friends, Kay with her endless antics, Marie's quick wit, Alice's quiet but ever-present humor. These were the moments she'd hold onto long after the trip was over. It wasn't just the indulgence of the spa or the beauty of their surroundings. It was this—the laughter, the lightheartedness, the shared experience of being completely in the moment together.

Leaving the Fairmont, the crisp evening air wrapped around them as they climbed into their car. As they wound their way back to the Sinclair Winery, the laughter from earlier had quieted, each of them lost in thought. The winery, so full of charm and warmth in the daylight, now seemed shrouded in shadows as the day's events settled heavily in Leigh's mind.

The decision to return to the main house hadn't been a complicated one. They needed answers, or at least some kind of clarity. One thing their group couldn't resist was a mystery that needed unraveling.

Inside, the warmth of the great room did little to remove the strangely hollow feel of the main house. The scent of aged wood and a lingering trace of wine filled the air, but the inviting ambiance they had experienced when they had first arrived had been replaced with something heavier.

Then the news hit. David had left town.

Leigh paced the great room, her brow furrowed. The subdued light of the wall sconces did little to chase away shadows of suspicion.

"Okay, so let's think this through," Leigh began, her voice steady but edged with urgency. She glanced at each of her friends, searing her own uncertainty reelected back at her in their faces. "David leaving could mean a hundred things, but given everything we've learned…"

"It's suspicious," Alice interjected, arms crossed tightly against her chest. Her expression mirrored the unspoken thoughts in the room. The skepticism in her voice was thick, a contrast to the usual lightness she brought to their conversations as she said, "Too suspicious to ignore."

Leigh nodded, but doubt tugged at her thoughts. David's leaving seemed abrupt, but guilt wasn't the only reason someone might vanish. She stopped pacing and looked at Kay, who sat perched on the edge of an armchair, phone in hand, scrolling through messages.

"Did David say anything earlier about leaving? Or give any sign?" Leigh asked.

Kay shook her head, her lips pressed into a thin line. "Nothing. He seemed on edge, sure, but I just assumed it was about Evelyn's accident. I mean… he worked for this family for years, right?"

Silence stretched between them for a beat too long. Leigh could see the same thought playing out in all their minds, what if David knew something? What if he wasn't running from guilt, but from something else entirely?

Marie frowned, and finally said what it seemed they were all thinking out loud, "Do you suppose he ran because he's guilty or because of something completely unrelated?"

"I'm not sure," Leigh admitted, her head filled with questions that didn't seem to have answers. The more they uncovered, the less it all made sense. The tension between Nicholas Sinclair, Olivia Sinclair and David Foster, the cryptic mentions of goblets, Evelyn's sudden death, it was all so tangled and intriguing. If there was one thing she was certain of, it was that they barely knew anything about the people caught up in it.

She thought back to Evelyn's office, a space they'd all seen more than once during their stay. Evelyn had struck her as the kind of person who valued transparency. She kept her office door open, her desk covered in neatly organized stacks of papers, as if she welcomed the world to see how things ran. On their first day, she had even walked them through her calendar and notes, showing them with pride how she kept track of every staff member and winery event. It wasn't just a workspace; it was a reflection of her.

Leigh bit her lip, turning to the others. "If there are

any real answers, they might be in Evelyn's office. She documented everything, schedules, notes, staff details. Possibly something in there will give us some clarity about what was really going on before she died."

Alice's eyes lit up with interest. "You're right. That office could be a treasure trove of information. And Evelyn practically invited us to notice everything, her notes, her schedule, even her staff list. She didn't seem like the type to keep secrets. If something doesn't add up, perhaps the answers were in plain sight the whole time."

Kay, who had been listening intently, grinned and held up her phone with a triumphant flourish. "It's time to channel our inner Elsbeth Tascioni and I'll be in charge of documenting anything we find," she announced, her eyes gleaming with determination. "Let's go."

Leigh smirked, shaking her head. "You're really pushing for this, huh?"

"Look," Kay said, slipping her phone into her pocket. "We're not snooping. Evelyn told us we were welcome anytime when she gave us the tour. She said she kept Sinclair family photos and albums in there and loved letting guests view them. So technically, we're just… taking her up on that offer."

Marie let out a soft laugh. "You do realize that's how every mystery novel starts, right? A well-intentioned visit that turns into something way bigger than expected?"

Kay shrugged, unfazed. "Then I guess it's a good thing we're quick learners. Besides, aren't you even a bit curious?" She gestured between them, daring them to argue.

Leigh exchanged glances with Marie and Alice. Of course, they were curious. That was never in question.

The air in Evelyn's office was heavy and still, like a room caught in suspended time. Leigh took in the space. Immaculate but warm, a perfect reflection of Evelyn herself. The polished wood desk gleamed under the soft glow of the desk lamp. Binders lined the shelves with precise order, and a faint trace of Evelyn's floral perfume lingered in the air. Framed photos of the Sinclair family adorned one wall, each carefully arranged, some dating back generations. If her winery was her life's work, her family was her heart, and this office was the place where both worlds met in perfect balance.

Leigh ran her fingers lightly over the papers on the desk, careful not to disturb anything too much. "This seems weird, right? Like, if we were in a movie, this would be the part where the audience yells at us to turn back."

"Completely out of character for all of us," Alice agreed, pacing near the window with her arms crossed. "I've never even snuck a peek at my kid's diary, and here I am, investigating a woman's office."

"Relax," Kay said, scanning the bookshelves. "We're not cracking a safe here. We're just… seeing if anything looks odd."

Marie, hovering near the desk, absently brushed her fingers against a neat stack of envelopes. Then—thud. A book shifted slightly on the shelf, sending a yellowed envelope tumbling to the floor.

"Well, that's a sign if I've ever seen one," Kay muttered.

"We should put that back together in a safer place," Alice urged, leaning forward.

Marie crouched down, gingerly lifting the envelope and letter, her eyes drawn to its contents. Evelyn's looping handwriting sprawled across the page, and as Marie read aloud, the room seemed to shrink around them. The letter revealed something they hadn't expected. David wasn't the villain they'd imagined. In fact, he had been working with Evelyn, trying to protect the winery and recover the stolen goblets. More than that, the letter hinted at financial troubles, a growing suspicion that someone within the winery might be responsible.

"She trusted him," Leigh said quietly, her heart twisting at how quickly they'd jumped to conclusions. "She wrote this like she planned to show information she had collected to someone, possibly the police."

Alice, who had been quiet, let out a shaky breath. "I really misjudged him," she admitted, her voice soft. "Honestly, I think I've been misjudging a lot of things lately. Realizing I assumed the absolute worst of this person I don't even know, I feel terrible. I know I've been in a bit of a negative space lately, but I don't think I even noticed how much I needed a mental reset."

Leigh reached out, giving Alice's arm a reassuring squeeze. "We all get overwhelmed. We all get stuck in our heads sometimes. But that's why we have each other. I hope you know you don't have to sort through anything alone."

Across the room, Kay spoke up, a flicker of relief crossing her face before she masked it with a wry smile. "Well, that explains why David was so nervous earlier," she said. "If he was working with Evelyn, perhaps he left to follow a lead or keep himself safe."

"Or maybe he worried he'd be blamed if he stuck around," Marie added, her voice tinged with sympathy and regret.

Leigh sighed. The letter answered some questions but left them with a dozen more. The gaps in their understanding only deepened the mystery. But one thing was clear. David wasn't the enemy they had made him out to be.

She caught Kay's eye and smiled softly. "Now I'm even more intrigued than ever to figure this out. For

Evelyn, for David, for everyone wrapped up in this. I'm still positive there's a good chance Evelyn's accident really was just that, an accident, but something strange is definitely going on at this winery."

The women exchanged looks, a shared determination passing between them. They weren't real detectives, but they weren't the type to ignore a mystery once it had found them, either. And with that, they stepped back into the hallway, each lost in thought, yet fully in this together.

# 16 REVELATIONS AT THE B&V WHISKEY BAR

After a day of twists and turns, the women made their way back to the guesthouse, their pace slowing as the sun dipped behind the hills. The little house shone like a small beacon in the early evening, with warm light spilling from the windows. Inside, the scent of spiced apple wafted gently from the diffuser on the mantel.

Leigh dropped her bag onto the couch and collapsed into one of the armchairs, pulling her sweater tighter around her shoulders. The thrill of the day still had her energized, but her body begged for a moment of stillness before getting ready for dinner. She rubbed her temples and released a long breath.

"You know," she said, glancing around at her friends as they settled in, "I don't get why I spend my whole life planning everything when I secretly love moments like this. That edge-of-your-seat feeling, the unknown. It's addicting, terrifying and exhilarating all at once."

Kay, in the middle of untying her sneakers, paused and raised an eyebrow. "You love it? The same woman who uses three different apps to organize her grocery list and highlights her calendar in seven colors?"

Leigh grinned, throwing a cushion at her. "That's what I'm saying! In my day-to-day life, I need everything mapped out. But on these trips? I'm someone else. Like I finally give myself permission to stop overthinking."

Marie was sprawled across the couch, her legs hanging off the edge as she tossed her shoes halfway across the room. "That's because these trips are magic," she declared, stretching. "No responsibilities, no orthodontist appointments, no middle-of-the-night panic about forgetting to sign a permission slip. It's like…we're living in an alternate universe."

Alice leaned casually against the doorframe, her expression contemplative. "You know what I think?" she said. "It's not only the break from routine. It's the fact that we don't have to constantly be tuned into other people's needs. We're not managing calendars or grocery lists or reminding anyone to pack their gym uniform. For once, we simply get to be. Like… what do I want today?"

Leigh sensed that one in her gut. They all loved their families, no question. She would walk through fire for her husband and kids. But this? This freedom, this time to actually listen to her own thoughts without interruption. It was rare. And precious.

"And we're Miss Marple and Kinsey Millhone wannabes," Kay chimed in, smirking. "Except we don't have their deductive skills, or their knack for finding murders and mystery around every corner, although we are coming close!"

The room erupted in laughter. "Seriously," Kay continued, "we get to be curious and bold and possibly even a little reckless here. No one's judging us for following hunches or poking around a wine cellar like a group of amateur sleuths on spring break. It's either we are a terrible influence on each other, or the best kind, depending on how you look at it."

"It's a group effort," Marie added, "and none of us are stopping the others. We go all in. One of us gets a hunch, and boom, we're suddenly all creeping down a hallway or sneaking glances at guest ledgers."

Leigh rested her chin in her hand, smiling as she looked around the cozy room. "So why don't we let ourselves be like this at home? Why does it take leaving everything behind to give ourselves permission to be this version of us?"

"Because," Marie said flatly, "if we acted like this at home, we'd become the talk of the PTA, the nosy neighbors' Facebook groups, and probably the neighborhood watch."

"Can you imagine?" Kay added with a laugh. "Omaha moms caught snooping in wine cellars—local mystery squad under fire for 'baking too many casseroles and asking too many questions.'"

"Fair point," Leigh said, grinning.

Her phone buzzed on the side table, breaking the moment. She glanced at the screen and let out a snort of laughter.

Matthew: Hey Mom, is it okay to microwave metal? Asking for a friend.

Leigh rolled her eyes and typed quickly.

Leigh: That "friend" better not be in my kitchen.

Matthew: Relax. I Googled it. The plate exploded, but we're good.

Leigh: "Good" as in no fire trucks?

Matthew: Probably. Alex and Emma say hi.

Leigh: All of you contributed to this disaster?

She set the phone down, laughing softly and shaking her head. "My kids are absolute menaces," she announced, the warmth of home flooding her chest. Before she could get too lost in the feeling, her phone buzzed again.

Tom: Everything's fine here. The kids are all home for the weekend and figuring out how to survive without you, and I'm hopeless as expected. But we love you. Have fun, babe.

Leigh smiled and sighed. Home was definitely be chaotic, but it was hers.

"All right, ladies," Marie announced, suddenly springing up from the couch with the urgency of someone who felt like she hadn't eaten since breakfast. "Let's get ready for dinner. I'm starving."

"Or a winery," Kay muttered, stretching her legs.

"Same," Alice said, shuffling toward the staircase. "Except perhaps just the cheese section. And a lot of bread. I don't care if it's carb overload."

As they headed to their rooms to freshen up, the sound of their banter echoed through the house, a comforting rhythm of friendship and familiarity. There was no need for polite small talk, no performance.

Later, at B&V Whiskey Bar & Grille, the air was rich with the inviting scent of roasted herbs and sizzling butter. The lighting danced off the exposed brick walls of the old Sonoma Creamery building, lending the space a sense of nostalgia. The women were ushered to a cozy leather booth tucked into a corner, the kind of spot that seemed tailor-made for secrets and laughter.

The menus were heavy in their hands, with descriptions so mouthwatering it was almost impossible to choose.

"Oh my goodness, everything looks so good," Marie said, her voice slightly higher-pitched from hunger. She tapped her menu furiously with a manicured finger. "I want the crab ravioli, but then I saw the gnocchi. This is torture."

Kay smirked and leaned over, invading Marie's personal space to peer at her options. "Get both. We'll share. I'm also going to add the herb-crusted sea bass because I'm a refined lady."

"You're a mooch," Marie shot back, elbowing her gently.

"Accurate," Kay replied, unabashed.

Alice sat back, cradling her glass of wine as she surveyed her menu. "Why do I even bother looking at these things? Homemade gnocchi is calling my name, like always."

"You're very predictable," Leigh teased, "but in a good way. I think I'll do the Paglia e Fieno." She paused, raising her glass of Pinot Noir. "To good food and good friends."

The women clinked their glasses, the toast ringing out softly over the din of the restaurant. But as Leigh glanced at Alice in the candlelight, she noticed something. Beneath Alice's poised exterior, there was a tightness around her eyes, a tension that no amount of wine or laughter seemed to soften.

Their meals arrived, each plate perfectly presented. The initial thrill of tasting and exclaiming over their dishes filled the table with chatter, but as the pace of the meal slowed, Leigh caught Alice absently pushing a piece of gnocchi around her plate.

"Alright, spill," Kay said suddenly, setting down her silverware with a soft clink. "Alice, you're doing that thing where you pretend you're fine, but look like the complete opposite."

The table fell quiet, all eyes turning to Alice. She sighed, setting her fork down and leaning back, the leather creaking softly.

"I wasn't going to bring this up, but… I guess I need to." Her voice wavered slightly, something so rare it made Leigh's heart ache. "It's life, it's school, it's my parents. Things have gotten… complicated."

She explained how her mom's health had taken a sharp turn earlier in the year. What started as a routine checkup spiraled into something so much more. "It was supposed to be nothing, one of those 'see you next year' appointments. But the tests came back, and everything unraveled. Surgery. Recovery. Physical therapy. And now she's tired all the time. Different."

She looked around, and continued, "And my dad... his memory's slipping. Little things at first. Names, appointments, forgetting what day it is. But it's getting worse. He won't admit it. Gets defensive. I'm terrified he'll forget to turn off the stove or take too much of something."

Alice rubbed her temples like she was trying to hold herself together. "I'm their only child. There's no one else. The few relatives I have called here and there, usually just to say what they would do if they were in my shoes. They mean well, I guess. But no one's really offering to help. Only advice I didn't ask for, or guilt for not doing more."

Her voice cracked again. "I'm constantly coordinating their doctor visits, dealing with insurance, making sure their bills are paid on time. And I love them, I do. But it's nonstop. I'm completely lost half the time. The details never end, tracking meds, calling back specialists, updating paperwork. Little things I never thought I'd have to worry about. And they're all piling up."

Leigh reached for her water, trying not to look too emotional herself. It was hard hearing this, all the invisible weight Alice had been carrying around, with barely a word.

"I had finally decided to go back to school," Alice said softly, eyes locked on the edge of her plate. "I'd been putting it off for years, and I was actually excited. History's always been my thing. I was going to do this one thing for me. I enrolled and started classes, but then my mom's surgery happened. Then my dad's forgetfulness became far more visible. And now I'm stuck between study guides and hospital visits, along with trying to keep up with things in my own household with the kids and Zach."

She looked up, eyes glassy. "It's like I'm failing at everything. I want to be dependable. For my kids, my husband, my parents, my professors… even myself. I want everyone to think I can handle it, that I've got it all under control. But I don't. I'm stretched so thin it seems like I could snap. I can't even complain, because it's not like I'm the one going through the health crisis. I'm simply the one holding it all together."

A silence fell over the table again, but it wasn't awkward. It was deep, empathetic. The kind of silence that happens when your friend finally took off a mask and let you see the messy, human part underneath.

Leigh reached across the table, placing a hand over Alice's. "Oh, Alice," she said softly. "Why didn't you tell us sooner?"

Alice shook her head, her eyes brimming with unshed tears. "Because you all have your own lives," she said, her voice cracking just enough to make Leigh's heart twist. "I didn't want to unload all this. I didn't want to be the one who brings the trip down. And honestly? I don't even know what I need. People keep offering advice, wanting to help, but I don't have a clue what would really help. It's like I'm fumbling around in the dark, and the guilt of it all keeps piling up."

Her words spilled out in a rush, as if she'd been holding her breath for weeks. The guilt, the exhaustion, the pressure of pretending to be okay when she wasn't. It was all right there, raw and real.

Leigh blinked against the sting behind her eyes. She'd

been so swept up in the fun of the trip, so focused on keeping everything light. She hadn't seen how heavy things were for Alice. Sure, she'd noticed the forced smiles, the way Alice sometimes went quiet when the rest of them were joking around. But she hadn't asked. Hadn't pressed. And now it was painfully clear: Alice had been struggling alone.

She glanced around the table. Marie's usual sharp wit was nowhere to be seen. Her face had softened, brows drawn together in a look of genuine worry. Kay looked like she was already forming a battle plan.

Marie leaned in, resting her elbows on the table, her wine forgotten. "Alice," she said, voice low and steady. "You aren't obligated to do this alone. You're allowed to need help. Heck, you're allowed to fall apart if you want to. That's what friends are for. We're not only here for delicious food and cute photos, we're here for the mess, too."

She gave a small shrug. "You're like family. And family doesn't walk away because things get hard."

Kay nodded, her voice full of warmth. "And if someone offers to help, take them up on it. I'm serious. Even if it's something small, like picking up groceries or driving your mom to an appointment. You don't need to be a one-woman show. No one expects that of you except, apparently, you."

Leigh smiled at that. It was very Kay, calling things out while wrapping them in enough care to make it land.

Alice let out a small laugh, shaking her head. "It's hard. It seems like if I don't do it, it won't get done right. And then I … spiral. I've been juggling so much that I don't even know where to start."

Marie leaned forward, already slipping into her "take charge," voice. "Well, that's what you have us for. Let's talk this out until we've got an actual plan. Something real and doable. Who's offered to help, and what did you turn down?"

Alice hesitated. "Zach's offered to step in more with the kids, but I hate asking him to handle things after a long day at work. And my Aunt… well, she's not super available, but she's tried. I have no idea what to delegate. Like, should I let Zach take over bedtime routines or school emails and homework? I keep thinking I'll have more time the next week, and I never do."

She glanced down, fiddling with the hem of her sleeve. "My friend Melissa even offered to bring freezer meals. I said no because I wanted to avoid being a burden. And there's a neighbor who volunteered to walk the dog during my mom's chemo days… but I figured I could squeeze it in."

Kay reached over and gently tapped her forearm. "Alice, those people aren't offering because they have to. They're offering because they care."

"Exactly," Marie added. "Let's write it all down. We'll make a 'Yes, Please' list and a 'Delegate or Die Trying' list."

Leigh pulled out her notes app. "And I'll make it pretty. Because nothing says self-care like a color-coded to-do list."

Alice exhaled, her shoulders relaxing a bit. "Okay. Let's try."

Kay leaned back and crossed her arms, looking every bit the strategist. "Okay, here's the deal. Zach can handle more than you think. Seriously, he wants to be there for you. Let him. You don't have to carry everything just because you always have. Start small: give him bedtime duty or let him pick up groceries. I promise, the world won't crumble if someone else buys the wrong almond milk." She gave a shrug, like it was the simplest math in the world. "And your aunt? Whether she's around a lot or not, she's still your family. Don't write her off before she has a chance to show up. Tell her what you actually need and let her decide what she can step up for. You're not assigning chores, you're opening the door."

Marie nodded fervently. "And don't forget us. We're just a text away, Alice. If you need to vent, call me. If you need help brainstorming, you've got Leigh." She shot Leigh a teasing glance. "Miss Planner over here can map out a schedule for you in five minutes flat."

Leigh gave a little snort but nodded. "She's not wrong. I can help. Honestly, Alice, you're not a burden. We love you, and this is just what friends do. You've been there for us. Let us return the favor."

Alice's shoulders dropped, but this time with a noticeable release, like someone had quietly taken a brick out of the load she'd been carrying. "You all make it sound so easy."

"It's not really easy," Kay said, reaching for her glass. "But maybe it doesn't have to feel impossible either. Break it down. Let some things go. Let people help. You don't have to fix every part of it all at once. Heck, I'll even take your mom to one of her appointments if you want. We'd have a blast. I might even convince her to do karaoke on the way back."

Alice burst into laughter, shaking her head as she pictured the chaos. "Goodness help her. She'd never recover from an afternoon with you."

The table erupted into giggles, the tension lifting like steam from a cup of tea. They spent the next hour brainstorming practical ways to ease Alice's load. Marie suggested setting up a shared calendar so everyone, family, friends, and even the kids could see where help was needed.

Kay offered to research local community resources and support programs, convinced there had to be something out there that could lend a hand, someone to help shuttle her dad to appointments, or even a school counselor who could offer flexibility with Alice's workload. "There's no way you're doing all this alone," she added, her tone light but firm.

Leigh leaned in, her voice softer. "And I'll send you that book list about managing stress and life events planning I mentioned. There's one on balancing caregiving with family life that I think you'll really like. It even has tips for managing time when you've got school stuff and kids' schedules flying at you from every direction." She paused and added, "I remember it had wonderful advice about how to make space for the people you live with, even while you're caring for others."

As the wine flowed and their plates emptied, the conversation shifted back to lighter topics, inside jokes, ridiculous stories from the past, and playful jabs at Kay's inability to whisper when she'd had more than two glasses of wine. Alice began to relax, her laughter coming more easily now. Leigh watched her, so grateful for the way their little group could rally when one of them needed it. It wasn't just about giving advice, it was the way they all showed up, without asking, when one of them could use a little extra help.

By the time they left the restaurant, the cool Sonoma night air greeted them like an old friend. The short drive back to Sinclair Winery was filled with a peaceful silence. They walked down the long drive towards the guest house in a cluster, arms brushing, voices low but warm. Kay joked about tripping over her own feet in the darkness, and Marie recounted an embarrassing moment from earlier in the day when she'd nearly walked into a wine barrel during the tasting.

Once back at the house, Alice released a deep sigh, one that sounded like she'd been holding it in for weeks.

"Thank you," she said quietly as they settled into their rooms for the night. "For everything."

She paused in the doorway, her voice shaky but steady enough. "I didn't realize how much I needed this. I've been carrying around so much, trying to figure it all out on my own, like I was supposed to have it all together by now. Like I had to be the adult who never needed help. But just saying it all out loud... not being judged... you helped me take tiny steps forward. And I didn't even know how stuck I was."

Leigh looked at her from across the room, heart full. "That's what we're here for. Now get some sleep. That's an order."

As the house fell silent, the warmth of their friendship wrapped around Leigh like a blanket. She lay awake a little longer, watching the moonlight stretch across the ceiling, thinking about how lucky she was to have these wonderful women in her life.

# 17 ECHOES OF THE PAST IN WINGO

They woke up the next morning to surprising news delivered casually by one of the staff dropping off fresh linens. David had returned to the winery. Though no one seemed to have actually seen him yet, the ripple of gossip had spread quickly among the Sinclair staff.

Leigh sipped her coffee by the kitchen window, gazing out at the beautiful landscape as the morning fog rolled away. The mist, which had clung to the hills, was slowly giving way to sunshine. Her thoughts worked overtime while staring out at the peaceful view.

Why would David leave so suddenly and return just as abruptly, where even everyone who worked at the winery was confused? He had seemed to be Evelyn's right hand, the person who knew as much as she did on how to run the winery. You would assume he would make sure there was someone in charge if he was gone. The question lingered in her mind, and judging by the confused looks and hushed murmurs among her friends, she wasn't alone in her curiosity.

"This keeps getting stranger," Marie muttered, leaning against the counter, tugging gently at the end of her scarf. She always looked perfectly put together. Even now, half-awake, she had the effortless elegance of someone who was able to turn a grocery run into a fashion editorial. "First, he disappears like it's no big deal. Now he's back, but no one's seen him? It's like he's hiding out, haunting the winery."

She gave Leigh a knowing look. "A mystery author would be unable to write this better if they tried. It's like one of our favorite mystery plots."

Leigh couldn't help but smile at her. Marie had a way of joking about the mundane to sound like a grand conspiracy. But despite the humor, there was a small note of genuine confusion in her voice.

Across the table, Kay arched an eyebrow over her tea, her voice calm but clear. "Don't forget, he seemed really close to Evelyn. He assisted her with the vineyard operations, and from what we saw, he was helping her search for those old family goblets. Perhaps he's grieving, or overwhelmed."

She gave a small shrug. "I really don't think we should jump to conclusions."

Leigh nodded slowly. She appreciated Kay's perspective. Perhaps they were getting too tangled in theories and half-clues about something that wasn't even real. Still...something didn't sit quite right.

"I get it," Leigh said, setting down her mug. "And I'm not saying we go full conspiracy theorist on him. I simply think if we keep our eyes open, we might notice more than we expect."

And with that, she pushed the uneasy thoughts aside. They had a full day ahead, and she wasn't going to let mystery overshadow everything.

Before heading out, the women decided to explore more of the Sinclair estate. A walk seemed like the perfect way to ease into the day. They would be able to stretch their legs, clear their minds, and shake off the last traces of sleep. Leigh slipped on her sunglasses and took a deep breath, the air still carrying a slight morning chill despite the promise of another warm Sonoma day.

They followed a gravel path that wound past the guesthouse and behind the wine cellars, where the landscape subtly shifted. The neat lawn gave way to untamed grasses and scattered wildflowers. This part of the property appeared forgotten. Quiet in a way that made the sounds of crunching gravel underfoot and chirping birds seem louder. Leigh noticed a rusted wheelbarrow lying on its side in the brush, and an old iron gate hanging crooked on one hinge.

As they ventured farther from the main house, they stumbled upon a run-down building tucked behind the vines. The old structure seemed to have been forgotten by time itself, with its weathered exterior barely holding together. The wood was cracked and faded, and vines had crept up its sides, as if nature itself were trying to swallow it whole. But something caught Leigh's eye: a narrow path in the overgrowth that had been trampled recently, as if someone else had been there not long ago. Her curiosity piqued, she motioned for the others to follow.

Alice stepped forward, her voice low with wonder, as though speaking too loud might break the spell. "Look at this place. It's like a little hidden treasure."

Leigh pushed open the heavy wooden door, which let out a groan loud enough to startle a nearby bird into flight. The air inside was dense, layered with the scent of dust, aged paper, and something slightly sour, mildew, perhaps, or simply the ghost of years gone by. The room was tight and cluttered, a forgotten storage space packed with cardboard boxes, rusting file cabinets, and stacks of yellowed documents teetering in every corner.

Sunlight filtered through a cracked window,

illuminating the chaos of what looked to be forgotten history. It was like stepping into another time, and despite the dust and damp, there was something oddly thrilling about it. "Alice, you must feel like a kid in a candy store," she said, smiling faintly as she reached for the nearest pile of papers on a rickety desk. Alice had a soft spot for anything that looked like it came from a bygone era—and this room appeared like it could be filled with forgotten stories.

As Leigh sorted through brittle newspaper clippings, faded letters, and old winery invoices, she saw something that didn't belong. A property deed, crisp and strangely new compared to everything else. The name "Sinclair Vineyards - Copy of Nicholas Sinclair" was written in elegant, looping script, and in the margins were scribbled notes, sharp, messy, and in a different hand. Possibly Nicholas's.

"'Meeting with Yates, proposal for partial sale,'" Leigh stated aloud, her voice tinged with disbelief. "Discussed east parcel options for development. What on earth?"

Marie, who had been hovering behind her, leaned in, peering over Leigh's shoulder. "Wait, Nicholas was looking into selling parts of the vineyard?" Her voice pitched higher, her expression shifting from curious to genuinely puzzled. "That doesn't make any sense. Evelyn was so passionate about keeping the land intact. She literally called this place her family's heartbeat. Remember when she gave us that little tour on the first day? She went on and on about how proud she was that the vineyard had never been divided or sold, that it had stayed in the family, untouched."

Kay picked up another paper from the pile, flipping it over with a frown. "This one mentions a surveyor. Looks like he was doing his research, mapping things out. Do you think Evelyn knew about any of this?" She sounded concerned, her usual calm demeanor replaced with a hint of unease.

Leigh pressed her lips together and gave a small shake of her head. "If she did, she hid it really well. Evelyn loved this place. She talked about it like it was her legacy. Not just for the family, but for the town, for the wine lovers, even for the staff. She was so proud to show us those old Sinclair family photo albums and journals, remember? She kept them right here in this office, like she wanted people to connect with the family's history. She was so open. Which makes this," she tapped the deed, "even weirder. Why wouldn't Nicholas talk to her about it? Or at least wait until she wasn't still running everything?"

She sat back on her heels, the document still in hand, her mind turning over what Olivia had told them the other day. At the time, it had seemed dramatic, really far-fetched, but now? It suddenly didn't sound so outlandish. Olivia had warned them, hadn't she? About how things seemed wrong behind the scenes, how Nicholas wasn't exactly playing by the rules.

"Perhaps Olivia had more reason to be upset than we thought," Leigh said quietly. "She knew something was off. She said Nicholas was acting odd. Now it makes sense. If he was quietly planning to sell land out from under Evelyn, of course he would be secretive."

Alice, who had been quietly thumbing through a ledger, looked up from the pages. "Lots of people have mentioned that the vineyard was struggling financially and Evelyn was on a mission to save it. Maybe Nicholas had plans that he knew Evelyn didn't agree with. Who knows?"

Kay looked thoughtful, then said, "So possibly Nicholas thought he was saving the place in his own way… selling off a piece to keep the rest afloat."

"But without Evelyn's blessing?" Marie said, her tone still thick with disbelief.

Leigh considered their words. It made sense, but the thought didn't sit well. Why would Nicholas be secretly planning to sell part of the vineyard? How could he, while Evelyn was still there? Could he have just been planning for the far off future or did he know Evelyn's wishes would not be an issue soon?

They stood in contemplative silence for a moment, this new discovery and what it could mean settling over them. Finally, Marie sighed and rolled her eyes. "Well, we're not going to figure this out standing in this dusty shack. Let's shelve our probably-made-up mystery for now and get to our excursion. The ghost town of Wingo awaits."

Leigh looked around one last time, making sure everything was left exactly as they found it. There was nothing here they hadn't technically been allowed to see, and it wasn't like they'd uncovered anything illegal, just a few too many unanswered questions that now itched at the back of her mind.

"Yeah," she said, exhaling as the tension started to lift from her shoulders. "Let's talk about it more later while we're exploring. But for now… I'm ready to let it go."

She smiled at Marie, who already had keys in hand and was marching back toward their car like the world's most stylish tour guide.

"Lead the way, Marie," Leigh said, her tone light again as they stepped back into the California sun.

The drive to Wingo took them through winding roads lined with endless vineyards and eucalyptus trees. As they rounded a final bend, the landscape changed. Gone were the lush grapevines. Instead, a weathered sign barely clinging to its last post marked the turnoff. They slowed to a crawl.

"Welcome to Wingo," Marie read aloud, her voice taking on an eerie tone. "Population: probably ghosts."

By the time they parked, the late-morning sun had cast a warm, golden hue over the forgotten town. Wingo was filled with a scatter of sagging wooden buildings, roofs bowed under time's weight, rusted out machinery leaning like exhausted relics, and pathways nearly swallowed by weeds and dry brush. It didn't just look abandoned; it seemed like the town itself had been holding its breath for decades.

Leigh stepped out of the car and paused, taking it all in. The stillness was the kind that pressed against your skin and made you question whether you were truly alone. Her skin prickled, and despite the sun, she shivered.

Alice looked around and gave a low whistle. "Well, this place is cheerful."

"This is straight out of a horror movie," Kay said, snapping a photo of a weathered saloon sign barely hanging on by a rusted nail. "Cue the creepy piano music."

"Remind me again why we thought this was a good idea?" Marie asked, arms crossed as she scanned the empty windows. "We came all the way out here to walk around a haunted ghost town?"

"Well," Leigh said, glancing toward a collapsed general store front, "some people say Wingo was once a thriving stop along the rail line. There aren't any documented ghosts, but I did ask someone at Sinclair Winery what they had heard. They said there's a local story about a woman who used to walk the tracks at night looking for her husband. Some people say they still see her, especially around sundown."

Marie laughed nervously. "Okay, but like we say we like this stuff, but do we really want to see a ghost?

Because I love a creepy vibe in theory, but if something whispers in my ear, I'm out."

Leigh chuckled, and said, "It's the thrill of possibly seeing something, without actually seeing something. Like roller coasters. We want the rush, not the reality."

"It's a love-hate relationship," Alice agreed, kicking at a patch of gravel. "I want to be scared, but in a controlled, daylight kind of way."

Kay turned to them with a grin. "Well, we've got daylight and control. Let's poke around, take some photos, perhaps summon the friendly kind of ghost. And if things get weird, we've got snacks in the car and a quick getaway route."

The wind howled through broken windows, creating a haunting whistle that seemed to follow them. As they explored, they found an old general store with shelves still lined with dusty jars, their labels faded beyond recognition. A creaking barn nearby revealed a collapsed roof and remnants of long-forgotten tools.

In one abandoned house, Marie opened a door, only to have it swing shut on its own. "Okay, that's creepy," she said, stepping back quickly.

Kay smirked. "Clearly a ghost doesn't want you snooping."

Leigh rolled her eyes but couldn't suppress a shiver. "It's just the wind."

"Sure, skeptic," Marie teased. "Until the ghost of Wingo's old bartender comes for you."

They wandered further into the town, their footsteps crunching against gravel and broken glass. A loud bang startled them all, but it turned out to be nothing more than a loose shutter slamming against a window frame. Still, the adrenaline sent them into fits of nervous laughter.

"Admit it," Kay said, pointing a finger at Leigh. "You

jumped."

Leigh crossed her arms. "I flinched. Big difference."

Alice clutched Marie's arm, eyes wide. "No, but seriously, did any of you see that?"

"See what?" Leigh asked, her tone still light, but something in Alice's face gave her pause.

Marie nodded slowly. "I saw it too. Something or someone behind the old saloon sign. Just for a second. Like a figure. Not moving, just watching."

Leigh followed their gaze, but the building looked empty now. Its paint chipped, its windows cloudy with years of dust. "Could've been a shadow," she offered, though her voice wasn't fully convinced.

"No," Alice said. "It had a shape. And I know how this sounds crazy, but it looked like someone wearing old-fashioned clothes. A long skirt. Pale face."

Marie gave a little shiver. "I swear I sensed something too. Like the air got colder for a second. Not spooky-scary, just sad."

Kay smiled, amused. "Well, you two just made this stop way more interesting."

Once they wrapped up their visit, the eerie charm of Wingo had thoroughly worked its magic. The little ghost town was quiet again, just weathered buildings and the whisper of wind rustling through the tall grass.

"You know," Marie said as they walked back to the car, "before this trip, I would've thought Wingo would be the place with the most secrets and eerie happenings. But compared to Sinclair Winery, this place is just a cute ghost town, with a couple of ghostly residents who just seem lonely."

Kay nodded, glancing back over her shoulder one last time. "Yeah, the real mystery is definitely back at the vineyard."

For lunch, they stopped at the Folktable Restaurant, a

rustic farm-to-table spot tucked into the corner of the Cornerstone marketplace. The open dining area was filled with natural light, wooden tables adorned with small bouquets of wildflowers. The warm, inviting atmosphere was a welcome contrast to Wingo's haunting stillness.

Leigh studied the menu, pleasantly overwhelmed by how good everything sounded, just as their server approached. She was young, with curly hair pulled back in a scarf, and carried the kind of cheerful energy that made you instantly feel like a regular.

"What's your favorite dish here?" Marie asked, leaning in with her usual effortless confidence, the kind that always managed to charm strangers within thirty seconds.

"Oh, the fried Pacific oysters on toast are a must," the server replied enthusiastically. "And the crispy chicken schnitzel is another crowd favorite."

Leigh opted for the open-faced summer BLT, intrigued by the promise of heirloom tomatoes and smoked bacon. Kay ordered the lobster roll with green goddess dressing, while Marie chose the schnitzel. Alice went for the oysters, her eyes lighting up when they arrived, golden and perfectly crisp.

The table was filled with conversation as they dug in, the flavors of their meals earning murmurs of approval. Leigh's BLT was perfection, each bite bursting with freshness. She sipped on a Farmer's Cup, a refreshing cocktail with hints of elderflower and cucumber, while Kay raved about her lobster roll, claiming it was almost too good to share.

"So," Marie said, raising her glass to her lips, "are we all in agreement that Wingo is officially haunted?"

Kay laughed, shaking her head. "I think it's just old and creaky."

Alice grinned. "You're no fun. Let me have my

ghosts."

After lunch, they decided to explore Cornerstone Sonoma, where the Folktable restaurant was located. The marketplace was full of charm. Quaint boutique shops nestled among lush, art-inspired gardens where vibrant flowers spilled over in a riot of colors. Statues of abstract forms peeked from behind towering trees, their smooth surfaces glinting in the sunlight, and little fountains trickled peacefully, providing a soothing soundtrack to the scene.

Leigh paused in the marketplace, her eyes wide, taking in the mix of sights and sounds. The lunch they'd just finished had left her full in the best way. Good food, great conversation, and that soft, wonderful sense of being with people who knew you inside and out. Now, walking through this little pocket of paradise, she felt like she'd stepped into a live Pinterest board. Couples strolled hand in hand, their faces lit with contentment, while children ran through the gardens, their laughter bright and carefree, chasing each other between the towering sculptures. Tourists, cameras in hand, tried to capture the magic, though Leigh doubted any photo could do it justice.

Marie was already ahead, her eyes caught by the glimmer of a delicate silver bracelet in a nearby shop window. "This is perfect," she said, tapping the glass as if making it hers. Without even waiting for a response, she darted inside. A few moments later, Marie returned with a small bag, her face beaming with that satisfied look Leigh knew all too well. "It's mine," she said with a grin. "Couldn't resist. It just called to me."

In another shop, Kay wandered toward an old Sonoma wine poster displayed in a dusty corner. "I've been looking for something like this for ages," she said with a satisfied sigh, holding it up to her chest. "This will look perfect in the kitchen. Plus, it's got that vintage charm I can never resist."

Leigh stepped into the darkened interior of an antique shop. The smell of old wood and leather filled her senses. She moved slowly between the stacks of forgotten treasures, her fingers trailing over the edges of shelves, and then she saw it. A worn leather-bound book that looked like it had been pulled from the depths of a long-forgotten library.

She smiled as she ran her hands over the cracked cover. It was beautifully aged, its pages thick and yellowed with time. "Oh, this is so going home with me," Leigh muttered to herself, as if the book had already chosen her. The weight of it in her hands brought her back to Savannah, to their trip to the Magnolia Mansion, and the feeling of excitement, curiosity, and nostalgia that had hung over them like a shadow.

She glanced at the others, holding up the book with a raised brow. "This reminds me of our trip to Savannah. Remember that old house with all the secrets hidden in the walls?"

Kay chuckled, shaking her head. "How could I forget? The place was a creepy maze of hidden doors and odd things. I half expected a ghost to pop out around every corner."

"Or offer us her journal. Oh wait, she did," Alice added, her eyes twinkling with mischief. "That place had Nancy Drew mystery written all over it."

Leigh laughed, the familiar sound of their banter settling her mind, which had been swirling with thoughts of the Sinclair Winery again and all its unanswered questions. "I think this book is my new favorite thing," Leigh said, clutching it to her chest. "I may even start a collection. First, a haunted house journal, now this. It's a vacation thing now."

Alice smiled warmly. "I can see it now, 'Leigh's Library of Forgotten Tales.' Perhaps we should open a bookshop and start a club. Only, you'll have to promise not to write in the margins of every book you find."

Leigh raised an eyebrow, mock scandalized. "Who, me? Never."

Marie, now sporting her bracelet, looked up grinning from admiring it. "You're right, and we can discuss our books and club with the mugs Alice just picked out. I can see us all sipping hot cocoa from them while we read our ghostly journals."

Alice, holding up the set of handmade ceramic mugs, grinned. "Actually, I was thinking these will be perfect for cozy mornings at home. Coffee in one hand, a book in the other. Although I'm always up for hot cocoa and ghost stories too!"

They wandered deeper into the marketplace, their spirits light and carefree. They paused to sit on a weathered bench in the center of the square, watching the world go by, savoring the joy of the moment.

"I love this," Leigh said softly, her voice filled with contentment. "These days, these moments... I don't want them to end."

Alice raised one of her mugs in a mock toast. "Here's to good friends, good times, and whatever adventure comes next on our day's itinerary."

# 18 A BALLOON RIDE WITH A SHOCKING VIEW

The group left the bustling marketplace, their shopping bags filled with little treasures—a delicate scarf Marie had insisted Leigh try on, an assortment of lavender-scented soaps Kay claimed she'd gift but probably wouldn't, and Alice's splurge on a vintage cookbook she declared "absolutely necessary." The sun hung lower now, stretching long golden beams across the sidewalks. Leigh trailed a few steps behind everyone, taking one final glance at the lively streets they'd just wandered through. The laughter of her friends floated back to her, light and familiar, which made Leigh smile and rush to catch up.

Chatter and occasional laughter filled their drive to their next adventure. Kay, sitting in the passenger seat, waved her hand as she recounted their interaction with a particularly eccentric shop owner. "He said I have the perfect energy for Sonoma," she announced, still delighted. "Do you think that means I should move here? Start fresh?"

Marie snorted as she glanced over from the road. "Or he just wanted you to buy the $200 hand-carved wine stopper."

"Details," Kay shot back, her grin infectious. She turned around in her seat to the others in the back. "But can't you picture it? Me running a quirky little bookshop-slash-coffee-bar-slash-vineyard-slash-everything?"

Leigh chuckled from her spot behind Marie, the idea oddly not too far-fetched. "Only if you serve lavender lattes and host dramatic readings of wine labels every Friday night."

Kay gave a regal nod. "Obviously. And only if you come co-manage with me."

When they arrived at the next stop. Leigh stepped out of the car and sensed a flutter in her stomach as she peered over at the hot-air balloon launch site. The vast field was alive with activity, crews preparing the massive balloons, the occasional roar of a propane burner sending waves of hot air into the colorful fabric above. She walked slowly behind the others as they made their way toward the launch site, gravel crunching beneath their feet.

The sight of the enormous, half-inflated balloon ahead took her breath away, but not in the poetic way she hoped for. Her heart thudded a little harder, and she forced herself to take deep, calming breaths.

Up ahead, she caught glimpses of her friends in motion, Alice's confident, no-nonsense stride, Marie's sensible sneakers kicking up dust with each step, and Kay bouncing with excitement, already angling for the perfect pre-launch picture.

They didn't seem nervous at all. If they were having any pre-flight worries, they were hiding it impressively well. Leigh envied that.

It's just one more adventure, she told herself. You'll survive this, just like you survived the ghost tour when you thought someone was actually tapping your shoulder.

But that had been pretend scary. This was real heights, real wind, real open-air floating.

As she neared the balloon, its vibrant panels swaying in the breeze, she muttered, "What was I thinking?" The wicker basket looked so fragile, like it might unravel if someone sneezed too hard. Booking this from her cozy living room, wrapped in a blanket with a cup of coffee in hand, had seemed spontaneous and magical. Standing in front of it now, she wasn't so sure.

But she didn't stop walking.

Marie stopped a few feet ahead, her hands on her hips. She tilted her head and squinted skeptically at the setup. "Are we seriously trusting our lives to a wicker basket? What's next, a parachute made of napkins?"

Alice smirked as she adjusted her jacket. "Oh, come on. It's not like they just throw you up there and hope for the best. There's, you know... ropes or something."

"Something?" Leigh echoed. "That's comforting."

Kay turned to face them, her eyes sparkling with the kind of energy for adventure Leigh wished she could summon right now. "This is perfect," Kay declared, practically vibrating with excitement. "I've been in such a rut lately, teaching, planning, repeating. I don't even know what I'm looking for, but perhaps it's this. Something that makes my heart race, you know? Something that reminds me I'm still alive!"

Marie raised an eyebrow. "So a 2,000-foot drop in a picnic basket is your idea of shaking things up?"

That cracked everyone up, the laughter bubbling out of them in that perfect, giddy mix of fear and thrill.

Leigh found herself smiling, the knot in her stomach loosening slightly. Maybe Kay was onto something. Perhaps this wasn't just a wild stunt. Possibly it could be a reset.

She decided to embrace Kay's attitude as her own,

fake it 'til you float, or whatever the saying would be in this case. Possibly this fluttery, stomach-turning sensation wasn't fear. Maybe it was anticipation. Because the truth was, every time Leigh pushed through the panic and did something that terrified her, she came out the other side stronger, clearer. Braver. If this insane balloon ride helped her feel that way again, she was all in.

Even if it did mean putting her life in the hands of a giant picnic basket.

Their pilot, Gus, strode toward them with the confidence of a man who had spent more time in the sky than on solid ground. He had salt-and-pepper hair, paired with an easy smile and the kind of tan that spoke of years spent outdoors, along with an air of trustworthiness. The clipboard he held looked almost comically official for someone whose job was to send people floating into the heavens.

"Ladies, welcome!" he greeted, his voice warm and rich, instantly disarming. "Ready to fly? And don't worry, I've been doing this for twenty years. Haven't lost a passenger yet."

Marie, standing with her arms crossed, cocked an eyebrow. "Yet?" she asked, her voice dry as a desert.

Gus let out a booming laugh that echoed across the field. "Relax," he said, his grin widening. "The most dangerous part of this is you all fighting over the best spot for selfies. Trust me."

"Selfies?" Alice asked, pretending to look scandalized. "We're way more sophisticated than that. We'll be fighting over who gets the artsy vineyard shot."

"Speak for yourself," Kay interjected, flipping her hair. "I'm going full-on Instagram influencer. Hashtag balloon life."

Leigh couldn't help but chuckle, though her stomach was still doing somersaults. She followed the group into the wicker basket, which, to her surprise, was sturdier and roomier than she'd anticipated. But the moment it swayed beneath her feet, her breath hitched.

"Just breathe," she whispered to herself, gripping the edge as if that could tether her to the earth.

Meanwhile, Kay leaned precariously over the side, her excitement infectious. "Oh my gosh! Look at the vineyards! This is unreal!" Her voice filled with exhilaration and disbelief, like a kid discovering candy for the first time.

As the ground slowly fell away, Leigh felt the familiar rush of panic, but it was overtaken by something unexpected, a creeping calm. From above, the world looked peaceful, like someone had pressed pause on the chaos of life. The vineyards below stretched in tidy rows, their greens and golds glowing in the soft light of the late afternoon. Leigh exhaled slowly.

"This is incredible," Alice whispered, her voice barely audible as she rested her arms on the basket's side.

Gus, standing at the helm, gestured toward the horizon. "You think this is good? Wait until you see it at sunset. Best view in the world, bar none. I've flown over mountains, oceans, you name it, but there's something about this valley. It's magic."

"Magic," Kay sighed, clasping her hands dramatically. "That's what I need. Should I quit teaching and become a hot-air balloon pilot? What do you think, Gus?"

"Ah, I dunno," Gus replied, stroking his chin like he was deep in thought. "Can you tell a story like me? That's half the job, you know."

"Oh, we love stories," Marie said, resting against the basket and crossing her arms. "What've you got?"

Gus grinned, clearly in his element. "Well, there was this one time a couple got engaged up here. Real sweet moment. Until the guy drops the ring right out of the basket."

"No!" Leigh gasped, her eyes wide.

"Yep," Gus said, chuckling. "The whole crew spent hours combing the vineyards for it. Found it, too, on top of a vine like it was waiting there. The guy said it was fate."

Kay clutched her chest and let out a dreamy sigh. "That's it. I'm manifesting a high-flying romance of my own. Swept off my feet, literally and romantically. Preferably by someone with a vineyard and good hair."

Marie rolled her eyes. "Please. You wouldn't last a week without your kindergartners."

"Excuse me," Kay said, mock-indignant. "Of course they would be with me. I'd be the world's first hot-air balloon teacher. Field trips in the sky. Can you imagine? 'Today, kids, we're studying clouds, up close!'"

The entire basket erupted in laughter. Leigh's knuckles, still white from clutching the edge, finally relaxed as she joined in. This—this ridiculous, joyful banter between them was keeping her grounded even as they floated higher into the sky.

As they drifted lazily over a patchwork quilt of golden vineyards and lush greenery, Leigh found herself leaning against the basket, her eyes scanning the horizon. A flicker of recognition sparked, and she squinted, shading her eyes from the afternoon sunlight. "Hey, isn't that the Sinclair property?" She pointed toward a cluster of buildings below, their cozy guesthouse now resembling a dollhouse, complete with its miniature wraparound porch.

Marie, standing beside her, followed her finger. "Good eye," she said, adjusting her sunglasses. "Looks like home sweet home… but wait, what's all that?"

Leigh leaned in further, her curiosity piqued. At the far edge of the Sinclair property, just past the familiar rows of vines, bright survey flags dotted the landscape, fluttering in the breeze. Vehicles were parked in a tidy row near the entrance, their real estate logos just barely visible from this height. But one car stood out. A sleek, yellow sports car that gleamed in the afternoon sun.

"That's Nicholas's car," Leigh said, her voice sharpening with certainty. "I'd recognize it anywhere. He's been tearing up and down the winery roads in that thing since we got here, like it's some kind of racetrack."

Alice let out a loud laugh. "Oh my God, yes! I've been wondering if he's trying to audition for the next Fast & Furious. I swear I saw him fishtail in front of the guesthouse yesterday!"

"Exactly," Leigh said, her brow furrowing. "So what's it doing parked out there with the real estate crowd?"

Kay groaned dramatically and rolled her eyes, throwing her head back against the basket with flair. "Can we please just enjoy this vacation without creating or stumbling into a random mystery? I mean, seriously, ladies. Right now, I'd like the biggest intrigue to be something manageable, like how Marie manages to keep her hair perfect even in this humidity."

Marie gave a mock bow. "It's called hair serum, darling. I'll share the secret for a price."

Alice, perched quietly on the other side of the basket, chimed in, her voice thoughtful. "It is kind of odd, though. Evelyn definitely didn't mention anything about selling the property, did she? The Sinclairs have been here forever, it's practically a landmark. Why would they want to leave?"

Before anyone could answer, Gus, who had been quietly manning the balloon with the calm of a Zen master, turned slightly. "Funny you should mention that," he said, his voice steady and conversational. "I've been flying over this valley for years, and I've never seen real estate folks out at the Sinclair place until recently. It's been pretty busy down there the last few weeks. I even saw someone with a clipboard walking the property lines the other day. Not your usual vineyard maintenance, that's for sure."

Marie furrowed her brow, sharing a look with Leigh. "Did you ever ask about it?"

"I did," Gus replied, his hands steady on the ropes. "Talked to Evelyn just last week. She seemed… put off when I brought it up. Not surprised, exactly, but kind of unaware. Changed the subject pretty quick. Seemed odd to me, considering how long the Sinclairs have been part of this valley."

Kay shrugged and tilted her head, brushing windblown strands of hair from her eyes. Looking at the concerned faces of her friends, she finally broke the silence and said, "Come on. I doubt Nicholas is secretly selling the property out from under everyone's nose. He probably just hired someone to get it appraised or cleaned up for insurance or taxes or whatever boring adult stuff vineyard owners have to do."

"Or," Alice added, her grin mischievous, "he's selling the vineyard to start a rival winery across the valley. You know, like a reality show where ex-lovers compete over wine."

"Or he's planning to disappear entirely," Leigh added, smiling. "Next thing you know, we'll find out he's a spy, and this is his cover story."

As their speculation grew more absurd, Marie theorized he was secretly fleeing tax trouble, while Kay insisted he was joining a secluded artist commune in France, the beauty of the landscape reclaimed their attention. Leigh inhaled deeply, letting the crisp, grape-scented air fill her lungs. Despite the joking, she noticed Kay growing quiet, her smile lingering but her brows knitting just slightly.

"It is a bit weird," Kay finally admitted, brushing a wind-blown curl from her face. "I mean, the whole situation. But whatever it really is," she added, her voice soft as her eyes swept over the rolling hills, "it can wait. This view is too perfect to waste."

The balloon began its descent with a series of gentle jolts that had Marie gripping the edge of the basket like a seasoned sailor bracing for rough seas. "This," she muttered, "is where it happens. The part where they write 'And then the balloon just… stopped working' in our obituaries."

"Relax," Gus said with a chuckle. "I've landed this thing hundreds of times. Trust me."

When the basket touched down with a soft bump, Alice and Leigh stumbled sideways, colliding into Kay. The three of them burst into laughter as they grabbed onto each other for support. "We survived!" Kay cheered, throwing her hands up in mock triumph.

Marie, on the other hand, stepped out smoothly and tossed her hair over her shoulder as if she'd never doubted their survival. "Piece of cake," she said, her smirk drawing groans from the others.

The group toasted their adventure with glasses of chilled champagne provided by Gus, their laughter ringing out against the hum of the balloon's burner. The wine sparkled in their glasses, reflecting the glow of the late-afternoon Sonoma sun. Leigh raised her glass and took a sip. Inside, she felt a quiet celebration bubbling up, a tiny victory against the anxiety that so often tried to dictate her experiences. Today she hadn't let it take over. She'd stepped into the moment, nerves and all, and come out smiling on the other side.

"Here's to hot air, potential real estate drama, and surviving another day with you three," she said, raising her glass.

"For now," Kay added with a wink, "the mystery of Nicholas and the Sinclair property can wait. But tomorrow?"

"Tomorrow," Leigh replied, her lips curving into a grin, "we make time for sight-seeing and investigating."

# 19 SPIRITS AT PETALUMA ADOBE

Settling in at Wit & Wisdom for dinner, Leigh felt the kind of exhaustion that only came from a day well spent, though it was tempered by an undeniable contentment. The tavern welcomed them, its warm, intimate lighting casting flickering shadows across rustic stone walls. The subtle crackle of the hearth oven mingled with the faint aroma of wood smoke and roasted herbs. The outdoor terrace tempted with its twinkling canopy of fairy lights and murmured laughter from happy diners, but the four of them were drawn to a quieter table near the fireplace, drawn to the quiet and warmth emanating from the glowing embers.

Leigh melted into her chair, pulling her scarf loose as she exhaled slowly. Across from her, Kay stretched her arms high above her head, her oversized cardigan puffing dramatically. "Now this is what I call ending the day right," she declared, looking perfectly at home and like she belonged on the cover of a cozy wine & lifestyle magazine.

"Careful," Marie teased, as she smoothed her linen napkin over her lap. "You appear so at home hers that someone might assume you're the heiress to a vineyard empire, not someone who hunted down free pours all day like it was her job."

"Oh, darling," Kay replied in a mock-posh accent, placing her hand delicately on her chest. "You know I don't only drink the wine because it's free, I curate my wine experiences. Tasting notes, hue, atmospheric vibes… it's a skill."

Leigh couldn't help but laugh. She opened her menu, and immediately, the scent of charred rosemary drifted up from the nearby kitchen pass, mingling with hints of garlic butter, toasted bread, and something sweet she was unable to place. Her stomach grumbled in agreement.

They were starving, borderline hangry, and placed their orders almost as soon as they sat down. Leigh's eyes widened at the sight of their entrées. The roasted chicken on her plate glistened, its golden skin crackling as it rested atop a bed of caramelized root vegetables. "Okay, this might be the prettiest meal I've ever seen," she admitted, practically salivating.

"Prettier than all those seafood dishes you gushed over in Savannah last summer?" Alice teased, leaning over her own plate of tomato-ginger glazed salmon. The sweet and tangy aroma wafted up as she grinned. "Although, I will say, this seems like winning the dinner lottery."

"Not so fast," Kay interjected, cutting into her own salmon dish with exaggerated flair. She paused dramatically after her first bite, her eyes fluttering shut. "Yep, I agree. Perfection."

Marie gave a doubtful look at them as she tasted her own roasted chicken. "You two can fawn over your fish all you want," she quipped, slicing another piece with deliberate elegance. "I'm just glad my dinner isn't staring back at me."

Their laughter rippled through the restaurant, earning

amused glances from nearby diners. Dessert, a cinnamon rice pudding topped with candied orange peel, arrived to a chorus of delighted murmurs, and Kay's hum of approval prompted the others to mimic her theatrics.

As they ate, their conversation meandered from lighthearted jokes to more meaningful topics, as it often did. Marie, swirling the last of her chardonnay in her glass, leaned back with a sigh that came from somewhere deep inside her. "You know," she began, her voice quieting, taking on that tone that said she wasn't making small talk anymore, "I love my job. I really do. But the travel… It's just, it's too much sometimes. It seems like I'm missing everything at home. The kids' games, quiet dinners with John. Even just being there when they're all hanging around the kitchen arguing over snacks and homework. I'm in airports more than I'm in my own bed."

Leigh watched, her heart tugging at the visible shift in Marie's expression. She'd always seen her friend as the one who had it all together, confident in a classic blazer and sleek heels, always hopping on and off flights like it was no big deal. But now, Marie looked smaller somehow, like the cracks in her perfect image were finally showing, and not in a bad way, in a real way.

Marie let out a soft laugh, but it didn't quite reach her eyes. "I've been to seven countries this year, but when it comes to planning a family vacation, we're lucky if we squeeze in one long weekend. It's like the more places I go, the more I realize how few of them I've shared with the people who matter most."

Leigh reached across the table, giving her hand a squeeze. "You've built something incredible, but perhaps it's time to rework the blueprint a little. What if you asked to limit travel for a while? Or at least focus more on regional work, stuff closer to home? That way, you're not gone so much, and it's not a complete shift, simply… a recalibration."

Kay, ever the cheerleader, leaned forward with a hopeful grin. "Yes! Or better yet, make it work for you. Like, bring the family with you on a couple of the trips. Even if it's only tagging on a weekend at the end. Business and vacation, all rolled into one. Think about the memories—and just imagine the photos! Your Christmas letter would be epic."

The group laughed, the mood lifting enough to take the edge off Marie's confession. She smiled, the first genuine one since the topic came up, and shook her head fondly. "You know… that actually might work. If I can frame it the right way, I think my boss might go for it. At least a couple of times a year."

"You're due for a shift," Leigh said gently. "You've given so much to your job, perhaps now's the time to ask for a little back."

Marie nodded slowly, her eyes a little shinier than before, but her posture more relaxed. "Maybe it is."

"Speaking of balancing things," Kay said with an exaggerated sigh. "I'm loving teaching, but you all know my heart keeps getting pulled toward photography. Sometimes I think… possibly it's time to take a leap."

Alice focused on her, pausing mid-bite. "You mean a 'quit your job and be a full-time artist' leap? Or on a slightly smaller scale of 'start selling your photos to fund your wine habit' leap?"

Kay let out a burst of laughter. "No idea!" she admitted, throwing up her hands. "But when Evelyn mentioned that first night that she might want to use some of my vineyard shots for the Sinclair brochures? It kind of lit a spark. I haven't been able to stop thinking about it. It'd be incredible to see my work printed, like really out there, not simply hanging in my hallway."

"You absolutely should!" Leigh leaned forward, her voice more insistent than she expected. "Kay, your pictures are stunning. You have this way of capturing the quiet parts, the little in-between moments that no one else sees. That's rare."

"Agreed," Marie said, nodding. "You've got an eye for detail, for emotion. Evelyn saw it too, clearly."

The appreciation that passed around the table wasn't only polite agreement, it was deeply rooted, like each word built a stronger foundation beneath Kay's confidence. Leigh could almost see it, the way their encouragement landed softly but firmly, like a gentle push forward.

This was what made these friendships so special, she thought, how they genuinely lifted each other. Not only with compliments, but with real belief. There was an unspoken understanding in moments like this, a kind of knowledge that came from years of knowing one another's dreams, fears, and hidden doubts. They weren't simply catching up on a vacation, they were helping each other become more of who they were meant to be.

As the evening wore on, the conversation loosened with another glass of wine, and the laughter came easily. They were almost through dinner when Kay pointed at her plate and announced, "Okay, I swear this salmon has spiritual properties. Like it's helping me see what my future is."

Leigh nearly snorted her wine. "What does that even mean?" she asked, wiping tears of laughter from her eyes.

Alice raised an eyebrow and deadpanned, "I think it means Kay has become one with the wine."

Even Marie cracked up, nearly dropping her fork. The moment was light and ridiculous and exactly what they all needed.

The meal was winding down, the kind that stretches

comfortably long after the plates have cleared and the wine has thinned. They teased each other, swapped stories, and as always, found those unspoken ways to hold space for one another. Leigh set her fork down, leaning back in her chair, savoring the heat from the stone fireplace nearby. She let her gaze wander across the room, taking in the mix of patrons, until her eyes froze on a figure at a distant table. Her breath caught in surprise. "Is that Nicholas?"

Her voice was quiet, but sharp enough to catch Alice's attention. Alice turned casually, her eyes narrowing like a detective spotting a suspect. "Oh, it's him, all right." Her tone dripped with curiosity as she noted Nicholas Sinclair sitting stiffly at a small table near the window. He leaned forward, his dark brows knitted into a stern frown as he spoke to a man in an impeccably tailored suit. Between them, a leather briefcase sat open, papers spilling out across the table. Whatever they were discussing, it didn't appear friendly.

"He seems to be everywhere but the winery," Alice murmured, her gaze unwavering. "Wouldn't that need the most attention with Evelyn gone?"

Leigh bit her lip. Her gut told her not to get pulled into another wild theory, but Alice already had that look. The one that meant she was three steps ahead in whatever storyline she'd already drafted in her head.

"Alice, don't," Leigh said, already knowing it was useless.

"Too late," Alice replied, flashing a grin that sparkled with mischief. "This is too good to pass up, and I'm feeling brave."

Before anyone could stop her, Alice began edging closer to the two men's table under the guise of examining the artwork on the wall. The rest of the group exchanged wary glances. Leigh gave a resigned sigh, then rose and followed with the others, as if it were the most natural thing in the world to suddenly appreciate a painting of Sonoma's rolling hills.

Nicholas's voice was low, but the occasional sharp word carried across the room. "…rushed sale… portion of the estate…"

Alice tilted her head as she leaned toward the conversation. She turned back to Leigh, her voice a whisper. "He's talking about selling part of the estate. Rushed, too. That doesn't sound good."

Leigh frowned. "And why do you care?"

Alice's brows lifted. "You're kidding, right? Evelyn's unexpected death, the odd vibes from Olivia at the vineyard, running into stories of Sinclair drama everywhere we turn and now this? It's all connected. I can feel it."

With a skeptical look on her face, Marie leaned in. "Or you just want it to be connected. Sometimes a cigar is just a cigar."

Kay laughed softly. "And sometimes it's a cigar haunted by the ghost of a murdered winery owner. I'm with Alice. This is fishy."

Leigh sighed. Her mind tugged in two directions. The logical side of her said they were just tourists spinning stories because they had too much wine and watched far too many mystery shows. But still… something didn't sit right.

"Are we really uncovering any real hidden truths," she asked, "or are we just spinning a mystery out of thin air?"

Kay gave a playful shrug. "Hey, if the clues keep showing up, I say we follow them."

As the server returned with the check, they reluctantly drifted back to their table. The conversation continued to revolve around Evelyn's odd behavior around Gus, the hot-air balloon pilot, and the tension David,

Nicholas, and especially Olivia, had exuded at the vineyard. "If nothing else," Leigh thought, "we're exceptionally good at imagining connections."

After dinner, the women emerged onto the dimly lit streets of Sonoma, ready for their next stop, The Napa City Ghosts and Legends Walks Tour. They had expected a standard ghost tour. Someone in a cape telling spooky stories under a flickering lantern. But instead, they were greeted by a small, energetic team of paranormal investigators who talked more like science fair finalists than haunted house actors. Their eyes sparkled as they passed out gear, talking about energy fields, cold spots, and hauntings. It wasn't cheesy or over-the-top, it was all very convincing.

Leigh blinked down at the copper dowsing rods she had been handed, feeling like she had just stepped into an episode of Ghost Hunters. "What am I supposed to do with these? Find water?" she asked, earning a grin from Kay.

"They're ghost detectors," one of the investigators said, earnestly. Their enthusiasm was contagious. Leigh could sense the skeptical part of her brain finally giving up as another investigator launched into an explanation about how copper could react to subtle electromagnetic changes in the atmosphere.

The women couldn't help but get caught up in it.

Marie tilted hers experimentally, only for the rods to swing wildly in opposite directions. "Great. Mine's broken."

"User error," Alice teased, already fiddling with a handheld EMF detector.

While they walked through the historic streets, the guides spun tales of eerie happenings and tragic fates. At the Whipping Tree, the group stopped as the guide recounted its grim history. "This tree was once a site of public punishment during the frontier days. Legend says the spirits of those who suffered here still linger, seeking justice."

The women shivered as the guide asked if anyone could sense anything. Leigh stayed silent, but Kay swore she sensed a sudden cold breeze. "Or more likely it's just Sonoma's weather messing with me," she quipped, though her uneasy expression betrayed her nerves.

Next was the Sebastiani Theatre, its grand façade glowing faintly under the streetlights. The guide spoke of a ghostly projectionist who still roamed the theater at night, adjusting reels and flickering lights. "They say you can hear faint music and see shadows moving across the screen, even when the theater's empty."

"That's oddly considerate for a ghost, supplying free entertainment for the masses," Alice said, grinning. "I'd haunt a popcorn machine instead."

Marie, meanwhile, kept pointing at the shadows cast by the trees, her nerves playing tricks on her. "That's definitely a ghost," she said at least three times, only for the group to discover it was a trick of the light, or in one case, a raccoon.

Still, the air was thick with tension, and by the time the tour ended, Leigh's unease had begun to grow. As they walked back to the car, Kay half-joked, "Do you think Evelyn's spirit is following us, trying to nudge us toward the truth?"

"Of course it's us who'd end up with a ghost on vacation," Marie quipped, trying to lighten the mood.

Leigh smiled faintly, but her thoughts were already swirling. The parallels to their last trip in Savannah, when they'd stumbled into uncovering Amelia's story, were eerily familiar.

When they returned to the Sinclair estate, the strange atmosphere seemed to intensify. Flickering lights greeted them as they stepped inside, and a sudden gust of wind rattled the windows. Kay glanced around nervously. "Okay, is it odd that I'm hoping that's just bad wiring?"

Leigh sighed, rubbing her arms as a chill settled over her. "Maybe we should have asked to keep some of those ghost detectors", she said with a nervous laugh.

But even she couldn't shake the sense that something, or someone, was trying to communicate with them. The night stretched on, filled with whispers of suspicion and half-joking fears. But deep down, Leigh knew one thing. There was no question they were definitely finding themselves in another tangled mystery.

# 20 LEGENDS IN NAPA VALLEY

Clear skies stretched endlessly overhead, and the early sun cast a warm glow on the windshield as the little red convertible cruised down the road. Leigh was at the wheel, her sunglasses perched on her nose, the breeze tugging gently at the strands of hair that had slipped free from her ponytail. She was trying, somewhat unsuccessfully, not to let her thoughts spiral back to Evelyn and Nicholas, but they lingered like background static, impossible to fully mute.

The soft hum of the engine filled the car as the other ladies chatted, their voices bubbling over with anticipation of the day ahead. Alice was recounting something hilarious she'd read on a wine-tasting blog, Marie was mid-rant about the audacity of someone wearing heels to a vineyard, and Kay kept mispronouncing the name of the castle they were headed to just to annoy her. Leigh caught their reflections now and then in the rearview mirror, flashes of faces she'd known for years, each one so familiar. Maybe more than ever, she realized how deeply grateful she was to have these women in her life. Friends who gave her space when she needed it, but still filled that space with their

"""

laughter and stories. And she made a quiet promise to herself right then not to take that for granted. Not ever.

When they pulled up to Castello di Amorosa, the car slowed, and all four women fell silent. The castle loomed before them, as if from another era, rising up against the backdrop of the rolling hills. Its stone towers reached high into the sky, surrounded by rows of meticulously manicured vineyards that seemed to stretch on forever. The grandeur was striking. As Leigh gazed at the scene, it was like she was momentarily transported to another time.

"This place is gorgeous!" Alice exclaimed, her voice filled with awe. She craned her neck to take in the full scope of the castle, her wide eyes taking in the towers, the turrets, and the massive iron gates. "I've always wanted to visit a castle! Maybe this is a dream? Like, someone's going to pinch me any second and I'll wake up in the car with a hangover."

Marie laughed and raised her hand. "I'll pinch you, but only if you promise not to scream so loud we get kicked out before the first sip of wine."

As they approached the entrance, Leigh's mind briefly wandered back to her thoughts in the car, the mess with Evelyn, the growing tension with Nicholas, and then she snapped back to the present. She couldn't let those thoughts take over on what promised to be an amazing day. As the castle's stone towers loomed overhead, she reminded herself that they were here to enjoy the moment, to soak up new experiences, eat too much cheese, and perhaps even sip wine like they knew what they were doing.

Inside the castle, the temperature dropped noticeably, and the scent of aged wood and old stone filled the hallways. Intricately woven medieval tapestries covered the walls, each one filled with knights, mythical beasts, and royal banquets frozen in time. It seemed like she was standing in a place where centuries had passed and yet nothing had changed.

Their tour guide, who introduced himself as Sean, stood near the entrance. Early 30s, scruffy beard, fitted jacket over a vintage wine-logo tee. He looked like the kind of guy who split his time between reading history books and home-brewing mead. "Welcome to Castello di Amorosa," he greeted warmly, "where we like our wine dry, our ghosts dramatic, and our staircases slightly uneven, just like in the 1300s."

Leigh grinned. She liked him already.

Sean led them into a winding corridor, one hand gesturing as he walked. "This isn't just a replica. Dario Sattui, the founder, was obsessed with authenticity. He spent years researching medieval architecture and building techniques, then worked with craftworkers to construct this castle using as many traditional materials and methods as possible. That includes chisel-carved stone walls, hand-forged iron gates, and no modern shortcuts." He ran his hand along a stone archway. "No concrete. No fake facades. Just an honest-to-goodness 14th-century-style Tuscan castle, built right here in Napa Valley."

Leigh's gaze traveled across the intricate ceilings, the uneven stones, and the iron chandeliers that hung overhead like gothic jewelry. The attention to detail was staggering. She could practically picture the masons of centuries ago, passing down their knowledge brick by brick.

As they stepped into a vaulted room filled with oak barrels, Sean paused near a wide arch that led into the shadowy wine cellar.

"Legend has it," he said, lowering his voice to a whisper, "that one of the original builders, who insisted on doing late-night inspections to make sure the barrel racks were perfect, walked into this cellar one night… and never walked back out. They searched everywhere. No signs. No struggle. Just… vanished."

The group leaned in, hanging on his every word.

Sean continued, eyes gleaming. "Now, some say he fell into one of the old secret passageways and got lost. Others claim his footsteps can still be heard echoing after hours, usually around midnight, when the wind picks up and the candles flicker."

Leigh glanced around the room. The dim lighting and thick stone walls certainly didn't help ease the sensation that someone, or something, might be lurking just out of view.

Alice's eyes widened as she elbowed her way closer to Leigh. "Great. Just great," she muttered, sticking close to Leigh's side. "I finally get to live out my castle dreams, and the first thing I hear is that it's haunted. I just want wine and to pretend I'm royalty, not ghost bait."

Leigh couldn't help but laugh. "Hey, I'm with you. We've met a lot of ghosts lately. But come on, if you're in a legit castle and don't get at least a little creeped out, are you even doing it right?"

Marie looped her arm through Alice's and gave her a playful nudge. "It's what makes it more authentic, Alice. Every good castle needs a spooky dungeon. Otherwise, it's just a fancy barn."

Kay, who had been trailing behind, shook her head with a smile. "I gotta agree. What's the fun in a castle without some creepy, candlelit cellars and ghost stories?"

Leigh grinned, sweeping her gaze across the arched ceilings and ancient walls. "Well, no ghost, or flickering light, is going to keep me from living my best queen life today with Alice."

They continued, weaving through the long hallways

and admiring the medieval architecture. The grand banquet hall was amazing, with its high beamed ceilings, an enormous fireplace that could roast an entire wild boar, and long wooden tables that looked like they'd hosted royal feasts filled with laughter, strategy, and perhaps a little backstabbing. Every detail, from the weathered candelabras to the faded banners, felt pulled from another century.

Sean pointed out a small courtyard visible through an iron gate. "Even the bricks out there were imported from Europe. Dario wanted this place to seem lived in, not like a museum. The artisans even used ancient techniques like lime plaster, medieval nails, and handmade tiles."

As they passed a row of old bookshelves in the gift shop at the end of their tour, Alice lingered behind. "I think I'm going to grab a couple of these books," she said thoughtfully. "Sonoma history and possibly one on local wineries, especially if there is one on this one. I need to know more about this place."

"Look at you, the historian in you can never stay hidden for long," Kay teased, nudging Alice with her elbow.

Alice smiled. "Don't act like you're not going to try to borrow it when I'm done."

Leigh chuckled, watching as Alice sifted through the books. It was comforting to see Alice like this, focused, curious, completely absorbed in her element. Not stressed or scattered like she'd been lately. Just… Alice. The shadows under her eyes had faded, as well as the quiet sighs when she thought no one was listening. She knew Alice was still struggling with working through all the issues at home, but it was wonderful to see that perhaps she had finally given herself some grace and energy for herself.

Before they left, they signed up for a grape-stomping

activity in one of the castle courtyards. It was something Leigh hadn't planned for, but it sounded too fun to pass up. They were given protection for their clothes and rolled up their pant legs. As they climbed into the large barrels, the squishy sensation of the freshly harvested grapes beneath their feet made Kay squeal.

"This seems so wrong," Alice said, wobbling as she tried to get her footing, one hand reaching out instinctively for balance. Her voice was caught somewhere between discomfort and amusement.

Marie, already stomping enthusiastically, grinned. "It's the closest I'll probably ever get to being a winemaker."

Kay, whose apron was already splattered with grape juice, let out a laugh. "It's so satisfying. Like, I feel like Lucy Ricardo or something." She laughed as she took a quick break and snapped pictures of the whole thing. "This is going straight to the photo album."

Leigh was laughing so hard she could barely stand, but she loved every second of it. She caught sight of Marie's exaggerated stomping and Alice's wide-eyed expression, the way she kept trying to keep herself steady, and Kay snapping photos of them all. There was something so perfectly unfiltered about it. The way they were all letting go, acting like kids, drenched in sunshine and grape juice. It wasn't elegant at all, but it was real. One of those moments you didn't plan for but never wanted to end.

By the time they finished and rinsed off, their sides all hurt from laughing at how absurd it all was. "I can't believe I did that," Alice said, a grin spreading across her face. "This is definitely…a unique experience."

The ladies piled back into the car, all talking at once. Marie was fiddling with the radio, skipping past static-filled country stations and '80s throwbacks until they landed on something mellow and upbeat. Kay passed around mints she'd dug out of her bottomless purse, and someone made a joke about road trip snacks and wine not being a balanced diet.

By the time they rolled into downtown Napa and walked up to the Bounty Hunter Wine Bar, the mid-afternoon sun had warmed the sidewalks, and their appetites had fully kicked in.

The second they stepped inside the Bounty Hunter Wine Bar, the smoky aroma of BBQ hit them. Leigh's stomach grumbled in response, and her mouth watered as she took in the rich, savory scent. The space had a rustic-meets-refined vibe. Exposed brick walls, shelves of wine bottles stretching to the ceiling, and candlelight bouncing off polished wood. It was inviting, like a place that didn't try too hard but knew exactly what it was doing.

"Well, hello there!" a lively voice greeted them, pulling Leigh's attention to the man behind the bar. Their server, who gave his name as, was already in motion, sliding effortlessly between tables, like he was born for this. He made taking care of a room full of tables seem easy and fun. Leigh admired that, people who brought their whole heart to what they did always stood out.

Joey led them to a booth near the window and handed out menus with a flourish. "Now, if you're up for the BBQ Bowl, let me say, you won't regret it," Joey said, a playful wink punctuating his words. "But, for the true connoisseurs, the pulled pork sandwich is what dreams are made of. Pair it with the spirits flight, and you've got yourself the perfect meal."

Leigh didn't need convincing. Her eyes skimmed the menu, but she already knew what she wanted. "I'm going with the BBQ Bowl," she said, grinning as she closed her menu. "You had me at 'won't regret it.'"

Kay nodded. "Yep, same. I'm not even going to pretend I'm considering anything else." She flipped her menu shut with a snap. "Meat, BBQ sauce, and a drink flight? Sold."

Alice made a face and held her menu out in front of her, squinting at it like it was a calculus problem. "Ugh, I was going to get that, but now it seems like I'm copying everyone. I need to mix it up."

Marie, never one for indecisiveness, said good-naturedly, "Just copy. No one cares."

It took them a few more minutes of teasing and playfully debating, but eventually, they all placed their orders. Joey disappeared into the kitchen, and they settled into their booth, picking up where they'd left off, catching up on life, laughing about things only they would find funny.

When Joey returned with their drinks, balancing a tray of colorful cocktails with an impressive flair, the group cheered.

"All right, ladies," Joey said, his voice full of mischief. "Bold, smoky, and guaranteed to put a smile on your face."

Alice leaned back in her seat and quipped, "Sounds like a Tinder bio."

That did it, the table erupted. Laughter bubbled up and spilled over, loud and unfiltered. Leigh watched her friends, soaking it all in, Marie's wide grin as she wiped a tear from the corner of her eye, Kay's uncontainable belly laugh that made her whole body shake, Alice trying (and failing) to play it cool while her shoulders shook with giggles.

Leigh smiled and let herself fall into the moment. For a second, it was like time rewound itself. She could almost see the younger versions of themselves. To when they first met, all full of energy and new dreams and late-night talks over what their futures would be. That carefree feeling, and the one of being known and seen and loved, hadn't faded. If anything, it had grown stronger over the years, layered with all they'd shared.

"Shocking, Alice," Marie said, faking disbelief. "What do you know about Tinder?"

"Only what I overhear Zach's single friends talking about on his poker nights," Alice said, rolling her eyes and smirking.

As their meals arrived, Kay was already on it, her camera poised and ready. Capturing each moment with an artist's eye. The vibrant colors of their plates, the smoke curling from the grill, the rustic charm of the bar. She didn't miss a single detail.

"This looks so delicious," Kay said, her grin infectious. She snapped a picture of Alice holding up her drink, eyes sparkling with mischief. "That's the perfect pose. You're a natural."

Alice, embracing the persona of a show woman, struck a red-carpet-worthy pose, her drink held high like a victory. "Anything for a good shot," she said, laughing as she sipped her drink.

The meal was everything they'd been promised, smoky, tender, and delicious. They dove into the food with the same enthusiasm they brought to everything. After all, they were women who appreciated the finer things in life. Like BBQ. And good company. And even better conversations.

Later, they wandered through downtown Napa, the day still warm and golden around them. The streets were bustling with tourists and locals alike, but it was the quirky little shops that caught their attention. They popped into one that seemed like it hadn't changed since the '70s. Cluttered shelves lined with everything from vintage knick-knacks and faded postcards to oddball sculptures and random trinkets that made them all stop and stare in amazement.

Kay tried on a vintage hat, one that looked like something from an old silent detective film. "How do I look?" she asked, spinning around like she was auditioning for a movie.

"I think you've found your new look," Alice said, deadpan. "Add a mustache and magnifying glass and you're good to go."

Leigh doubled over in laughter. "Honestly, Kay, it honestly works for you. You should keep it, but perhaps skip the mustache unless you're committing to full character."

But Alice wasn't done yet. She wandered deeper into the shop, her eyes lighting up as she discovered a peculiar ceramic statue of a chicken holding a wine glass. "What even is this?" Alice asked, holding it up like it was an ancient artifact.

"It's art," Kay replied, her voice completely straight. "Modern art. I am an expert in these things."

Alice snickered, shaking her head, and Leigh laughed along with them, her cheeks actually hurting a little from how much fun they were having.

They continued to explore, popping into a tiny bookstore that smelled of old paper and adventure. Alice, of course, headed straight for the history section, scanning the shelves with determination. She always had to know more, and now she was on a mission about Sonoma history. Leigh smiled, watching her. Alice might not have been the loudest of the group, but when she was passionate about something, she would talk about it for hours.

They stepped back out into the street, still chatting, still teasing one another. Their voices blended with the sounds of downtown. The passing cars, soft music drifting from a nearby patio, someone whistling a familiar tune. They were making memories. Not the kind that came from big events or perfectly planned moments, but the ones that sneak up on you, spur-of-the-moment adventures, inside jokes about wine-drinking chickens, and old hats that suddenly seem like new personas.

# 21 UNVEILING TRUTHS AT BERINGER VINEYARDS

The friends eagerly headed off to Beringer Vineyards, their next stop in what was quickly becoming a marathon of wine, views, and as much local lore as they could soak up. It was a sprawling estate renowned not only for its world-class wines but for its haunted past. As they pulled into the gravel driveway, the towering, ivy-draped Rhine House rose before them like something from a storybook. Its gabled roof, arched windows, and ornate trim looked straight out of a Gothic mystery. Leigh leaned forward in her seat, eyes wide. The way the sunlight hit the old stones made the house glow softly, as if it held secrets.

"Wow," Marie said, stepping out of the car and shielding her eyes from the sun. "If there aren't at least three ghosts haunting this place, I'm going to be seriously disappointed."

"Four ghosts," Kay chimed in, "and I bet one of them is a disgruntled winemaker still critiquing the blends."

As they began to walk the property, the vineyards stretched out across the hills, the vines a deep green contrast against the golden earth. The air held not only the fruity scent of ripening grapes, but something older, deeper, like weathered oak barrels and sunbaked stone. It was easy to imagine the history embedded in every inch of the estate. Leigh lagged slightly behind, marveling at the Rhine House's intricate architecture.

Alice had come prepared. She stopped abruptly, holding up a finger like a tour guide preparing for a dramatic reveal. "Okay, listen to this," she said, eyes dancing. "The Rhine House is rumored to be haunted by the original Beringer brothers, Jacob and Frederick. Some say they never really left. There've been reports of footsteps echoing on the stairs when no one else is in the house, and lights flickering in empty rooms. One employee even claimed to have seen a man in an old-fashioned suit looking out a second-story window... and then he vanished."

Leigh raised an eyebrow. "Wait. When did you have time to read about all this?"

Alice grinned, her mischievousness on full display. "One of the books I grabbed this morning was about this vineyard. I had to sneak a peek in the car."

"You were reading? In the car? While still managing to chime in on every single one of our conversations?" Leigh blinked. "That's not multitasking. That's... supernatural."

Alice smirked. "What can I say? I have many talents. Multitasking is one of them."

Kay jumped in with a laugh. "Yeah, like the time you claimed you would make lasagna, balance the checkbook, and teach yourself French all in one weekend?"

"Hey, I still remember how to say 'cheese' in French," Alice shot back, grinning.

"Oh, oui oui, Madame Overachiever!" Kay teased, making an exaggerated bow.

Leigh laughed so hard she snorted, which only added

to the uproar.

As they continued their walk, Alice's energy shifted. She paused by a row of vines, gently running her fingers over a cluster of deep purple grapes. Her voice softened.

"You know," she said, "it's been so good to get everything out. All the swirling thoughts, the stress I didn't even realize I carried. This trip, and finally… letting go and talking to you all… it's been like taking a breath I didn't realize I needed."

Kay gave her a gentle nudge. "Seriously, it's been amazing seeing you more relaxed again. We've missed you." Her tone was soft and sincere.

Marie nodded thoughtfully. "We all pile so much on ourselves. Like, we're supposed to carry everything quietly and figure it all out solo. But that's not how this works. None of us would ever want to let the others fall apart alone."

Leigh's throat tightened unexpectedly. "Exactly. And yet… I catch myself doing it anyway. Like asking for help is this big admission that I've failed. Which is ridiculous, because I'd never think that about any of you."

The group fell into a thoughtful silence. The only sounds were the breeze gently rustling the leaves and the soft crunch of gravel under their feet. It was one of those rare, quiet moments where vulnerability hung in the air…not heavy, but real.

Leigh looked around at her friends. They were all walking side by side, heads a little higher, shoulders a little lighter. This honest moment was something they'd all needed more than they realized.

Finally, Marie broke the silence with a laugh. "Okay, now we've officially had our Oprah moment. Can we please not cry before the wine tasting?"

"Speak for yourself," Kay said, fanning her eyes dramatically. "I'll cry before and again after the wine tasting. You know, when we realize we can't afford a single bottle in the gift shop."

"Or when Leigh finds out they don't sell Chardonnay," Alice quipped.

"Hey!" Leigh protested, laughing. "I can broaden my horizons. Probably."

Their tour led them into a sun-dappled courtyard, the kind of space Leigh could picture on the glossy pages of a wine country travel magazine. The kind she'd flip through in waiting rooms and dream about. A cluster of bistro tables, some dotted with half-finished wine flights and little plates of olives and cheese, sat tucked beneath a leafy canopy of grapevines.

At the far end of the courtyard, an elegant older woman stood beside a long wooden table artfully arranged with wine bottles and polished glassware. She wore a flowing linen dress in a soft sage green that fluttered gently in the breeze. Her silver hair was swept into a loose bun, one of those effortlessly chic styles Leigh always admired but could never quite replicate without looking like she'd just rolled out of bed.

The woman's smile was as warm as the golden afternoon light. "Welcome, ladies," she said, her voice carrying the refined lilt of someone who'd spent years perfecting the art of hospitality.

Leigh glanced at Kay, who mouthed, "Fancy," before approaching the wine table.

"Wait a moment," she said, her smile widening. "Are you all the ladies staying at the Sinclair winery?"

Leigh exchanged a quick look with Marie, who winked and whispered, "We're famous," before edging closer to the wine table. Leigh couldn't help but laugh quietly as she stepped forward.

Realization dawned on her. This must be the same woman she had spoken with when first planning the trip.

Back then, Leigh had spent a few evenings curled up on the couch with a glass of wine and her laptop, combing through travel sites, tour options, and winery events. She'd made a point to ask every single place how close they were to Sinclair and what they recommended for out-of-town guests. Most had given quick, standard answers, but not this one. This woman had lingered on the phone with her, sharing personal favorites, recommending little-known restaurants, even pointing her toward the best time to visit for fewer crowds and blooming wildflowers. And now here she was, remembering them weeks later.

"Yes, that's us," Leigh replied, a little more brightly now. She smiled, and added with friendly curiosity, "Do you know the Sinclair family?" She tried to sound casual, but she could hear the eagerness for more information in her voice.

"Oh, yes," she replied, her laughter warm and fond, as if recalling a cherished memory. "I was devastated to hear about the accident at the winery. Evelyn was a dear friend. I'm Margaret St. James, but please, call me Maggie. Evelyn and I spent countless afternoons in this very courtyard, solving the world's problems over a glass of Merlot."

Leigh smiled, picturing Evelyn seated right where they were now, perhaps laughing and leaning in close to Maggie to share a secret. "That's lovely," Leigh said, her voice gentle with sincerity. "It sounds like you two were really close. I'm so sorry for your loss."

"Thank you, we were," Maggie said, her smile dimming but still tender. "Evelyn was fiercely passionate about the winery. She poured herself into every vine, every bottle, every event. But she always worried that her children didn't share that same love. She confided in me once that Nicholas's ambition made her uneasy. He always had big ideas, too big, sometimes, and she feared he was more interested in what the winery could do for him than what it was. And Olivia…" Maggie sighed, swirling the wine in her glass. "That girl had a spark, but Evelyn said she was restless, always looking toward the next thing instead of rooting herself here."

Leigh caught Alice's eyes flick up, her expression alert with interest. The group stayed quiet for a moment, letting Maggie's words sink in.

"But Evelyn wasn't only concerned about that," Maggie continued, her voice dipping. "She felt like something wasn't quite right at the winery. Secrets, she called them. Not things she could pin down, just a heaviness. Like there were things happening behind the scenes that she wasn't being told. She used to say her instincts always kept her one step ahead. But this time… she wasn't sure where to step."

Leigh glanced at her friends. Alice was leaning in, hungry for more details, while Marie stood back, her arms crossed, analyzing Maggie with her usual quiet intensity. Kay, on the other hand, was already eying the samplings of wine and giving Maggie a wide grin.

"Maggie," Marie said, breaking the silence, "did Evelyn ever talk about those secrets? Or what she planned to do about them?"

"Oh, she was quite the planner," Maggie said, a hint of mischief in her tone. "Always had a backup plan, sometimes three. She told me, a few months ago, that she'd made an unusual change to her will. Something about ensuring that decisions and profits would be shared with more relatives if the winery was ever sold. Not only her kids. There was a name… David Foster. A distant cousin, I believe. I'd never heard her mention him before and believe me, we talked about everything. It struck me as odd. Like perhaps he had a role in something she wasn't ready to explain."

The group exchanged a series of pointed looks. There it was again, a sense of being pulled along by something bigger than them. Something Evelyn had started before they even arrived in Sonoma. The woman may have been gone, but it was like her presence lingered in every conversation, every place they visited, every shadowed hallway they passed. Like she was still nudging them forward, daring them to look closer.

Leigh's heart raced as Maggie casually poured small samples of a vibrant zinfandel. It was starting to seem like Evelyn had left them a trail of clues, whispers hidden in casual conversations, notes tucked behind smiles and wine labels. She wasn't just their host or a friendly face from the past. She was the start of a story they hadn't even known they were going to be a part of.

"Interesting," Alice said, her voice measured. "That definitely explains some things."

"Like why Nicholas seems less interested in what makes the winery work, grapes, the land, the people, and more into what's buried in the filing cabinets," Kay said, raising an eyebrow.

"Or why there appears to be so much mystery around David," Leigh said quietly. She stared into her sample glass, the ruby liquid swirling as her mind churned with possibilities. "Everywhere we go, it's like the Sinclair name follows us. Not just as a brand or a family, but as something... unfinished. It's like Evelyn planted little pieces of herself all over this place, just waiting for someone to put them together."

And somehow, Leigh couldn't shake the thought that they were the ones meant to do it.

Maggie seemed to sense the shift in the mood. She picked up the last glass, raising it slightly as though offering a toast. "Come now, Evelyn wouldn't want all of you to waste a beautiful day at a winery thinking about anything but the beauty that's around you," she said with a small smile. "There's so much more to see. The actual Rhine House is just beyond the courtyard, and it's full of history, and a little mystery, too, if you're curious."

"We're very interested," Marie said, her tone dry but her eyes sparkling.

The women followed Maggie toward the stately Rhine House, their chatter picking up again as they walked. Kay nudged Leigh with her elbow. "I think Evelyn might've been a closet detective," she said, grinning. "I mean, secret clauses? Hidden motives? She'd fit right into one of our mystery novels we love so much."

Leigh nodded. "You're not wrong. But it seems a little too real right now."

Inside the Rhine House, the grand halls were filled with ornate woodwork, oil paintings of stern-faced ancestors, and chandeliers that sparkled like something out of a period drama. Maggie led them through each room with the grace of someone who'd walked these halls a hundred times.

"During Prohibition," she said, pausing in front of a bookshelf that swung open to reveal a narrow hidden door, "the Beringer family used these tunnels to smuggle wine to trusted locals. Of course, the authorities knew, but no one dared to intervene. Too many secrets tied to this place."

Kay leaned toward Leigh. "Smuggling tunnels. Secrets. Ghosts. This is basically Disneyland for grown-ups who think they are amateur sleuths."

"Haunted Disneyland," Alice corrected, snapping a picture of the hidden door.

The tour continued into what Maggie called "the blending room," set up with tall stools, long wooden tables, and rows of wine bottles, beakers, and pipettes.

Each of them received a little tasting notebook and were encouraged to create their own custom wine blend. Leigh stared at her small beaker, carefully measuring tiny pours from a Cabernet, a Merlot, and a splash of Zinfandel. She felt like a mad scientist, or a very hopeful winemaker.

"This is like high school chemistry class," Kay said, her tongue poking out as she concentrated. "Except I actually care about the results."

"Don't drink your experiment!" Alice scolded, laughing as Kay feigned taking a sip straight from the beaker.

Leigh's blend ended up surprisingly good, or at least, that's what the others claimed after a few generous sips. The activity offered a lighthearted reprieve, but Maggie's revelations of Evelyn's thoughts lingered.

As they wandered into a grand dining room filled with antique furniture, the group huddled close.

"If what Maggie says about Evelyn is true, then that changes quite a bit," Kay murmured. "If Nicholas knew about that clause…"

"He'd have a motive," Alice finished, her voice grim.

Leigh let out a slow breath. "So would Olivia. And David, honestly. They were both weirdly on edge anytime we saw them." She paused, tugging her sleeve down over her wrist, a small habit she'd picked up when her nerves flared. "It's just… the more we learn, the more it seems like everyone has something to hide."

She groaned, running a hand through her hair. "This definitely makes it seem like there is something going on. No turning back."

"But do we even have anything solid?" Marie asked, her voice low. "We can't exactly go to the police and say, 'We're pretty sure the brother's shady because he gives us the creeps.' I mean, we barely even know these people."

Kay snorted. "Right. What would we even say? 'Hi,

Detective, we're just four nosy women with a gut feeling and too much time on our hands.' We'd sound like an episode of Monk gone wrong."

"Or Diagnosis Murder," Alice added. "Only we're not nearly as clever as Dick Van Dyke."

"I disagree," Kay teased. "I'm the Dr. Sloan of this group."

Leigh shook her head, smiling despite her worries about Evelyn. "Look, we have to admit there's still a very real chance Evelyn's death was just a horrible accident. She was sneaking around, maybe stressed, and maybe something just… went wrong. Not everything has to be a grand conspiracy."

The group fell silent, their gazes darting between each other and the darkened corners of the Rhine House. The mysteries of the estate swirled around them like the rich red wine in their glasses. Whatever truth they were uncovering, Leigh knew one thing for sure: they were in it together, for better or worse.

If Evelyn's ghost was watching, Leigh hoped she was somewhere in the corner of the Rhine House with a glass of Merlot in hand, raising an amused eyebrow at their amateur sleuthing.

# 22 CONFRONTATION AT THE DEERFIELD RANCH WINERY

The friends returned to their cozy guest house at Sinclair Winery, arms filled with tote bags stuffed full of local treasures from their day's adventures. The house smelled faintly of the lavender sachets Kay had picked up at a boutique, and the hum of their chatter blended with the soft jazz playing from a speaker someone had left on earlier. Leigh dropped her bag near the door and let out a long, exaggerated sigh. "Alright, ladies," she said a moment later, pushing her hair back and standing up with mock authority, "it's time to get serious. We're making a case board."

Alice, who sprawled across the overstuffed armchair, gave an incredulous snort. "A case board? What are we, detectives now? Do we get badges? A theme song?"

"Yes!" Kay said without hesitation, her eyes sparkling with excitement. She bolted to her room and returned seconds later with an armful of colorful notepads, gel pens, and a nearly unused pack of glitter markers that Leigh was pretty sure she bought, hoping for moments like this. Kay dumped the supplies onto the coffee table with a flourish. "Detective Leigh and her band of merry women. This is happening." She grabbed a pen and started furiously doodling a magnifying glass on a yellow sticky note.

Within minutes, the coffee table was buried under a rainbow of Post-its, pens, and index cards. It looked more like a preschool art project than an investigative operation, but they were having too much fun to care. Marie took charge of the chaos with the efficiency of someone used to directing models and managing wardrobe disasters backstage.

"Kay, for the love of Chardonnay," she scolded, "stop drawing on everything. We need facts."

Kay leaned back in her chair, feigning outrage. "These scribbles set the mood! You can't solve mysteries without a good aesthetic." She smirked and stuck a bright pink Post-it onto the edge of their board. It read, in loopy handwriting, Motive: Family Drama = $$$. Next to it, she'd drawn a figure wearing a fedora and peeking out from behind a bunch of grapes.

"Classic Kay," Alice muttered, raising her wineglass to her lips. "If this was a real case, we'd already be kicked off it for excessive use of glitter pens."

Leigh tried to regain control, but the scene had devolved into laughter. Alice held up a Post-it that simply said Secret Will??? in Kay's neon marker and waved it in the air. "We're grown women. And here we are, acting like we're starring in Law & Order: Napa Valley."

Leigh cracked a smile, though she still tried to muster some seriousness. Even with their makeshift board and Kay's doodles of sneaky grapes and dramatic arrows pointing to nothing, a part of her felt like they were onto something. "Okay, perhaps this isn't exactly how we should be spending our evening," she admitted, sitting back down and crossing her arms. "But admit it, we're onto something."

Marie wasn't listening. She'd pulled out her phone and was angling for the perfect shot of their "case board." "Hold up, hold up," she said, gesturing for the others to pose in front of it. "I'm sending this to my boys. They predicted this would happen the second I said we were going on another vacation. They're going to lose it."

The women scrambled to strike dramatic poses. Kay leaned forward, pointing at a Post-it with all the intensity of a movie detective solving a triple homicide. Alice adopted a "thinking face," chin in hand and brows furrowed. Leigh, unable to resist, grabbed a sticky note with the word CLUE scribbled across it and struck a Sherlock Holmes stance.

Marie snapped the photo, laughing so hard she could barely hold her phone steady. "Oh, they are never going to let me live this down," she said, typing a caption with exaggerated glee. "'Wine, laughs, and a potential murder mystery. You guys called it!'" She hit send and fell back onto the couch, still chuckling to herself.

Leigh looked around at her friends, their laughter echoing off the walls of the guest house. For a moment, she let herself soak it all in, the wine, the silliness, the joy of being surrounded by the women who could turn any situation into an adventure. Fun. And part of her loved the moment for exactly what it was: four friends letting loose, making memories, and turning a vacation into an adventure.

But as she stood there, sticky note still in hand, Leigh couldn't help the flicker of unease twisting in her gut.

What if they weren't being dramatic? What if this wasn't simply a coping mechanism for Evelyn's accident, something to focus on besides the sad reality of it? Because that's what it was, wasn't it? A tragedy. Evelyn had been kind, warm, generous with her time. And then she was… gone. Everyone said it was a horrible accident. But the things they'd noticed and heard, what if they weren't imagining patterns where there were none?

Were they making a game out of something that was actually dangerous?

No one had said that out loud. Not really. But Leigh could sense the unspoken thoughts.

They all wandered to their rooms to rest before dinner, the mood shifting slightly. Leigh curled up on the soft quilt of her guest room bed. The window cracked open to the cool Sonoma breeze, and let her thoughts wander.

Perhaps they were overthinking everything. They were wine-sipping tourists with too much imagination and a lot of time on their hands. Possibly, making a mystery out of a tragedy was their way of processing it, of protecting themselves from something that seemed too senseless to understand.

Later that evening, the women began to get ready, each transforming from the day's casual explorers to the picture of evening elegance. Leigh stood in front of the mirror, adjusting her blouse for what seemed like the hundredth time. "Flats," she muttered to herself, glancing down at the pair of black, shiny flats she'd swapped for her usual sneakers. "A step up, right?" She looked over her shoulder at Kay, who was twisting her hair into an elaborate updo.

Kay smirked, expertly placing a final pin. "You look adorable, but if you keep tugging at that blouse, you are going to have to iron it again."

Marie breezed in from the bathroom, smelling faintly of gardenia and wearing a wrap dress that somehow looked polished and effortless. "We're going to be late if you don't stop primping, ladies," she teased, grabbing her clutch. "Leigh, you're fine. Just let the flats do their magic."

Alice strolled in wearing a bold red jumpsuit and heels high enough to qualify as a safety hazard. "If I break an ankle tonight, you're all carrying me," she announced, grabbing her purse from the counter. "But hey, I'll look fabulous doing it."

The drive to Deerfield Ranch Winery was filled with chatter and laughter as they teased Alice about her heels and debated whether Leigh's flats were "fancy enough" for the occasion. Leigh rolled her eyes at their banter, but secretly loved it. They were always able to pull her out of her head, even when she was overthinking everything, from her outfit to the murder mystery dinner they were about to walk into.

When they arrived, the winery's candlelit dining room took their breath away. Wine barrels stacked floor to ceiling gave the space a rustic charm, while long wooden tables draped in deep burgundy linens added a touch of luxury. Leigh looked around, taking in everything. This wasn't just dinner, it was an experience. A perfect setting for the fun murder mystery play they'd been looking forward to. "Wow," she said, adjusting her blouse again. "It's like I've walked onto the set of a movie."

Kay nudged her. "A murder movie," she whispered dramatically, wiggling her eyebrows.

As they settled into their seats, actors in elaborate costumes began mingling with the guests, weaving dramatic whispers and hints of suspicion into their conversations. Leigh kept her head low, pretending to be absorbed in the menu. "I swear I just want to blend in," she muttered to Kay. "If one of them asks me to participate, I'm going to die."

"No, you won't," Kay said with a grin. "You look way too nice to be a wallflower. They'll sniff you out immediately."

Before Leigh was able to reply, an actor in a bowler hat and suspenders approached their table. His mustache twitched as he pointed directly at her. "You ladies," he declared, "you have the look of detectives who might crack a case wide open."

Leigh's stomach did a flip. "Oh, no," she began, shaking her head. "I'm just here to …"

But it was too late. The actor had already gestured for her to rise, and the room broke into applause and encouragement.

Against all logic, and maybe influenced slightly by the second glass of Pinot Noir she hadn't yet finished, Leigh stood. She glanced at Alice, who gave her a thumbs-up that was anything but helpful.

"What just happened?" she hissed at Kay as the actor gently took her arm and led her toward the front of the room.

"Your curiosity betrayed you," Kay called after her, laughing as she aimed her phone at Leigh to capture every second. Across the table, Alice and Marie were no help whatsoever. Both of them were hunched over, wiping tears from their eyes from laughing too hard.

At first, Leigh stumbled through her role as an impromptu detective, awkwardly wielding the faux magnifying glass and avoiding eye contact with the crowd. But as the night went on, something shifted. The wine helped, of course, but so did the infectious energy in the room. She leaned into the role, pointing dramatically at suspects and barking out accusations. "Don't lie to me, Mr. Davenport," she said, channeling her best police procedural voice. "I know you were in the wine cellar at 9 p.m.!"

The crowd erupted in laughter, and Leigh found herself grinning. She spotted her friends at the table, Marie clapping wildly, Alice whistling, and Kay shaking her head while recording the whole scene on her phone. Leigh forgot her earlier hesitation and just enjoyed the ridiculousness of it all.

After the murderer was revealed, she returned to the table, her cheeks flushed and her hair slightly askew. Alice slid a fresh glass of wine toward her. "Hollywood's next big detective," she said, smirking. "I can see it now, Leigh, Private Investigator. Coming to Netflix soon."

Leigh laughed, shaking her head. "I'm sure you would rather stick to your books," Kay teased. "But seriously, you killed it."

The evening took another twist when, on their way out, they spotted Nicholas, once again tucked in a corner, deep in conversation with a group of business executives. His posture was tight, his gestures sharp.

Marie frowned. "What's he doing this time? He doesn't seem interested in being at the winery at all."

Leigh watched him closely. He didn't see them yet, or if he did, he was pretending not to. "How is he always where we go? It's like he's following us," she murmured, a chill running down her spine despite the lingering warmth of the afternoon. "Or at least keeping tabs.".

Before they could decide what to do, Nicholas looked up and spotted them. His face twitched, then he excused himself abruptly from the group and strode over. The way he moved, tight shoulders, clenched jaw, set Leigh on edge.

"I know what you've been doing," he said without preamble, his voice low and clipped. "Asking questions. Stirring things up."

Marie stepped forward, folding her arms across her chest. "We can't help it if people talk to us," and Nicholas's face turns ghostly pale when she starts detailing what they've heard. Leigh noted the slight tremor in his voice as she brought up the secret will clause and Evelyn's apparent ignorance of some of the winery's dealings. He stumbled over his words, finally confessing his desperation to sell the winery. "But I didn't do anything to her!" he blurted out, his voice cracking. "If someone did, then it had to be David Foster. He had more to gain than anyone if there really was a secret will with changes!" He looked around, eyes darting as if someone might be listening. "You should stop digging. Some things are better left alone."

Leigh's stomach twisted. There it was, not a threat exactly, but a warning. A subtle suggestion that they might be getting too close to something dangerous.

Kay crossed her arms, skeptical. "David? Evelyn trusted him. He was helping her!"

Leigh and Alice exchanged glances, confusion settling between them. Nicholas's story was riddled with holes, but his insistence that David was involved was unnerving. Leigh rubbed her temple, trying to piece it all together. "Something's not adding up," she murmured as they walked toward the car.

Kay let out a worried breath. "What I want to know is how we're the ones trying to solve this mess. Are we sure the professionals are not needed here?"

Alice frowned. "You mean the ones who thought Evelyn tripped over a crate of wine and 'accidentally' hit her head? Sure, Kay. They are definitely going to be all in with our theories and ideas."

As they climbed into the car, Marie shook her head. "Honestly, Nicholas's whole dramatic confession seemed like something out of a soap opera. I half-expected him to clutch his chest and fall onto a fainting couch."

Leigh started the car, glancing back at her friends in the rearview mirror. "You think David actually could be guilty of something? Or is Nicholas just grasping at straws?"

Kay snorted from the passenger seat. "I think Nicholas is losing it and feels guilty so he's willing to throw suspicion on anyone he can."

Alice chimed in, "I really can't see David being the villain of the story." She paused. "Then again, every mystery needs a plot twist."

They all sat in silence for a beat, thoughts tumbling faster than they could keep up with. It was all starting to seem a little too real. Theories tangled with actual concern.

"We're probably just getting in over our heads," Leigh said slowly. "This might just be about money. Inheritance. Family drama. Sneaky business dealings, sure, but not murder. Not danger. Not… us."

"Right," Marie said with a nod. "And if it does start feeling dangerous, we go to the police. No matter how ridiculous we think we sound."

"Agreed," Kay said, a bit too quickly.

Alice exhaled, finally leaning back. "Let's not spiral. We've had a weird day. We're tired. And stressed. Let's just assume Nicholas, Olivia, and David are fighting over who gets the wine barrels and call it a night."

The air in the car lightened, the tension slowly dissipating. Leigh turned down a quiet street toward their guest house, grateful for the shift.

Marie leaned forward, resting her chin on Leigh's seat. "Speaking of drama, Leigh, I died when you pulled out the 'Don't lie to me, Mr. Davenport!' line during the dinner. Where did that come from?"

Leigh groaned. "I don't even know. My mouth and brain stopped communicating about halfway through."

Alice cackled. "Oh, we know. You practically channeled a cop from a 1950s detective flick. It was glorious."

They pulled into the driveway, finally back at their rental. As soon as they stepped inside, shoes were kicked off and dresses traded for flannel pajamas and oversized sweatshirts. Marie was the first to raid the fridge, emerging with a block of cheese and crackers. "Ladies, our charcuterie board for the evening," she declared with a mock bow.

"Classy," Kay deadpanned. "What's next, canned olives and string cheese?"

"Don't tempt me," Marie said, grinning as she popped a cracker into her mouth.

Alice sank onto the couch, tucking her legs underneath her. "Kay, find us something good to watch. None of that boring news stuff."

Kay began flipping through the channels, her finger hovering over the remote until she stopped suddenly. "No way," she said, her face lighting up. She pointed at the screen, where Adam Sandler and Jennifer Aniston stood in formalwear. Murder Mystery.

Marie gasped and plopped onto the couch, spilling popcorn in the process. "It's a sign!" she declared, handing out bowls of snacks. "This is meant to be."

Leigh settled into the corner of the couch, cup of hot cocoa in hand. "I mean, if the universe wants us to be amateur detectives, who are we to argue?" she said.

As the movie played, the women narrated it themselves, comparing the bumbling suspicious characters to Nicholas and David and debating whether they could pull off Jennifer Aniston's wonderful wardrobe. Kay, channeling her inner critic, provided commentary on the detectives. "See? Even he knew to check the alibi," she quipped, shaking her head dramatically.

By the time the credits rolled, they were a tangled heap of blankets and laughter, their heads resting against one another's shoulders. Leigh sighed contentedly, looking around the room. Despite the strange past few days and the growing mystery surrounding Evelyn's death, this moment was perfect.

"You know," Alice said softly, "maybe there's no real mystery to solve. But we sure have one heck of a story to tell."

Marie raised her bowl of popcorn in a mock toast. "To mystery! And to Leigh's starring role in the next crime drama."

"Don't hold your breath," Leigh said, laughing as she tossed a kernel at Marie.

The uncertainty still hung around them like fog on a vineyard morning, but in that moment, surrounded by friends, Leigh let it drift to the background. Whatever tomorrow brought, tonight at least they were okay.

# 23 BETRAYAL BENEATH THE VINES

The next morning, the women lingered over coffee and conversation as they prepared for the day, each gathering her things with the leisurely energy of travelers who had no deadlines. Leigh sipped from her mug on the patio outside their rental, savoring the comforting aroma of strong coffee swirling around her. She could get used to mornings like this… no agenda, no emails, no real-life responsibilities knocking. Simply friends, sunshine, and a loose plan for breakfast.

By the time they stepped into Dierk's Parkside Café for breakfast, the delicious scent of something buttery and sweet and sizzling bacon enveloped them. The restaurant was intimate and charming, with checkered tablecloths that clashed perfectly with mismatched chairs, giving the space a wonderful eclectic vibe. Large windows framed the busy sidewalks outside, and a handwritten blackboard listed specials like "Lemon Ricotta Pancakes" and "Farmer's Market Omelet."

Leigh's stomach growled audibly as she watched a server whisk by with a tray laden with fluffy biscuits and glistening hollandaise. Kay gave her a knowing glance, smirking. "Guess it's time to fuel up, huh?"

Once they were seated, Marie scanned the menu, her fingers idly drumming on her coffee cup. "Homemade corned beef hash for me," she declared with certainty. "I mean, come on, anything labeled 'homemade' is a no-brainer."

Leigh nodded appreciatively, already imagining the crispy potatoes and savory beef. "I'm going for the country benedict," she said, her mouth watering at the idea of hollandaise sauce and perfectly poached eggs atop buttery biscuits.

Kay declared, "I need something big enough to keep me going until dinner. Boulevard burrito, for sure."

Alice, who always seemed to weigh her options a little too seriously, tilted her head thoughtfully. "The warm poached egg salad is calling my name. I've been eating like I'm prepping for an eating competition this whole trip, I think I owe my arteries a little grace."

Kay raised an eyebrow. "Grace? You ate both mine and your bowls of ice cream last night."

Alice didn't miss a beat. "And I'd do it again. No regrets," she replied with a grin, snapping her menu shut.

Leigh shook her head, amused. These moments, full of easy banter, were exactly what she'd needed. Especially with everything going on. The strange undercurrent that had started to run beneath their otherwise perfect trip. There was still so much they didn't understand about what had happened to Evelyn. And what was it that kept nagging at the back of her thoughts?

Their server, a cheerful woman named Jenna, approached with a pen poised. She gave a warm chuckle at their lively banter as they ordered. "Great choices, ladies. Coffee all around?"

"And orange juice for me," Leigh added. "Gotta keep my vitamin C levels high."

The group chuckled as Jenna jotted down their orders

and disappeared into the bustling kitchen.

As they waited for their food, the conversation ebbed and flowed with the ease of lifelong friends. They spoke freely, pausing only to sip their drinks or lean in when something juicy came up, each word spinning effortlessly from one story to another.

"So, David Foster," Kay began, a shy grin tugging at the corners of her mouth. "What is everyone's opinion? Mysterious good guy or secret troublemaker?"

Alice couldn't hide her amusement. "Definitely mysterious. But you seem awfully interested in figuring him out. What's your angle, Kay?"

Kay shrugged nonchalantly, though her eyes sparkled with mischief. "He's… interesting. And handy. You know, taking care of everything at the winery."

Leigh chuckled, setting down her cup. "Only you, Kay, could turn 'handy' into a selling point."

Still, as she teased, a quiet thought stayed in the back of her mind. Kay had been quick to speak up for David more than once this week. She'd brushed off suspicions, offered explanations, even laughed off things that had made the rest of them pause. It wasn't like Kay to hold back, not about someone she found attractive or suspicious. But here she was, walking a line between fascination and defense. Perhaps she saw something in David that the rest of them didn't yet. Or maybe… she was ready for her own romantic adventure, even in someone wrapped in mystery.

Their meals arrived, the server sliding plates onto the table with practiced ease, and the conversation slowed to a contented lull. Leigh's country benedict was exactly as she'd hoped: a decadent plate full of poached eggs, crispy bacon, and fluffy biscuits drenched in golden sauce.

Across from her, Alice picked at her egg salad before pausing, a small, genuine smile forming. "I talked to Zach last night," she said softly, almost like she wasn't sure if she should. "He was so happy. He said it was the first time in weeks I didn't sound like I was frustrated trying to explain why I needed to do everything myself or apologizing for being stressed and overwhelmed." She took another bite, slower this time. "I believe I've finally found some peace. A few avenues for help. Honestly… thanks to all of you."

Marie, mid-bite of her corned beef hash, nodded. "I feel better too. I've remembered how much I genuinely love traveling, exploring new places, meeting new people. I'm going to take everyone's advice and talk to my employer about turning some of my work trips into opportunities to stay a little longer and explore. Try to coincide them with family vacations. Blending work and family would be amazing."

Leigh smiled as she listened to her friends share their reflections. These moments of unexpected clarity, tiny decisions, and sparks of courage were why she loved planning these trips.

She looked out the café window as she took another sip. Once upon a time, she'd been spontaneous. Brave, even. The kind of girl who'd say yes to a last-minute trip simply to chase the sunset. But somewhere in the tangle of motherhood, anxiety, and practical choices, she'd started playing it safe. She clung to lists and plans, mistaking them for control. And yet… here she was, sensing the old version of herself stir.

She hadn't erased her anxiety, but it wasn't driving anymore. These trips, this time with her friends, it was like medicine in disguise. The more she leaned into the unknown, the quieter that anxious voice became.

She raised her orange juice, her heart full. "Here's to us, and to more trips that remind us who we are and what we are capable of."

The women clinked their glasses, their laughter blending with the noise of the café.

Their plates slowly emptied, conversation turning quieter and more thoughtful, and before long, they were leaning back in their chairs, filled not only with food, but with something deeper. The kind of full that lingered long after the check was paid.

The afternoon sun shone down on them as they strolled through the Sonoma Botanical Garden, its tranquil paths winding through a kaleidoscope of colorful blooms and towering trees. The hum of bees and the soft rustle of leaves accompanied them, creating an almost magical atmosphere. Leigh lagged slightly behind the group, letting the serenity of the place wash over her. She took in the bursts of color from clusters of dahlias and the way the sunlight filtered through the canopies, casting shadows on the ground.

Everything was quiet here, peaceful. And yet… her mind wouldn't let go of the nagging sense that something was off. Evelyn's accident, the staff and neighboring wineries' whispers, and the odd tension she couldn't quite name, occupied her mind. Beautiful as the garden was, it seemed like a pause before something shifted. Like the breath before a page turns.

Ahead of her, Kay was fully immersed in conversation with a man they'd met along the path, a professional photographer named James, who was friendly, knowledgeable, and just eccentric enough to be instantly likable. Leigh had seen the spark in Kay's eyes the second he mentioned he taught weekend workshops.

"So, if I want to capture this fern," Kay asked, crouching beside a vibrant patch of greenery, "what's the best way to make it pop without losing the background?"

James smiled patiently. "Use a shallow depth of field. Lower your f-stop to blur the background slightly while keeping the fern sharp."

Kay adjusted her camera and snapped a photo, her face lighting up as she reviewed it. "Look at that! I'm basically Ansel Adams now."

Alice peeked over her shoulder. "Or at least his lesser-known cousin."

Unbothered, Kay laughed. "I'll take it."

Leigh smiled, watching them. She found herself marveling at how Kay could throw herself into a moment, always eager to learn something new. It was a trait Leigh admired but had trouble emulating. While her friends often embraced spontaneity, Leigh found herself clinging to control.

The group continued to move slowly, pausing to admire everything from delicate orchids to an intricate Japanese maple, its crimson leaves fanned out like lace. Marie pointed out a tiny hummingbird flitting between blossoms, its wings a blur. "See him go! How is something so small, so full of energy?" she marveled.

Leigh chuckled, her gaze following the bird. "That's how I feel about this trip and the others I've been taking lately. It's like my energy has been refilled in these little, beautiful bursts."

James led them to a serene koi pond tucked into a shaded grove. The still water mirrored the surrounding foliage, broken only by the gentle ripples of colorful koi gliding beneath the surface. "This is one of my favorite spots," James admitted. "It's so still, but there's always something happening if you watch closely."

Leigh knelt by the edge, watching the fish dart and circle below her. She felt a quiet kind of awe, the kind that crept up on her in places like this, surrounded by nature and possibility. These trips were always meant to be about connection and renewal, but they also stirred something deeper within her, a reminder of who she was before life had settled into its predictable rhythms.

Alice called out from a short distance, waving her hand in front of a tree covered in delicate, bell-shaped flowers. "Guys, come check this out. It's beautiful!"

The group gathered around, marveling at the tree as James explained its origin and significance. Leigh listened, but found her focus drifting. She was glad to be here, glad to be surrounded by these women who reminded her of her best self. After a few more appreciative murmurs and camera snaps, they thanked James warmly and said their goodbyes.

The car ride back to Sinclair Winery began with light conversation about the beautiful gardens they'd just visited. The colors of the flowers, the peaceful trickle of fountains, and the cool breeze of the late afternoon.

But it wasn't long before their conversation shifted, and, predictably, the topic turned back to Nicholas.

His smug demeanor, the way he always seemed to have a convenient excuse for everything, and the way he avoided direct eye contact, it all screamed dishonesty. The weight of his secrets, and the unease they had about what they'd uncovered, pressed its way into the conversation like an unwelcome guest. Leigh sighed. These really weren't simply idle rumors, they were pieces of a puzzle that someone needed to be told about. Whether intentional or not, it seemed like Evelyn had been trying to rid the winery of its secrets before her tragic accident.

Marie broke the silence, her voice quiet and determined, echoing Leigh's thoughts. "Someone else needs to know. Not only us. People connected to this place deserve the truth."

Leigh nodded, her fingers tightening around the strap of her purse. "Exactly. Too many pieces aren't adding up, about Nicholas, about the sale of pieces of the property, about the will. Even if it's not… sinister, it's still wrong to keep this to ourselves."

"I don't trust Nicholas as far as I can throw him," Kay muttered from the front seat, crossing her arms. "He's slimy, like one of those guys who always has a 'great investment opportunity' only for you, but you end up broke and wondering how the heck you fell for it."

"Or a guy who smiles too much while lying through his teeth," Alice added.

Leigh released a nervous laugh. "He's definitely not winning any awards for trustworthiness."

Marie jumped in and added, "Olivia and David definitely need to know. If they don't already."

Leigh thought about that for a moment and agreed. Olivia had opened up to them, sharing her fears about Nicholas, the pressure he'd been putting on her, how something didn't seem right. That kind of vulnerability wasn't something you gave lightly, especially not to a group of guests you barely knew. But Olivia had done it anyway. Trusted them.

And David? Leigh remembered how fondly Evelyn had spoken of David on their first night, and how she'd written about him in those letters they had found. It hadn't been an official endorsement, but the warmth in her voice and written words had said enough. Evelyn had trusted him. And if she'd seen something in him, then perhaps that was worth leaning on now.

"I agree," Leigh said finally. "That way, they can be as informed as possible to take their next steps."

The car settled into a thoughtful silence, the road winding ahead of them.

When they pulled up to Sinclair Winery, the air seemed almost electric. The group spotted Olivia standing near the main building, motionless, her back straight but her expression tight. It was as if she'd been standing there for hours, waiting for something, or someone.

"It's like she knew we were coming," Kay whispered, barely moving her lips. "We were just saying we needed to talk to her."

"Perhaps it's fate," Leigh murmured, her gaze lingering on Olivia. Up close, she looked more fragile than ever, her slender frame dwarfed by the large, weathered doors of the winery. Her cream sweater hung loosely on her shoulders, her arms wrapped tightly around herself, not for warmth, but like she was trying to keep from falling apart. Her face was pale, her eyes shadowed, as if the burdens of the past days had hollowed her out.

Leigh felt a pang of something sharp, sympathy? Caution? She wasn't sure. She just knew that Olivia looked like someone who had reached the edge of something. She exchanged a glance with her friends, and they silently agreed. It was now or never.

They approached slowly, their footsteps crunching on the gravel path. Leigh couldn't shake the idea that Olivia looked like a porcelain doll, beautiful, but breakable. Yet, beneath that fragility, there was something almost steely in her gaze as they drew closer.

Leigh wasted no time. "Olivia, we've learned some things about Nicholas, about a clause in Evelyn's will, and what might have been going on behind the scenes here. We want to tell you everything, and then we suggest you should talk to Officer McBride about it."

Olivia's posture didn't change, but her expression flickered, just enough to reveal a spark of alarm.

Kay stepped up beside Leigh, her voice steady but gentle. "If you aren't comfortable going to the police yourself, we can do it for you. We don't have all the answers yet, but what we do know seems important. Let the authorities decide what to do with it."

For a moment, Olivia was silent, her face an unreadable mask. She blinked, seeming to process the words, and perhaps the weight of what they meant. The wind tugged a strand of hair across her cheek, and she brushed it away absently, her hands trembling.

Leigh softened her tone. "We're not trying to cause more trouble for you. But you deserve to know the full truth about what Nicholas has done. Your mom even had her suspicions that something horrible may have been happening. There was a clause Evelyn added to her will where she included David in her final revision. She didn't tell Nicholas or you, did she?"

That landed. Olivia flinched, almost imperceptibly.

"No," she said quietly, almost to herself. "We had no idea. Nicholas and I… we thought it was just the same old document." Her lips pressed into a thin line. "This is all such a mess."

Kay took a step closer. "We're going to talk to David next. Your mother trusted him. We think he's closer to figuring this out than anyone thinks."

Then, her expression darkened, and the air around them seemed to shift, thicker somehow, like the weight of her words had already begun pressing down before they were even spoken. Olivia stood there, still and trembling, yet with a strange defiance burning behind her eyes. She looked like someone unraveling and clinging to the thread that might hold her together, determined, but undeniably broken.

"You think Nicholas is the one behind all of this?" she said, her voice rising sharply, edged with something dark. "He's not innocent, but he's not the mastermind either. That would be me."

The words hit Leigh like a physical blow. Her mind struggled to make sense of what she'd heard. She blinked, trying to read Olivia's face, but it was a storm of fury, guilt, and something close to relief.

"I needed the winery to sell," Olivia said, her voice tightening with every word. "I've been stuck here my entire life. Every birthday, every holiday, every summer, this place has held me like a prison. I had no choice in my future, it was all planned out for me before I could even walk. My mother didn't understand that. She thought tradition and heritage were enough to keep someone happy.But for me, it was a cage."

She took a small, shaky step forward, like her body was still deciding whether to run or stand her ground.

"I didn't want her dead," she said quickly, pain flashing across her face. "I just wanted out. I wanted her to understand how bad things had gotten. I needed her to let go."

"I had to find a way to push her out of the way, but it was only supposed to be figuratively, not literally," she said quickly, her expression twisted with pain. "I encouraged Nicholas and his ridiculous schemes. He's always been greedy. I simply gave him more ideas, more reasons to think his plans would work. I exaggerated the losses, created fake financial reports, and made sure certain shipments didn't go out on time. We needed the books to look desperate. Hopeless."

Leigh stared at her in stunned silence, every word revealing a deeper betrayal.

"I planted ideas, rumors, whispers," Olivia continued. "Talk of bad luck, spirits, of the winery being cursed. I began setting traps, subtle things at first. A broken step here, a flickering light there. Just enough to make it seem unsafe, to keep guests uneasy. I was planning something bigger. I even told Nicholas that the next staged accident would make people think this place was a danger zone. A liability."

Her voice cracked, and she swallowed hard, her hands now trembling at her sides. "She wasn't supposed to be there that night. I swear. I was going to fake a fall the next day during one of the tours, just to sell the illusion. Show people how dangerous it was getting. I didn't know Mom would be going there. I never meant for her to... Once everyone agreed it was an accident, I thought we were safe, but afterward David wouldn't stop asking questions. I thought I had come up with a task that would keep him away from the Winery for a while, but he was so intent on getting back that he finished it in record time. I didn't expect him to actually care that much." Her voice broke off, brittle and desperate.

Leigh's stomach twisted. She could see it all now, how Olivia and Nicholas must've scrambled after Evelyn fell. Together, they'd probably gathered anything that looked like tampering. Cleaning up the tangled mess Olivia had created and then lost control of.

"You set the trap," Leigh said, her voice low but firm. "You built the lie, convinced Nicholas to help you rob the place blind, and tried to run David off when he got too close to the truth. This wasn't simply a scare tactic gone wrong, this was sabotage that cost your mother her life."

Kay's arms were tightly crossed, her brows drawn. "So you stirred up all this chaos, and what? You were just going to walk away and act like it never happened? Like her death was simply collateral damage?"

Olivia crumbled into a nearby chair, her composure finally shattering. She buried her face in her hands, her shoulders shaking. "I didn't know what else to do," she whispered, muffled and hollow. "I never thought it would go that far. I wanted, actually needed, to escape. But every day since mom's accident... I feel like I'm drowning."

Leigh exchanged a look with her friends. The shock in their eyes mirrored her own. Finally, she spoke, her voice steady despite the whirlwind of emotions inside her. "We're calling Officer McBride, Olivia. This lying has to stop."

There was no argument. Olivia didn't even look up. She simply sat there, hands still covering her face, too defeated to protest. She had nothing left to say.

When the police arrived, the weight of it all seemed to finally catch up to her. Her earlier sharpness was gone, replaced with weary honesty. She confessed in full. How she and Nicholas had been draining the winery's accounts for months, how her plans to devalue the business had spiraled into something she hadn't been able to control. Nicholas tried to maintain his usual smug smirk, but as the truth poured out, his expression cracked, revealing something uglier, panic.

As the officers led them away, Leigh felt a strange mix of relief and sadness. No one had wanted it to end like this, and they were sure, least of all, Evelyn.

As they walked back to the guest house, Alice shook her head, her voice heavy with disbelief. "Well, that went a bit differently than we expected."

"That's putting it mildly," Kay said. "We really are magnets for chaos, aren't we?"

Leigh let out a slow breath, and the tightness in her chest finally eased. "Maybe," she said, glancing at the women beside her. "But I wouldn't want to face it with anyone else."

Marie slipped her arm through Leigh's with a tired smile.

And together, they stepped back towards the guesthouse, leaving the tangled web of Olivia and Nicholas' secrets behind them.

# 24 THE FINAL PIECES

Later, after Olivia's tearful confession and the last of the police cars finally rolled down the long drive, the friends found themselves wandering the expansive grounds of the Sinclair Winery estate, needing something, anything, to come down from the adrenaline rush still running through them.

The late afternoon sun stretched across the endless rows of vineyards. The ripe grapes were heavy on the vines, their rich, fruity scent mingling with the earthy aroma of the soil. Leigh's sandals crunched softly against the gravel path. She tried to focus on the serene beauty of the estate, but her mind wouldn't settle.

The sadness kept creeping back in, no matter how she tried to shake it. Poor Evelyn. A woman who had worked so hard to build something lasting, something beautiful, only to be failed by the very people who should've cared for her most. Leigh's heart ached thinking about it. The selfishness of Evelyn's children had led to her being alone in that cold, dark cellar the night of her accident. And it didn't have to happen.

Her thoughts spun around and around the same questions. Why had Evelyn gone to the cellar so late that night? What had been so important that it couldn't wait until morning? Was she searching for something? Fixing something? Was she supposed to meet someone else down there? The possibilities clung to Leigh like cobwebs she couldn't brush away.

The others had walked ahead, and now their chatter broke through Leigh's thoughts.

"I still can't believe we're just… back to normal after everything," Kay said, pulling out her phone to snap a picture of the vibrant flowers spilling over a crumbling stone wall. She frowned at her phone like she couldn't quite believe the colorful, peaceful scene in front of her matched the day they'd just had. "It's like we're in some surreal alternate reality."

Marie's laugh floated back, light and a little tired. "You mean the kind where clueless tourists accidentally stumble into a full-blown mystery? Because that's definitely us."

"Speak for yourself," Alice quipped, adjusting her oversized sunglasses as she twirled on the path. "I'm practically a licensed detective now. Someone get me a badge." Her antics broke the tension and earned a round of laughter from the group.

But even as her friends joked and tried to find their footing again, Leigh couldn't let go. The question gnawed at her. She slowed her steps, and they all moved closer together.

She finally voiced her concerns. "What was Evelyn doing down there? No one had expected her what would've been needed so late at night that couldn't have waited? Why the cellar, and why go when it was so dark?"

Looking at her photos, Kay tilted her head. "Perhaps she was trying to find something? Hide something? It really doesn't make sense."

Alice's eyes lit up with that familiar gleam of curiosity,

the one that had gotten them into plenty of trouble (and a few memorable adventures) before when they were younger. "The cellar's open again, isn't it? I mean, now that the police have cleared it? What if we... went back? Just to see?" she said, lowering her voice even though they were the only ones around.

Marie crossed her arms and looked doubtful. "I'm not thrilled about revisiting the scene of... everything, but if it helps piece this together or put this behind us, count me in."

Leigh hesitated, glancing toward the shadowy pathway leading to the place where Evelyn had been found. Her stomach fluttered nervously, but she nodded. "Let's do it. Perhaps it'll give us some answers Evelyn deserves."

The group made their way to the cellar entrance, the heavy wooden door groaning in protest as Marie gave it a hard tug. It swung open slowly, revealing a set of brand-new wooden steps leading down. As they descended, the air grew noticeably cooler, and the damp scent of stone, earthy and old, surrounded them. Leigh shivered slightly, adjusting her cardigan as they stepped into the dimly lit space.

At the bottom, the main area stretched out before them, much more polished than Leigh remembered from their first day. There was no longer any evidence that anything terrible had ever happened here.

"This is where tourists go to sip their Chardonnay and marvel at 'rustic charm,'" Kay said, gesturing dramatically. "But I swear there's something eerie about this place, and it's not just because of Evelyn's accident."

Alice wandered toward the darker, dustier rooms at the edges of the cellar, her sharp eye scanning every nook and cranny. Her footsteps echoed against the stone floor as she moved slowly, scanning the dusty walls and old crates stacked haphazardly.

"Hang on," Alice said, pausing near a cluster of old barrels and half-collapsed shelves. She crouched low, brushing aside a web that clung stubbornly to a crate corner. "Look at this."

The others joined her, huddling close as she pointed to a patch of floor where the dust had been recently disturbed. Alice's fingers worked quickly, pushing aside crates and revealing a heavy linen bundle tucked behind them. Her hands trembled slightly as she picked it up, the fabric stiff and scratchy with age.

"What is that?" Marie asked, leaning in.

Alice carefully peeled back the layers of coarse fabric, her movements slow and deliberate. As the cloth fell away, a glint of silver caught the lantern light. The group inhaled sharply as a set of intricately designed, jewel-encrusted goblets emerged, their surfaces shimmering in the low light.

Each goblet shimmered under the lantern glow, adorned with tiny, glittering gemstones and fine, delicate carvings, roses, vines, and what looked like little crests or shields. They looked almost unreal, like something out of a fairy tale or a museum exhibit.

"Oh my goodness," Kay breathed. "Are those... the Sinclair heirlooms?"

Her heart pounded as Leigh nodded. "They have to be. Evelyn must have been hiding them that night."

Nestled alongside the goblets was a neatly folded note. Leigh unfolded it, her hands trembling as she read aloud. Evelyn's handwriting, looping and precise, filled the paper. It was a letter addressed to David. Evelyn explained how she had recently rediscovered the goblets, hidden away after being lost for decades. She wrote that it had been a hunch, a gut feeling that led her to an old stone building tucked away on the edge of the property.

It was a place most people overlooked, half-covered in ivy and half-forgotten, but she remembered hearing her grandmother talk about it once as a child. If the old family rumor about Edward stealing the goblets was true, maybe he'd hidden them somewhere no one would think to look. She confessed that she had hoped the goblets' immense value would be enough to save the winery from bankruptcy, to prevent the estate from being sold off to strangers. But more than that, she admitted she had begun to suspect that someone close to her was stirring up trouble, someone she loved.

She wrote that it broke her heart even to know it might be her own children. She wasn't sure who to trust anymore. That's why, she explained, she was hiding the goblets for now, keeping them safe until she was absolutely certain she could hand them over to David, the only person she truly trusted. Perhaps, she wrote with a shaky hopefulness, once they showed these to them together, they would finally make her children see how much the winery was worth saving. It was so much more than land and buildings.

"She was trying to protect her family," Leigh murmured, her throat tightening with emotion as she lowered the note. "She thought she could fix it all and stop her children from trying to throw the winery away. Only she had no idea how far they had already gone to try to be rid of it. She just didn't want to see their legacy fall apart in front of her eyes."

Alice ran her fingers over the delicate engravings, her expression softening. "These are more than just goblets. They're pieces of their history... and Evelyn's last genuine hope to save it. She was carrying the weight of it all on her shoulders."

The group fell silent for a moment, the gravity of the discovery settling over them. It was one thing to joke about mysteries over glasses of wine, but standing here, holding a woman's desperate hopes in their hands, was something entirely different.

Finally, Kay broke the heavy silence with a soft, almost guilty laugh. "Okay, but seriously, this is our second mystery on vacation. I'm starting to suspect we're either really lucky... or some mischievous spirits have decided we're their favorite detectives."

Leigh smiled faintly, tucking the note carefully back with the goblets. "On our next trip, we're picking a boring destination," she said firmly. "No old cellars, no family heirlooms, no hidden messages. Just sunshine, lounge chairs, and lazy beach days."

"We have to tell David," Marie said. "Evelyn wanted to give these to him, and we don't want to leave them for someone else to find."

Alice nodded, clutching the wrapped goblets. "She trusted him. She said it herself in her note, if anyone would do right by the winery, it would be David."

Back in the bright light of day, Leigh and her friends gathered in David's study, their excitement barely contained as they laid the goblets and the note on the polished mahogany table and explained everything in a rush. The sunlight streaming through the tall windows illuminated the intricate carvings on the goblets. Leigh glanced at David, waiting for his reaction.

His face, always so composed, shifted from stern curiosity to an expression of stunned disbelief. Without a word, he sank heavily into the leather chair behind him, running a trembling hand through his hair, as if trying to process everything at once.

The room fell into complete silence, the only sound the faint ticking of the grandfather clock in the corner. Then David spoke, his voice filled with emotion. "Evelyn... she was always thinking of everyone else. She wanted so badly to fix things, to save this estate. Even when… even when others didn't deserve her kindness."

Leigh swallowed the lump in her throat. She remembered Evelyn's warm smile, the way she welcomed them and had opened up to them immediately when they first met her. To imagine someone like that working quietly behind the scenes, trying to protect a legacy that others seemed so willing to destroy, was almost too much.

He paused, rubbing his temples. "She and I were working together to quietly find out if Nicholas was really trying selling off pieces of the estate. She was so upset when she heard the rumors about his plans. But Olivia? We had no idea she was involved. Evelyn just wanted to protect what this place stands for, without dragging the family name through the mud." His voice broke a little, and he quickly cleared his throat, but the pain in his eyes was unmistakable.

Leigh exchanged a glance with her friends, the unspoken sorrow hanging between them. There was so much betrayal wrapped up in what David was saying, so many people who should have cared about this place, about Evelyn, and instead had nearly destroyed it. She could see he was still coming to terms with it, the arrests of Nicholas and Olivia probably feeling like a nightmare that hadn't ended yet.

Kay stepped forward, her voice gentle. "She loved this place. It was obvious the moment she began to speak about it. She believed in the winery's value. You can see it in every decision she made. She had faith in it, and obviously in you." Leigh admired how Kay had a knack for saying the right thing, even in moments like these.

David exhaled deeply, his shoulders relaxing for the first time since they had met him. "She did. What you've found here… it means more than I can say," he said, his voice thick with gratitude. "Thank you for this." Despite all the horrible revelations of the day, the deceit, the arrests, the cracks in a family that had once seemed so perfect, there was something good here too. Evelyn's final wishes had been fulfilled. The goblets had been found and given to David.

Moved by the emotion of the moment, David insisted on treating them to lunch at La Casa Restaurant, and before they knew it, they were stepping through the arched doorway into a vibrant, bustling dining room that instantly lifted their spirits. Leigh immediately sensed her mood lighten as the warm colors of the walls, sunset orange and golden yellow, seemed to embrace them. Strings of papel picado swayed gently overhead, and the lively hum of conversation was punctuated by the soft strumming of a guitarist wandering between tables.

Sliding into a cozy corner booth, they wasted no time diving into bowls of crisp tortilla chips that were surrounded by vibrant guacamole, smooth queso fresco, and three kinds of salsa that looked almost too good to eat, almost.

Kay scooped up a generous helping of guacamole onto a chip and sighed dramatically. "This guac deserves its own fan club," she declared, sending a ripple of laughter around the table.

Marie rolled her eyes at the dramatics, but smiled as she reached for her own bowl, scooping up a heaping bite without hesitation.

Without needing to say a word, there was an unspoken agreement among the group to steer the conversation toward something a little lighter, a little warmer, Evelyn. They didn't want to cloud the afternoon with sadness; instead, they leaned into celebrating her. Between bites and sips, they peppered David with questions, not just about Evelyn as they had met during their brief time here, but about the woman she had been across the years, and the generations she was a part of. Stories about the Sinclair family flowed easily, tales full of laughter and the kind of tiny details that painted Evelyn in an even richer color. Leigh found herself soaking it all in, feeling a bittersweet joy at getting to know their hostess even more through the people and places she had loved.

The main dishes arrived with a flourish: sizzling platters of chicken fajitas, grilled salmon glistening with a citrus glaze, and fish tacos piled high with slaw and crema. Each bite was better than the last, and the table buzzed with compliments and exaggerated groans of delight. "I'm never eating a boring sandwich again," Alice announced between bites of her chipotle chicken salad.

The drinks, however, were the true showstoppers. Marie's watermelon basil margarita was the envy of the table, its vibrant pink hue catching the light. "This," she said, raising her glass like a trophy, "is summer in a glass."

David, seated next to Kay, leaned over to admire the photos she had taken on their trip. "These are incredible," he said, scrolling through her phone. "Would you ever consider letting us use some for advertising? You've got a genuine talent."

Kay's cheeks flushed, not with her usual quick-witted sass, but with a real, unmistakable excitement. She tucked a piece of hair behind her ear, her voice a little breathless. "Are you kidding me? I'd love that! I'll give you all my contact information. Just let me know what you need, and I'll send over the high-res versions."

She hesitated for a second, then added, "You know, Evelyn actually said something really similar when we first met her. She told me she loved my pictures and how they captured the spirit of the place. She even mentioned wanting to possibly use some of my pictures in marketing. Honestly, it got me thinking... perhaps it's time to start something. Like, a real business. And I can't imagine a better first client than Sinclair Winery."

Leigh smiled at Kay's excitement, sensing a little jolt of pride for her friend. It wasn't every day you watched someone stumble into a dream they didn't even realize they had.

Leaning back in her seat, Leigh let herself soak in the moment, experiencing peace in every sense of the word. The warmth of the restaurant, the laughter of her friends, and the sheer absurdity of their adventure filled her with a deep contentment.

After lunch, they set off to wander Sonoma Plaza, their pace slow and easy, like people who had nowhere better to be. The historic square was brimming with charm and life, musicians strumming guitars under the shade of sprawling oaks, little kids chasing pigeons, and shopkeepers chatting with locals outside colorful storefronts. The cobblestone paths were lined with vendors selling everything from handmade pottery to artisanal soaps. Leigh was drawn to a boutique filled with rare trinkets, her eyes drawn to the delicate designs on an antique locket. Across the way, Alice stood in an antique shop, holding up a vintage hat and striking a ridiculous pose that made Marie dissolve into laughter.

While exploring, they struck up conversations with other tourists, including a couple who seemed hopelessly lost. "The wine-tasting room you're looking for is down that alley," Kay said, pointing. "And trust me, order the pinot noir. Life-changing."

Their final stop was Wine Country Chocolates, a shop that Leigh swore was crafted by angels. The air was thick with the smell of rich cocoa, and the display case glittered with truffles, barks, and caramels. Leigh bit into a dark chocolate truffle filled with raspberry ganache and groaned aloud. "If this chocolate had a face, I'd kiss it," she said, earning a laugh from the others.

Marie held up a bag of chocolate-covered espresso beans. "Fuel for our next adventure," she said with a grin.

Leigh laughed, feeling lighter than she had in weeks. "Remember, next time we're picking a no adventure destination," she joked as they waved goodbye at David getting into his car and piled into their own car.

Alice smirked, tossing her bag of chocolate onto the seat. "You'd be bored within five minutes. Chaos suits us."

Leigh leaned back against the seat and looked around at her friends, their faces glowing from the sun and the chocolate and perhaps a little from just being together. Their laughter filled the small car, bouncing off the windows, weaving through all the spaces between them. She smiled to herself, heart full. No matter how crazy things got, or how crazy they made things, these were the moments that mattered.

And she wouldn't trade a single second of it.

# 25 BITTERSWEET FAREWELL TO SONOMA VALLEY

For their final evening in Sonoma, the friends gathered around a rustic wooden table nestled in a quiet clearing at the heart of the winery. Long strands of twinkling café lights were strung between low-hanging oak trees, casting a warm golden glow over their faces. The sun had begun to dip below the hills, leaving the sky streaked with watercolor shades of lavender, rose, and apricot. Surrounding them, the vineyard stretched in gentle rows; the grapevines rustling softly in the breeze. The air was cool and earthy, scented with a mix of damp soil, crushed leaves, and a faint sweetness from the grapes ripening on the vines. Somewhere a frog croaked, and the soft crackle of a nearby lantern flame added a comforting touch to the evening's soundtrack.

They all raised their glasses of Sinclair Winery's Pinot Noir, the deep red wine shimmering in the fading light. "To Evelyn," Kay said, her voice filled with the weight of their shared memories. "And to the adventure we'll never forget."

The others echoed the sentiment, their glasses

clinking in quiet unison. Leigh's gaze moved around the table, settling on each of her friends. Kay, with her easy laugh and side comments that had kept them all laughing, her fingers tapping absently on her glass stem like she was still half in a story she hadn't told yet. She was the kind of person who found fun anywhere, even in a ghost story or a forgotten trail. Alice sat tall, her posture always confident, but tonight there was a softness in her shoulders, a calm that hadn't been there all week. Perhaps it was the wine, or maybe it was the closure that came with letting go a bit. Either way, she looked peaceful. And then there was Marie, thoughtful, constantly in motion, always a few steps ahead of everyone else, whether solving a mystery or simply picking up on the moods in a room. She wore a quietness tonight, like she had finally discovered the joy of doing nothing for a change.

Leigh looked down into her glass and smiled. It was hard to imagine this group of women, so different from one another, had come together in such a perfect way. The bond they shared had been forged in laughter, in tears, and in plenty of wild, unforgettable moments from their younger years that would stay with them forever.

They each took turns exchanging gifts, thoughtful mementos from Sonoma that captured the spirit of the week they'd shared together. These weren't only souvenirs, they were bits of memory, tokens of laughter and late-night talks.

Marie had chosen a set of elegant Sinclair Estate wineglasses for each of them. The glass was etched with the vineyard's crest, fine and delicate, just like their time in Sonoma, a nod to the elegance of the vineyards as well as a memory of Evelyn. "These are for the next time we gather," Marie said, grinning as she carefully passed them out. "For when we're reminiscing about this trip, and trust me, that'll be often."

Leigh smiled as she turned the glass in her hand, the rim catching the light. She imagined pouring something rich and red into it during one of their future get-togethers, a wonderful little piece of Sonoma.

Alice's gift came next, a surprise wrapped in soft tissue. Each of them unrolled handwoven scarves dyed in colors that immediately brought the valley's sunsets to mind. Deep oranges, purples, and soft pinks.

"I saw them and thought of all of you," Alice said, her voice soft, almost shy. "The colors are all different but mix so well together… just like us."

When it was Kay's turn to give her gifts, she handed the ladies beautifully crafted small wooden serving trays, polished and sleek, with intricate vine designs etched into the edges.

"For all those amazing wine and cheese nights, we are going to continue to have once we get back home," she said with a grin. "And so no one ever forgets I'm the charcuterie queen."

Marie looked at the tray, her face softening with affection. "This is gorgeous, Kay. Thank you. It'll be a perfect reminder of our time together."

Finally, Leigh took a breath and handed out her gifts. Each one was a hand-poured candle in the base of an actual wine bottle from Sonoma Valley that had been cut down. The wax was a blend of lavender and sage. "I figured we all could use something to bring a little bit of Sonoma's calm into our daily lives," she said. "It's a little reminder to keep the chaos to a minimum."

Alice held the candle up, the fragrance immediately filling the air with its earthy, calming scent. "You're right, Leigh. This will be wonderful. Thank you."

The group smiled, exchanging appreciative glances. One by one, they turned to each other, not with dramatic speeches or teary eyes, but with genuine thank-yous, small nods, warm squeezes of hands.

As they relaxed, their conversation shifted to the challenges they'd faced on the trip and beyond. Wine glasses sat half-full on the table between them, forgotten as the tone of the conversation deepened.

Alice, who had finally opened up about her personal struggles, spoke with quiet pride. "I've been working on finding peace and knowing it's okay to ask for help," she said, her voice steady but filled with emotion. "And I feel like this trip, this whole experience, has helped me realize I'm in a better place than I imagined I was. I'm stronger than I give myself credit for."

Leigh looked over at her, heart tugging with empathy. She remembered the tight smile Alice had worn when they first arrived, the way she always seemed to be holding something back. But here she was now, sitting open and honest among friends.

Marie chimed in, her expression thoughtful. "And you know, for me, it's been about stepping away from thinking work always comes first. I've been running myself ragged for so long that it seemed impossible to slow down. But talking with all of you… has shown me how important it is to take a breath, think creatively for new ideas, and simply be present. I'm ready for more of that."

Leigh smiled at her friends, her heart swelling with affection. "It's amazing to see how much we can accomplish when we put our heads together," she said, turning with a playful grin toward Kay. "And Kay, there even looks to be something new going on with David Foster."

Kay's eyes sparkled with excitement, her voice brimming with possibility. "You know what? I've been thinking about it. We did talk a lot about work, but there's something else there, too. I'm looking forward to what comes next. Perhaps this will be more than simply a professional relationship." She winked, her cheeky grin suggesting she was open to whatever came her way.

They exchanged knowing glances. There was no denying the connection between Kay and David, and though they hadn't discussed it outright, everyone sensed the potential simmering right beneath the surface. Something was beginning there, something with possibility and risk and perhaps even romance.

And then, as they sipped their wine and relaxed into the warmth of the evening, a sudden sound of a twig snapping came from the grove of trees nearby, sharp and unexpected. The women froze for a moment, eyes wide, before bursting into nervous laughter. Still, the sound had stirred something, and the conversation drifted to the odd, unexplainable things that had happened over the past few days at the winery.

"I'm certain I saw Evelyn one time," Alice said, her wineglass pausing halfway to her lips. Her tone was mock-serious, but her expression said she wasn't entirely joking. "I thought she was standing right there in the hallway near the library. I even said her name. But then, poof, gone. Like she dissolved into thin air.

Leigh smiled and leaned back. "I thought I saw her reflection in a mirror one day when I was wandering the house," she admitted. "It wasn't clear, but I swear I saw the shape of someone behind me. I turned around and, nothing. Maybe she's been with us the whole time, just watching us stumble through all this and hoping we could help her."

They all fell quiet for a beat, letting the possibility settle in the surrounding air. It wasn't fear they felt, it was something gentler. Something almost comforting.

Leigh's heart was full as she relaxed. They had uncovered so many secrets, Evelyn's presence, ghostly or not, had remained a part of the adventure, sometimes almost seeming to lead them in ways they couldn't quite explain. And perhaps that was the beauty of it all. They didn't have to understand everything, they just had to enjoy the ride.

As the last of their wine disappeared, the women stood, stretching and gathering their things. The cool evening air had settled in for good, and the promise of their early morning flight loomed. But no one seemed eager to rush.

They strolled slowly back toward the guest house, shoes stepping softly on the stone path. The moon lit their way, silver and still, while the vines whispered beside them in the breeze.

Back inside, they moved through their usual motions, shoes kicked off, teeth brushed, phones plugged in. But there was a quiet reverence in it tonight, as if they all sensed the weight of goodbye coming too quickly.

Leigh paused in the hallway before heading to her room. She glanced once more toward the main house beyond the trees, where Evelyn's story had unfolded.

"Goodnight," she whispered, not sure if she was speaking to her friends or someone else entirely.

The next morning, Leigh stood in front of her open suitcase, sunlight spilling through the gauzy curtains of her room. The familiar ache of homesickness tugged at her, mingling with that strange, wistful pull of not quite wanting to leave. She folded her clothes methodically, the fabric still carrying the faint scent of the vineyard's breeze and lavender from the estate's gardens.

She smiled to herself, her hands pausing over a soft sweater as her thoughts wandered back home. She couldn't wait to share every detail of the trip, the ghost tours that had sent chills down her spine, the heavenly meals that had left them dazed in the best way possible, and of course, the wild turn their vacation had taken with the mystery at the Sinclair Estate.

Carefully, she nestled the gifts she'd picked out into the corners of her bag: decadent truffles from Wine Country Chocolates for Alex, because he had a serious sweet tooth and zero self-control; a bottle of deep, velvety Pinot Noir for Tom that the winery owner had claimed was a perfect pairing for grilled steak, which was his favorite; a leather-bound journal for Matthew, who'd probably pretend not to care, then end up writing in it late at night; and for Emma, a delicate, hand-painted ceramic bowl that Leigh had found at the artisan market. Its soft, earthy glaze reminded her of the sunset. Each item was like a little snapshot of the trip, a pocket-sized piece of the moments she wanted to share with her family.

Down the hall, the shuffle of suitcases and muffled voices echoed. Leigh zipped her suitcase shut and paused, glancing around the room one last time. The rich wooden beams of the ceiling and the floral bedspread were now familiar. She smiled, bittersweet. It was strange how quickly a place could go from new to comforting, how fast something temporary could start to seem like a second home.

Outside, the group had gathered in the driveway, and what should've been a quick task, loading up the car, was already spiraling.

"How did we end up with so much more luggage than we came with?" Kay asked, holding up a tote bag filled with bottles of wine.

Marie groaned. "Blame Alice and her 'just one more bottle' philosophy."

"It's not my fault Sonoma has excellent wine," Alice quipped, trying to wedge her suitcase into the trunk. "Besides, I only bought four bottles. The real question is, who's responsible for this?" She held up a large, unwieldy bag stuffed with various souvenirs.

Leigh raised her hand sheepishly. "Guilty. But in my defense, they're all gifts!"

"Sure they are," Kay teased, pushing the bag into the already packed car. "Remind me to never let you shop unsupervised."

By the time they'd finished, they were laughing so hard that tears streamed down their faces. Somehow, they managed to fit everything in, though the trunk was precariously close to bursting.

Before leaving, they made their way back to the main house to say their goodbyes. The staff greeted them warmly, offering hugs and heartfelt thanks for their visit. One of the servers even slipped a tiny jar of local honey into Leigh's hands with a wink and whispered, "For sweet memories."

They also spotted Will and Pamela, the warm and witty couple from New Orleans they'd bonded with over wine flights and ghost stories. Leigh made a beeline for them.

"We better keep in touch," Pamela said, wrapping Leigh in a tight embrace that smelled faintly of jasmine and sunblock. "Next time y'all are down South, you better let us host you."

"Only if we get more of your ghost stories and that bread pudding recipe," Leigh laughed.

They all laughed, trading phone numbers and promising to stay connected, even if it was just through photos and texts about wine and weird happenings.

David stood off to the side, talking quietly with Kay beneath the shade of a tall olive tree. Leigh couldn't make out their words, but the way Kay's eyes lit up as she spoke told its own story.

Leigh raised an eyebrow, glancing at Kay and David.

"You think there's something there?"

A smirk crossed Marie's lips. "Oh, there's definitely something brewing."

Leigh grinned. "Good for her. She deserves a little excitement, and not just of the haunted winery variety."

Outside, they gathered for a group photo in front of the winery. The view behind them looked like something out of a postcard. The rows of grapevines seemed endless, their golden leaves fluttering in the breeze. They posed with arms draped around each other, their laughter bubbling over as Alice tried to strike a vogue pose, one hand on her hip, the other in the air like she was ready for the runway.

"Can we get one serious picture?" Kay said, rolling her eyes but smiling.

"This is serious," Alice replied, tossing her head.

The camera clicked, capturing the moment, the warmth of their friendship, the beauty of the vineyard, and the joy of an unforgettable trip.

"Another one for the memory book," Kay said, glancing at her phone.

The car ride to the airport was quiet. Everyone was tucked into their seats, each of them staring out the windows, letting the last views of Sonoma soak in.

Leigh leaned her head gently against the cool glass, her gaze sweeping over the landscape as it rolled by. Golden fields dotted with sleepy farmhouses and rows of grapevines that looked like they went on forever. A weathered sign for a fruit stand flashed by, its paint faded and peeling. In the distance, a hawk soared over a line of trees.

"This place was magic," she said softly.

The others murmured their agreement, each lost in their own reflections. No one needed to say much. They were all holding tight to their own pieces of the trip.

For Leigh, the trip had been more than a vacation, it had been another journey of rediscovery. She was enjoying finding more and more of herself again. Not the version of her that worries too much or overanalyzed every decision she makes. But the version that had space to breathe. To notice. To experience things in real time instead of always bracing for what was next.

And she realized that in letting go of all that inner noise, she'd finally been able to really see the people around her, too. She'd noticed when Alice got unusually quiet and needed someone to draw her back in. She'd sensed Marie's stress before Marie had even spoken it aloud. She'd caught the flicker of something unreadable behind Kay's smile and just sat beside her in that moment, no questions asked. That was something she definitely wanted to carry back with her, this ability to be more present. More open. More in tune.

She thought of the bucket list she was mentally compiling, filled with more places, not just to capture on a phone or check off a plan. She wanted to walk more unfamiliar streets, try dishes she couldn't pronounce, and meet people who made her laugh unexpectedly. And she wanted to keep showing up for her friends, not just as the one who remembered the sunscreen or booked the hotel, but the one who truly noticed.

As the airport came into view, Leigh had a quiet contentment settle over her. She'd once again sensed that she had learned so much about herself on this trip, more than she ever expected. They'd come to Sonoma thinking it would just be a fun girls' trip, wine, laughter, a little adventure to spice things up. But what they got was so much more. A reminder of how resilient they were, how deeply rooted their friendship really ran, and how healing it could be to just escape the noise of everyday life for a few days.

As they pulled up, Leigh let out a small sigh and glanced back one more time, hoping to catch a final glimpse of the rolling hills. "Goodbye, Sonoma," she thought with a smile. "Back to the real world."

And with that, she grabbed her bags, adjusted her sunglasses, and stepped out of the car, ready for whatever came next.

## 26 EPILOGUE

Weeks later back home, the group gathered for the first time since returning from Sonoma at their favorite coffee shop in Omaha, a place that felt like a second living room after all these years. The familiar, worn leather of the corner booth welcomed Leigh as she slid in, the warmth from her latte radiating through her chilled fingers. She glanced out the frost-edged window, where the Nebraska weather had pulled one of its classic tricks, coating everything in a shimmering blanket of snow, even though it was technically still autumn. The gray sky made her miss the sun-drenched days in Sonoma more than ever. There, the breeze smelled like lavender and grapes. Here, it smelled like salted sidewalks and winter coats. Still, there was something comforting about being home, too. Familiar.

"I still can't believe I screamed so loud during that dungeon tour," Alice began, her hands flying up as she mimicked her own panicked reaction. "It echoed forever! I'm pretty sure I scared myself more than anything down there."

Marie was laughing so hard that she had to set her cappuccino down before it toppled over. "Scared yourself? You scared me! I thought we were under attack. I still say that scream could wake the dead."

"I think it did," Kay teased, brushing a stray strand of hair behind her ear. "That tour guide looked like he was going to start handing out earplugs."

Alice feigned offense, narrowing her eyes at them. "Oh, and you were so composed? I seem to recall someone, Marie, being absolutely convinced that David was some kind of underground crime lord."

Marie rolled her eyes, but her grin gave her away. "That's because you made him sound like he was hiding bodies in the vineyard! The way you talked about him, how could I not suspect him?"

Leigh couldn't help but smile at the memory. David, the friendly winemaker they'd met, had indeed given off a very mysterious vibe at first, and Alice definitely had a talent for storytelling that made everyone seem like a suspect.

"I'll admit," Marie continued, "he turned out to be pretty great. She paused just long enough for Leigh to wonder if she was about to change the subject, and she did. Her tone shifted subtly, and her expression softened as she leaned forward on her elbows, drawing everyone's attention. "Speaking of great... I finally had that conversation with my supervisors."

The laughter paused, replaced by a quiet anticipation. "And?" Leigh prompted.

Marie's smile grew. "I told them I needed more balance, more time to travel, more space to actually live outside of work. And you know what? They surprised me. They didn't push back. They were excited, actually. They said they've been looking to make the brand feel more family-focused, more real. They want me to bring my family along sometimes, on shoots, for market testing. They said I'm exactly the kind of voice they've been missing."

"That's wonderful," Kay said, her voice filled with excitement for Marie as Alice nodded.

Leigh grinned. It was easy to picture Marie's two boys going to fashion showrooms, awestruck as their mom worked her magic and directed a photoshoot or helped a new designer bring their ideas to life. "It's going to be perfect for you," Leigh said warmly.

As the group soaked in Marie's good news, a thoughtful expression crossed Alice's face. She cleared her throat gently, and everyone turned toward her.

"So," she began, a little more hesitantly, "I've been making changes too. Our talks during the trip… they really helped me. I realized it's okay to say I've been carrying too much. Always trying to be the one who has it all figured out—for my parents, my classes, my husband and children. But I really don't have to do it all. I've finally started letting people in."

She paused, her fingers tracing the rim of her mug, then looked up at Leigh with a steady gaze. "I asked my Aunt to take over Mom and Dad's medical paperwork, she has worked in the field and knows so much more. I let Zach and the kids help with the grocery shopping and meal planning, it's now more of a game than anything else but at least it's off my plate. And I even, believe it or not, accepted a classmate's help with a huge research project I've been stuck on for weeks."

She looked around, her gaze steady. "It's not easy, but it's worth it. I've started giving myself permission to not have all the answers for everyone. Life feels… so much lighter now."

Leigh took a sip of her latte. "Well," she said, setting her cup down with a soft clink, "I guess it's safe to say that trip in Sonoma was anything but ordinary. I think it gave all of us a feeling of something new, something better than what we felt before the trip."

Just then, the smell of freshly baked scones wafted over, warm and buttery, mingling with the rich aroma of coffee. Leigh looked up to see Marie's son, Hunter, approaching the table with a plate piled high with the pastries. His grin lit up the room as he carefully placed the plate in the center of the table. "So, ladies," he teased, brushing a crumb off his shirt, "I hear your 'relaxing' vacation was anything but."

Leigh raised an eyebrow, smirking as she reached for a scone. "What have you heard?"

Hunter's grin widened. "Oh, you know, I've just heard overheard little details like, ghosts, a haunted winery, a murder mystery. Totally sounds like a calm, normal getaway."

"Don't forget the wine," Kay interjected, raising her coffee cup in mock toast.

"And David," Alice chimed in with a mischievous wink in Kay's direction.

At that, Kay blushed, an actual, full-face blush that had her setting her mug down carefully, as if it had suddenly grown too heavy to hold. "Well," she began, her voice quieter than usual, touched with a bit of shyness that was rare for her, "speaking of David…"

Hunter immediately started backing away, hands raised in mock surrender. "And that's my cue to get back to work," he said with a good natured grimace, clearly relieved to make his escape before things got too mushy. Leigh couldn't blame him, no teenager wants to hang around while his mom's friends start dissecting romantic moments.

The table waved him off, and the energy shifted. Everyone leaned in, chairs creaking slightly as the circle drew closer, fully invested in whatever Kay was about to say. Her hands fluttered for a moment, then stilled as she began to describe her conversations with David—how they'd gone from casual to unexpectedly meaningful. They'd talked about everything from winemaking techniques and the science behind fermentation, to bucket-list travels and the strange, beautiful surprises life tends to throw at you when you least expect it.

Leigh watched Kay closely, noticing the way her eyes seemed to shine, not just with excitement, but with something more. Something hopeful. Kay had never been the one chasing romance. She didn't pine or plan around it. In fact, she often joked that she had made peace with the idea that romance belonged in books and Hallmark movies, not in her day-to-day life. She was content with good friends, fulfilling work, and the occasional spontaneous adventure. But something had shifted. Getting to know David hadn't just been fun, it had felt... easy and exciting.

"We're all rooting for you," Leigh said warmly, reaching across the table to squeeze Kay's hand.

"I knew you would be," Kay replied, her smile wide and genuine. "I may have finally found the kind of excitement I've been looking for!"

Leigh exchanged a knowing glance with Alice and Marie, their shared joy in Kay's happiness unspoken but deeply felt.

Just then, Kay reached into her oversized tote bag, pulling out four beautifully bound memory books, each one a little treasure chest of their recent adventures. "By the way," she said, sliding one to each of them, "I made albums for all of us again. everyone loved the ones from our first trip to Savannah."

Leigh took hers, running her fingers over the textured cover. It was sturdy yet elegant, with delicate lettering that spelled out "Sonoma Memories". As she flipped it open, the trip came alive again in vivid detail: pictures of their late-night ghost tour, where Alice's exaggerated scream could practically still be heard; ticket stubs from the winery tours; pressed flowers from the vineyard; even scribbled notes of their inside jokes that had kept them laughing for days.

Little captions were scattered throughout in Kay's curly handwriting: "Leigh trying to sweet-talk the haunted mirror!" and "Marie vs. the bee = Marie 1, Bee 0."

"Oh my gosh, you kept this?" Alice exclaimed, pointing to a candid photo of herself mid-scream in the dungeon, her face a perfect blend of terror and hilarity.

"Of course," Kay replied, laughing. "It's iconic."

Leigh found a page with a small envelope taped inside. Curious, she carefully opened it and pulled out a handwritten note. As her eyes skimmed the familiar curves of Kay's handwriting, her heart swelled. The words were simple, but they hit deep. Kay had written about how Leigh had this quiet way of pulling people together, of making the trip feel effortless even when everyone knew it wasn't. She talked about Leigh's gift for planning, how she'd found just the right balance between adventure and rest, and how her calm presence had steadied them all during moments that could've gone sideways. Leigh blinked quickly, her throat tightening as she swallowed a lump of emotion. It was one thing to share a trip with your friends, it was another to have it reflected back to you like this, to be seen.

"These are amazing, Kay," she said softly, her voice thick with gratitude. "You didn't miss a single detail."

"Not even the ones we tried to forget," Marie quipped, pointing to a page with a picture of the four of them crammed into the car, souvenirs piled high around them like a comedic game of Tetris. Empty coffee cups, tote bags, and one very unfortunate bottle of lavender lotion that had leaked onto the backseat.

Laughter filled the cozy space again, their voices carrying over the steady hum of the coffee shop.

Then, as the conversation ebbed, Kay leaned forward, her expression mischievous. "You know," she began, "Will and Pamela, that couple we met at the winery? They completely sold me on New Orleans. Haunted mansions, live jazz, gumbo, it's officially on my bucket list."

"Oh no," Alice groaned, covering her face with one hand. "Another haunted city? I thought we agreed the next trip was going to be peaceful! No shadows moving, no doors creaking, no whispered voices from nowhere?"

"But think of the history!" Marie said dramatically, throwing her hands in the air like a fortune-teller predicting their future. "Old houses, secret courtyards, carriage rides, voodoo legends! It's a walking storybook, Alice."

"And the beignets," Leigh added, her lips curling into a smile as she imagined the warm, powdered sugar melting on her tongue.

"Okay, okay," Alice relented, laughing. "I might be swayed by the food. But if you make me scream in public again, Kay, we're going to have words."

"Deal," Kay said, still grinning. She paused, then added, "Oh, and by the way, I may or may not have spoken to Will and Pamela already. Just in case, you know, Leigh feels like planning our next adventure there."

All eyes turned to Leigh, who rolled her eyes, pretending to resist, though the spark of excitement was already catching fire in her. "Of course. Because what would you all do without me?"

"Absolutely nothing," Alice said with a wink.

As the group dissolved into laughter, Leigh let herself savor the moment. New Orleans, she thought, already picturing their next escapade, the jazz clubs, the swirling mystique of the French Quarter, and, inevitably, more ghostly tales.

She didn't know what was waiting for them next. But she knew one thing: it was going to be unforgettable.

# ENDNOTES- EXPLORE SONOMA

Greetings once more, dear reader! If you've joined Leigh and her friends for another unforgettable journey, this time to the vineyards, ghost towns, and luxurious spas of Sonoma Valley, then you already know this wasn't your typical girls' getaway. It was filled with laughter, rich wine, haunting history, and the kind of memories that only a place like Sonoma can offer.

So, whether you're planning your own real-life adventure or just daydreaming from your favorite reading nook, I present to you Leigh's Sonoma Valley Itinerary, a mix of charming spots, spooky fun, and wine country elegance. Like a good mystery, allow this to be your roadmap but not your rulebook. Sometimes the best parts of the journey are the detours you never expected.

Sip the wine, chase the ghost stories, relax in a hot spring, and let yourself be swept away in the beauty (and mystery) of Sonoma. Here's to unforgettable friendships, spine-tingling stories, and perfect pours!

Now pack your sense of adventure, Leigh's itinerary awaits…

# Leigh's Itinerary for the Sonoma Girls' Trip

## Day 1: Arrival and Introduction to Sonoma Valley

-**Arrival**: Welcome to Sonoma! Time to kick off the
girls' trip with some wine and fun.
-**Check-in at a charming guest house on winery
grounds**: Unpack and settle in, this is your cozy base
for the next few days of wine, laughter, and adventure.
-**The Sunflower Caffe**: Enjoy a delicious meal with
fresh, local flavors.
-**Sonoma Plaza**: Enjoy boutique shopping, historic
sites, and wine tasting rooms.
(Side Note: Don't forget to grab a souvenir!)
-**Mission San Francisco Solano**: Known for its
slightly eerie, old-world charm.
-**The Girl & The Fig**: Delicious farm-to-table dining
with an extensive wine list.
(Side Note: Pro tip, ask for their lavender-scented house
cocktail.)
-**Sonoma Plaza Ghost Walk Tour**: Learn about local
ghost stories and haunted locations around the plaza.
-**Sweet Scoops Homemade Ice Cream**: Cool down
with a sweet treat and maybe a spooky tale or two.

## Day 2: Historical Immersion

-**Buena Vista Winery**: The second oldest winery in
California, with a spooky history and beautiful old
cellars.
(Side Note: Wine and ghosts? Yes, please!)
-**Horseback Riding Tour at Jack London State
Historic Park**: Ride through literary history and take
in the serene scenery.
-**Tour The House of Happy Walls, an Interactive

Museum about Jack London**: Discover the wild stories behind this famous author.
-**Charles Schulz Museum**: A must for fans of Charlie Brown and Snoopy!
-**Jacuzzi Family Vineyards**: Known for its Tuscan-style setting and laid-back atmosphere.
(Side Note: Make sure to try the olive oil tasting,it's divine.)
-**The Depot Hotel Restaurant and Garden**: Casual dining spot which is known for its ghostly tales.

## Day 3: Spooky Adventures and Hot Springs

-**Gundlach Bundschu Winery**: Take a ghost tour of the winery, often rumored to be haunted.
-**Cafe La Haye**: Enjoy lunch with a chic, modern dining experience.
-**Fairmont Sonoma Mission Inn and Spa**: Relax at the spa's natural hot springs.
(Side Note: Wine, ghosts, and now hot springs? This trip just keeps getting better!)
-**B&V Whiskey Bar and Grille**: Cap off the day with whiskey cocktails in this cozy, laid-back spot.

## Day 4: Adventure Day and Wingo Visit

-**Wingo**: Head to this small, lesser-known ghost town. Explore its abandoned buildings and learn about the history of this once-bustling town.
(Side Note: Definitely the spookiest stop yet!)
-**Folktable Restaurant**: Farm-fresh cuisine in a stylish setting.
-**Cornerstone Sonoma**: Beautiful gardens, shops, and outdoor art exhibits, perfect for a leisurely stroll.
-**Hot Air Balloon Ride**: Soar over the vineyards with

breathtaking views.
(Side Note: Trust us, the sunset views are worth it.)
-**Wit & Wisdom Restaurant**: End your day with hearty meals and local wine.
-**Napa City Ghosts and Legends Walks Tour**: paranormal investigator tour.

## Day 5: Day Trip to Napa with Haunted Sites

-**Castello di Amorosa**: Tour this medieval-style castle and winery with rumors of hauntings and a dark dungeon.
-**Bounty Hunter Wine Bar & Smokin' BBQ**: Finger-lickin' BBQ and a solid wine list.
-**Beringer Vineyards**: Visit one of Napa's most historic (and allegedly haunted) wineries.
-**Deerfield Ranch Winery**: Enjoy dinner and possibly an interactive murder mystery detective show.
(Side Note: You get wine AND a mystery? Sign us up!)

## Day 6: Sonoma's Charm

-**Dierk's Parkside Cafe**: Enjoy breakfast in Santa Rosa.
-**Sonoma Botanical Garden**: Spend time relaxing and enjoying the beautiful garden.
-**La Casa Restaurant**: Classic Mexican dishes in a fun, lively atmosphere.
-**Sonoma Plaza**: One last stroll around this charming spot-perfect for last-minute shopping.
-**Wine Country Chocolates**: Grab some artisanal chocolates to take home.
-**Pack and Depart**: Say goodbye to Sonoma Valley and head home with wonderful memories.
(Side Note: Until next time, Sonoma. We'll be back!)

# ABOUT THE AUTHOR

Kelly Greer is a wife and mother of three who has always found joy in writing, reading, and creating. Her love for both storytelling and exploring new places began at a young age and has blossomed into a passion for crafting cozy mysteries in captivating locations. When she's not lost in the world of her characters, Kelly enjoys spending time with her family, exploring new locales, and indulging in her creative pursuits. Her blend of family life, love of an intriguing mystery and exploring hidden gems brings a unique warmth to her writing, making each story a charming escape for readers.